Orange, VA

A novel of political intrigue

Michael Abraham

Orange, VA

Pocahontas Press
Blacksburg, Virginia

Also by Michael Abraham

The Spine of the Virginias
Journeys along the border of Virginia and West Virginia

Harmonic Highways
Exploring Virginia's Crooked Road

Union, WV
A novel of loss, healing, and redemption in contemporary Appalachia

Providence, VA
A novel of inner strength through adversity

War, *WV*
A fight for justice in the Appalachian coal fields

For updates and ordering information on the author's books, excerpts, and sample chapters, please visit his website at:
http://www.bikemike.name/

The author can be reached by email at:
<bikemike@nrvunwired.net>

Orange, VA

ISBN-10 0-926487-76-0
ISBN-13 978-0926487-76-5

Cover design by Michael Abraham and Jill Darlington-Smith
Cover illustration by Thong Le

Author back cover photograph by Leslie R. Gregg
Maps by Bob Pearsall
Book design by Michael Abraham

Printed in the United States of America

Pocahontas Press
www.pocahontaspress.com

Acknowledgements

I am deeply indebted to many people who supported my effort. My editors worked countless hours to help me make my book readable, relevant, and grammatically correct.

Jane Abraham, Blacksburg, Virginia

Beverly H. Frederick, Alexandria, Virginia

Elizabeth T. Greer, Roanoke, Virginia

Flora Mason Diehl, Collinsville, Virginia

Pat McNally, Fulks Run, Virginia

Sally Shupe, Newport, Virginia

I am also indebted to the people who helped me understand the technical aspects of the book and gave me encouragement, support, and ideas.

Mark Bold, Lynchburg, Virginia

Wyatt Durrett, Richmond, Virginia

John Edwards, Roanoke, Virginia

Shantal Hover, Blacksburg, Virginia

Geoffrey Knobl, Blacksburg, Virgnia

Vivian Lingenfelter, Salem, Virginia

Harry McCoy, Blacksburg, Virginia

Karen Grossman Molzhon, Richmond, Virginia

Molly O'Dell, Christiansburg, Virginia

Bob Pearsall, Riner, Virginia

Liza Piedmont, Roanoke, Virginia

Jagger Rutledge, Check, Virginia

Isaac Sarver, Dublin, Virginia

Bonnie Smith, Christiansburg, Virginia

Sandra Smith, Orange, Virginia

Frank Walker, Orange, Virginia

I give special thanks to Thong Le who provided the cover and inside illustrations and Bob Pearsall who provided the maps.

Dedication

This book is dedicated to Robert "Bob" and Doris T. Abraham, who have provided me a lifetime of parental security, encouragement, and support.

Central Virginia and the environs of Orange

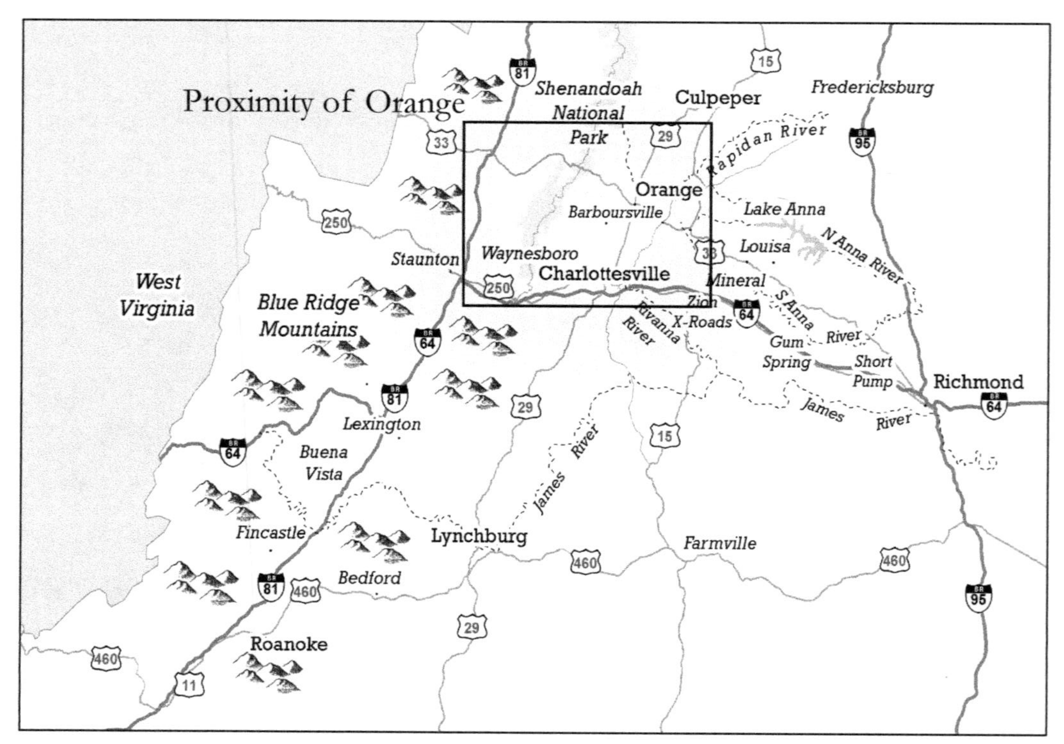

Proximity of
Orange, Virginia

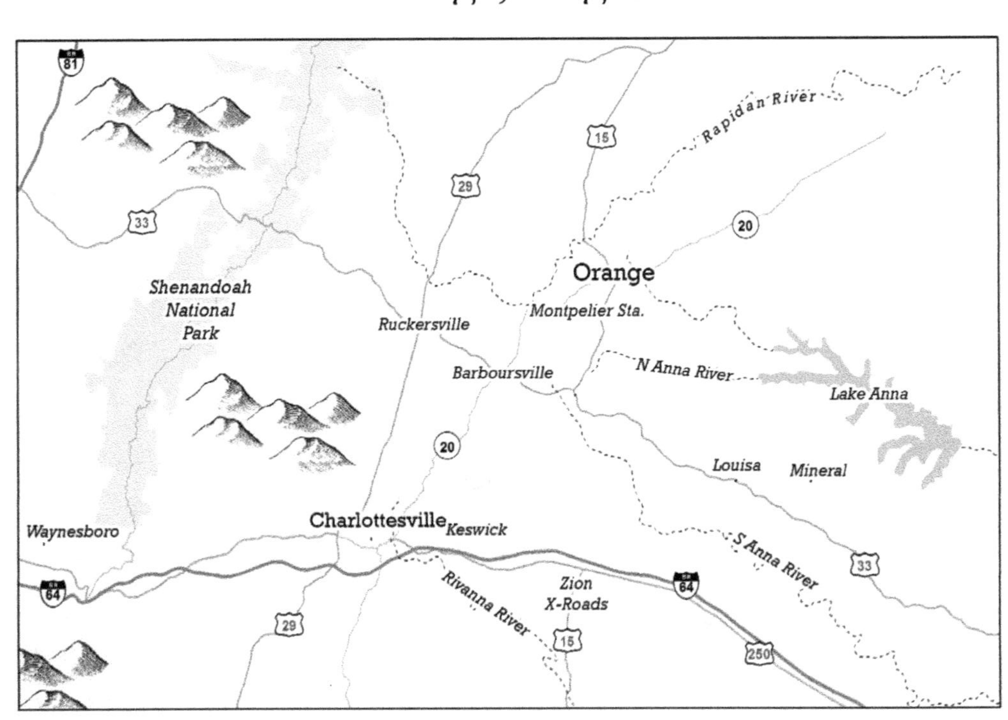

Orange, VA

One

Wednesday, November 1

"It's malignant," Dr. Paula Truesdell informed definitively. Behind her, a raven-haired Asian-featured nurse dropped her chin to her chest and sighed, painfully. The double-paned window in one of the older buildings at the University of Virginia Medical Center rattled in its moldings against the wind where browned leaves danced in the air. "I'm very sorry."

A brilliant red northern cardinal, perched in the tree outside, sang a high-pitched whistle, "Tear. Tear, psssss!"

The afflicted woman, Sally Taliaferro Bradley, took a deep breath and turned to her twin sister, Marjorie Taliaferro. Marjorie grimaced, and said nothing, but her heart felt as though it had been pierced by a dozen swords.

Marjorie spoke next, simply mentioning her name at barely a whisper, "Sally?"

Sally's auburn fading to copper hair, the same as Marjorie's, bounced on the lime-green paper gown, complementing the color nicely. Their hazel eyes met. For several moments, nobody broke the pall of profound dread.

"What's next?" Sally asked her doctor.

Truesdell began describing what would become a lengthy process to rid Sally of the rapacious, monster cells currently multiplying unchecked within her body, plotting a course to eliminate as many as possible and then render the rest impotent. Marjorie's mind wandered to the path that had taken her and her sister to this gut-check moment.

Ten days earlier — or was it eleven? — Sally had called, "Sis, I have a lump." She had done her breast self-exam and found it. Sally said she had just gotten off the phone with her general practitioner and had scheduled an appointment for three days later, on October 24. Both women knew that secrecy was vital to Sally's chances for success in the upcoming election. All those months of twelve- to fifteen-hour days would be wasted if the voters knew that this Democratic candidate for Virginia's Lieutenant Governor was stricken with such a potentially devastating disease. The pundits thought it would be a razor-thin margin anyway, so the sisters vowed to let as few people as possible know.

"If I can just get through Election Day…" Sally pleaded to no one specifically.

"Your health has got to come first," Marjorie yelled, knowing because of her twin's stalwart determination that her admonition might be fruitless. "Do you want me to come down?" meaning to Sally's home in Roanoke.

"I'll get through this one on my own. Then we can go from there."

As the sisters expected, Sally's general practitioner wanted her to see an oncologist. Knowing she didn't have support at home, Sally asked for a doctor at the UVA Center in Charlottesville, closer to Marjorie in Orange. It was the premier cancer center in the state anyway. An appointment was quickly made.

Marjorie's reverie was shaken by the oncologist's ongoing explanation. "… and after we dig out as much as we can, you'll recover from the surgery for a few weeks. Then we'll poison you." The nurse grimaced again, knowing too well the horrors that lay ahead for Sally.

"Poison?" Sally asked.

"Chemo. Chemotherapy is a treatment that involves mainlining some really nasty chemicals that impede the growth of rapidly growing cells."

"Meaning her hair will fall out," Marjorie concluded.

"Yes. The reason we do it is that we can never know we've gotten every cancerous cell. So if there are some, they continue to replicate. You have IDC, invasive ductal carcinoma. That means cancer cells originated in your breast duct but the cancer is now outside the duct into the other breast tissue.

"Your cancer appears to be hot, very active. We get what we can in surgery. Then the chemo attacks the rest, seeking out the malignant cells in your body. Unfortunately, the hair growth cells, the fingernail cells, and your digestive system cells are also fast-growing. So your hair will fall out. And you'll be nauseous. But that's all for later. Surgery is first. We should do this as soon as we can. Given your situation, what do you want to do?"

"Well, how fast is my cancer spreading?"

"Fast. But a few days won't matter. Do you need to get your things in order? It's a relatively routine surgery, but my standard disclaimer is that anything can happen."

"You know I'm running for office, for Virginia's Lt. Governor, right?"

"Yes, I do. How's the campaign going?" the doctor inquired, sympathetically.

"Our polling shows that it will be extremely tight. But that's if nobody knows I have cancer. I suspect thousands of voters don't want a stricken person in a direct successional line for the governor."

"What do you want to do?" Marjorie asked her twin.

Sally looked at Marjorie, then at Doctor T. and said, "Can we wait until after the election?"

"Yes, but not long after. My schedule stays pretty full. I'll send a staffer who will make the appointment with you."

The room was quiet again, anticipatory. Truesdell broke the silence, informing, "There is one more thing I feel compelled to say. There is nothing certain when we deal with cancer. Try as we might, we never really cure cancer. Even if we think it's in remission, it can still come back. Our goal as oncologists is not to cure you, but to keep your cancer at bay long enough to let you die of something else." That said, Truesdell took her leave.

When the staffer arrived moments later, they made arrangements to have the mastectomy done on Monday, November 20th.

Sally got dressed and the twins walked outside into a brisk, dazzling autumn Charlottesville afternoon. "Sit with me for a minute," Sally implored. Sally got into the driver's seat in her late-model Ford Fusion and unlocked the passenger side for Marjorie.

"Thanks for being here."

"Heck, I'm just doin' my job, ma'am," Marjorie quipped

in her best Joe Friday, attempting to inject some levity.

"Cancer!" Sally yelled. "Damn it! Why me? Why now?"

Quiet.

"Here's where we stand," Sally broke the silence. "Our guy looks good for the governorship. Westphall has really turned off a lot of women voters, particularly in the DC area. That loon Brady Pasdon is likely to win the Attorney General race. Can you damn believe anybody would vote for him? He was 'Senator No' in the Senate. And my race is anybody's guess."

Marjorie knew Virginia elected its three top offices separately, as opposed to a single ticket. What lunacy, she thought, that a Governor and Lt. Governor could be from opposing parties. It would be madness if, at the federal level, a Democratic President might be paired with a Republican Vice President, opposing him every step of the way. She wondered if Virginia was the only state still practicing such a regressive system. Nevertheless, she was impressed that her sister was still so focused on her race in the face of such horrific personal news.

"I've never asked, but are your personal affairs in order?" Marjorie ventured.

"When Russ was dying six years ago, we met with our trust attorney. I think everything has been spelled out. Karen is the beneficiary of everything we have, but I haven't heard from her since she stormed out of the house a couple of Christmases ago. For all I know, she's in a commune in Mongolia. I can't think about that now. I've got to get back to the campaign. I already missed three appointments being here, and I can tell them it's for 'personal reasons' for only for so long. People are going to start talking."

"Your secret is good with me," Marjorie said. "Liza and I have two more appointments I told your staff we'd do between now and Tuesday. Then we'll be coming down to Roanoke for the Victory Celebration on Tuesday night. What else can I do?"

"Nothing. I don't know. I'll let you know. Just be there for me."

Marjorie looked hard at her sister, seeing what she always felt was a mirror of herself. Sally was slightly thinner, typically with more makeup. Her auburn hair spilled from a stylish felt hat over her ears, festooned with curly copper earrings. Both women had faces filled with freckles, belying their age. Marjorie's features were more rounded and her nicotine-laced voice was more gravelly. Otherwise, even as their 63rd birthday loomed in February, they looked youthful and people had trouble telling them apart.

"Get out of here and let me go. I've got so much to do; I know you do, too," Sally said, taking a deep breath. "I'm going to beat this thing. I'm not a quitter."

Marjorie smiled a wan smile, bent over and kissed her sister on the cheek, and whispered, "Call me tomorrow. Whenever."

"Will do."

Marjorie exited her sister's car and walked towards her own, speed-dialing Liza Randolph on the way.

"Hey, sweetie," Marjorie's life partner answered. "How's Sally?"

"Bad. Of all the possible outcomes, we got the worst."

"Damnation! I'm sorry I couldn't be there for you both."

"I'm going back to Runnymede," Marjorie reached the door to her Mercedes C250. "Can you come up?"

"Dang, I wish I could," Liza apologized. "These days I don't have time to turn around. I'm taking out an interviewee tonight for that professorship we have open. We have that fund-raiser for Sally on Saturday here in town. Why don't you come to Keswick early and we can go from there?"

Even though Marjorie and Liza considered themselves life partners, Virginia law forbade them from getting married, as many other states were already doing routinely. Nevertheless they still lived apart, with Marjorie at Runnymede Meadow Estate outside Orange and Liza at her family mansion she'd inherited at Keswick, ten miles east of Charlottesville.

Marjorie said she would. She unlocked her Mercedes, sat inside, and lit a Marlboro with the car's lighter. Then she buckled her seat belt and drove into traffic as the afternoon rush hour ensued. Distracted by empathy for her twin, she nearly sideswiped a bicyclist and implored herself to concentrate on her driving. After several drags, she snubbed out her cigarette in the ash-tray and turned on NPR News.

Half-listening to a story about melting ice in the Antarctic, Marjorie drove northeasterly on SR-20, the "Constitution Highway," through Barboursville, past Montpelier Station with its restored segregation era railroad depot, and into the town of Orange. She waved at several people she knew walking Main Street in the quaint, historic town. She passed the Orange Church of the Redeemer whose sign-board proclaimed, "God answers knee-mail!" and she chuckled to herself. She turned left on Spicers Mill Road, headed west, and approached the Rapidan River before turning right onto the long, graveled, tree-lined driveway of her estate.

As she parked and emerged from her car, Boo and Radley, the corgis, scampered out to meet her. The litter-mates were now four, filled with energy and spirit. Boo, the male, was Creamsicle colored, with a rich tan back and mostly white underparts. Radley, the bitch, was tri-colored, with a white center-face, brown around the ears and eyes, a white chest, tan legs, and a black back.

Before she could stop them, they jumped on her navy blue slacks, muddying them. "Bullcrap," she muttered to herself in frustration. "Hey, you two! Let's get you some food." The dogs yipped excitedly. They followed Marjorie inside and filled their muzzles in the matching food bowls as she placed them on the floor.

It was nearing dark and the temperature was dropping by the time the sun began to set behind the distant Blue Ridge Mountains to the west. She fed herself, checked some correspondence, and sent quick love notes to Liza and Sally before showering for bed. It had been a long, emotional day, and she worried about her sister as she fell into a fitful sleep.

Thursday, November 2

Marjorie walked the dogs down the long driveway to get the paper, and returned to fix herself breakfast of fried eggs and potatoes. She had her first cigarette, and then fed the dogs, and they followed her as she went to check on the horses and other animals.

Tank, the youngest of her four Lusitanos, was still a bit lame and she gave him special attention. He was a male yearling, and she planned to geld him soon and needed to ensure that he was healthy. She already had a buyer for him, and he would bring a good profit. She was an astute businesswoman, and between her real estate dealings, her day-trading, and raising horses, she made a fine living.

Scooping out some grain to feed the horses, her mind swept back to her meeting and courtship with Liza and she flushed with emotion and lust.

Marjorie was a member of Orange's Daughters of Dolley Society, a women's historical club named after Dolley Madison, perhaps America's best known First Lady. Liza had been a guest speaker at their quarterly meeting, talking about her descendancy from Paul Jennings, the Madison's house slave who wrote, *A Colored Man's Reminiscences of James Madison*, one of the most impressive works in American history detailing slavery and the Negro experience during the nation's founding.

Liza's African-American blood had been diluted to the point that only a rippling in her dark brown hair indicated her ancestry. The white branch of her family had been extraordinarily accomplished with her grandfather being a Supreme Court justice from North Carolina nominated by Herbert Hoover. Her birthright from her mother's side was the Keswick estate. When Liza and Marjorie met, Liza was Associate Dean at Georgetown Law. Shortly thereafter, Liza won her dream job as Dean of the College of Law at the University of Virginia, and moved back to Keswick.

From the moment Marjorie had laid eyes on Liza at that meeting, she was smitten, drawn to Liza's long legs, expressive fingers, fine high breasts, golden-toned skin hue, and Southern expressions and mannerisms. As it turned out, Marjorie had planned a trip to DC the following week and when she told Liza, Liza invited her to dinner. They made love that evening and had been committed ever since.

When Liza got the job at UVA and made plans to return

to her childhood home, Marjorie was elated to have her lover closer, even if they'd still chosen not to live together, given the sensitivity of their situation and ownership and maintenance needs of their respective estates.

Friday, November 3

After doing her chores, Marjorie went to the Democratic Headquarters for the coordinated campaign in Orange and did phone banking for Sally. From the responses she got, she knew how tight things would be. But the differences between the political parties were like a yawning chasm. It would be an important election for determining the future of the state.

The Democrats of Virginia, in contrast to the Civil Rights era two generations before, were increasingly more inclusive and less racist.

The Republicans, in keeping with national trends, had gotten largely swept away in the anti-government fervor. While both sides agreed that the economy and jobs, as typical, were the greatest motivators of the populace, the Republicans believed that prosperity would come through eliminating regulations and reducing taxes, and in "getting government out of the way," as was their rallying cry, whereas Democrats felt that the economy could best be fostered by investments in roads, schools, and other public services, and didn't mind asking citizens, particularly wealthier ones, to pay for them.

The Republicans were also significantly more conservative regarding social issues including abortion, gay marriage, and gun ownership. Marjorie didn't think any of her lesbian friends were Republicans, but from the yard signs scattered about the neighborhoods and countryside of Orange County, seemingly everybody else was.

Saturday, November 4

By Saturday afternoon, the weather had turned decidedly colder and with the deciduous trees, common in the Virginia Piedmont, shorn of leaves, nature was moving into winter dormancy. Marjorie drove the half-hour trip from her home to Liza's in the early afternoon, enjoying the beauty of US-15, the two-lane "James Madison Highway," to Gordonsville and then SR-231 for the remainder of the thirty-mile route. She used the time to call Sally, hands-free, on the car's cell phone. Sally responded eagerly to her sister, as always, but Marjorie could hear the stresses of the final days of the campaign burdening her voice. Sally reminded Marjorie that she would be at a reception of her own in Alexandria, at the home of Tom Leathers, a popular former governor and current U. S. Senator. Each sister promised to spread regards to attendees at their respective functions.

Reaching Liza's mansion, Marjorie drove through the grand brick entrance pillar topped by marble balusters and listened to the reassuring crunch of her tires on the yellow stones of the driveway. The women went for a walk to the pond into which they threw granular food to watch the fish jump in joyous consumption. They took a nap in each others' arms before showering and dressing for the evening's reception at the opulent Jefferson Country Club.

The lovers drove separate cars to the event, primarily because Marjorie needed to return home afterward as nobody was available to care for the corgis, but secondarily because many people were still not aware of her homosexuality.

She and Liza habitually chose not to enter public functions together and never acknowledged their romantic tie.

The guest of honor was gubernatorial candidate Miller McGregor, Jr., from Richmond. Marjorie was nibbling a mini-quiche when his eyes caught hers, and he motioned her over. "Hello Marjorie! Have you met my wife, Ronnie? Ronnie McGregor, this is Sally Bradley's sister, Marjorie. I'm sorry Marjorie; I have forgotten your surname."

"It's Taliaferro. Hello, Mrs. McGregor. I'm a big fan of yours. I know you'll be a great First Lady."

"Thank you!" Ronnie McGregor then asked, "How's Sally doing with her campaign?"

Marjorie gulped, not knowing if McGregor knew of Sally's cancer. "I spoke with her earlier today. She's fine. She's optimistic. Virginia has never had a female Lieutenant Governor, but she's confident she can win."

"We are, too," the McGregors harmonized.

A boisterous man with a black turtle-neck shirt and a gray jacket burst forth to greet the gubernatorial candidate, and Marjorie retreated. Marjorie did her best to mingle with as many people as possible, knowing the benefit it would have for her sister. Marjorie had always been more introverted; making small-talk with strangers had always been difficult for her. But in addition to her eagerness to help her sister, she knew how high the stakes in the upcoming election were.

She approached a group of three women, railing about the Republican ticket. Liza was one of the three, but a blond woman, short even with high heels, held court. "These guys are maniacs! My granddad was a staunch Republican and worked for the Eisenhower and Goldwater campaigns. These Republicans are nothing like Ike or Barry. They want to turn back fifty years of social progress."

Another, a tall, dignified dark haired woman chimed, "My father was a legal assistant when Loving v. Virginia was fought. A white man was sentenced to prison for marrying a black woman! My state of Virginia, my beloved state, went all the way to the Supreme Court fighting to keep two people from marrying each other."

"Heavens to Murgatroyd," Liza exclaimed with pained exasperation. She looked fondly at Marjorie who was wondering if they'd ever be given the right to tie the knot in their home state.

Marjorie quipped, "What a bass-ackward irony that is!"

The blonde asked, "What?"

"That the case would be brought against a man named 'Loving'!"

Liza introduced her partner to the two other women, Allison Donovan and Zoe Inserra, and indicated that she knew them through her work with Planned Parenthood and Virginia's Rainbow coalition. Donovan was the Executive Director of the Charlottesville Planned Parenthood office and the state President. Marjorie thought Donovan looked familiar, with her angular face and jet-black, shoulder-length hair. Both women were tastefully attired in understated dresses.

Albemarle County Democratic Party Chairwoman Alex Mosby gathered the attention of the attendees and made her welcoming remarks. Then Charlottesville Mayor Jalaj Ramachandran officially welcomed, "Former Mayor of Richmond, Miller McGregor and his lovely wife, Ronnie."

Ronnie, dressed in a elegant blue-on-blue dress with a single-strand pearl necklace said, "I want to thank you for all the support you've given Miller. He has approached this race with the same indefatigable zest with which he does everything. If I don't get to bed by 10:30 p.m. every night, I'm oatmeal the next day. But Miller, I swear, he never sleeps. A week ago Sunday, his staffers insisted that he take one last day off before Election Day. You know what he did? He spent all day raking leaves and cleaning the basement. I've never known a harder worker in my life. I know if the people of Virginia elect him, he'll work tirelessly for them." She spoke about his dedication to their three children and his support for the military, which their eldest had recently joined. Introducing Miller, she gave him a kiss on the lips, transferring some of her gloss to him.

"Ladies and gentlemen, Tuesday is Election Day, and the stakes couldn't be higher. Our beloved state faces a clear choice. Over the past few months, I have been campaigning hard and explaining how stark the differences are between our party and theirs. In three days, this campaign will be over. Virginia will have elected its next Governor, Lt. Governor, and Attorney General. I want to thank our future Lt. Governor Sally Bradley for sending her twin sister, Marjorie Taliaferro, to be with us tonight." He gave her a friendly nod and she waved to the audience. "Representing our next Attorney General Lawrence Willis is his lovely wife Martha." A well-dressed black woman waved from the other side of the room.

"I also want to thank my mother-in-law, Grace Fitzsimmons, who has been traveling with my Ronnie for the past two weeks. Grace is here from Minnesota. Please give Grace a warm welcome."

People applauded.

"My opponent, and I'll only mention his name once," McGregor said, pausing, to the amusement of the audience, "my opponent, Adam Westfall, has made government the enemy. He has surrounded himself with people who believe government is incompetent and have set out to prove it."

There were a few chuckles from the crowd.

"He believes our best days are behind us, and he wants to take us back there. This election says a lot about Virginia's future. It says a lot about America's future. Because Virginia votes in non-Presidential years, America is watching what we do.

"Charlottesville is a red-purple-blue area. Elections are often hotly contested. If we go red, Virginia will likely go red. We cannot let that happen. Every precinct will count. Every vote will count. My opponent and his party will only win if we give this election to them. They want voters to stay home. If Democrats are apathetic, if they think we'll win anyway or their vote doesn't matter, then the other guys will win. Their voters come to the polls reliably and consistently. They count on our apathy, and they will do everything in their power to encourage non-voting on our side.

"Ladies and gentlemen, I want to take Virginia forward! If we are going to face the 21st century as leaders, we must have the best education available. We have to pay our teachers what they're worth. Right now, we're 46th in the nation in teacher pay, but 12th in per capita income overall. That won't get it done! We must have a 21st century infrastructure with roads, airports, and seaports that are the envy of the world rather than public safety risks.

"Most importantly, we must make sure every Virginian has access to quality health care. This will become my signature issue as your Governor. The federal government, as part of its new national health care initiative, has made millions of dollars available to the states to help uninsured people get coverage. This Health-Net program returns our tax dollars that we are paying to the federal government back to Virginia. The new program will put an additional 350,000 people on the health care rolls. How can we face an uninsured cancer sufferer and tell him that we're going to deny him the coverage his tax dollars have paid for? We are ethically and morally bound to act. I will devote every waking hour of my term, if necessary, to getting this done. I promise you, I will not let this legislation die.

"When you go door-to-door and make calls to your friends to get out the vote, remember that it's not just for me. We have an exceptional candidate for Lt. Governor, Sally Bradley of Roanoke! Sally will make a great Lt. Governor. We have an exceptional candidate for Attorney General, Larry Willis from Warrenton. We have a great candidate here in Charlottesville for the House of Delegates, Toddy Smythe.

"I want you to all close your eyes. Yes, right now. I want you to envision waking up next Wednesday morning and looking at the newspaper or the Internet for election results. I want you to think about how great it will feel if we've elected Larry Willis as our next Attorney General! How great it will feel if we've elected Sally Bradley as our Lt. Governor! And I hope you'll be happy if I'm elected the next governor of this great Commonwealth!"

The crowd let out a roar.

"We're down to the wire. If you want these good feelings to be reality, I know you'll work these last few days to make it happen. Make one more phone call for us. Go through your neighborhood and talk with your friends. Elections are won one vote at a time. As they say on the gridiron, leave everything you have on the playing field. We need this win!

Sunday, November 5

Mucking the stalls the next morning, Marjorie was overtaken with giddy irony that one day after appearing in public with some of Virginia's wealthiest and most influential people she was now shoveling horse-shit. Radley and Boo busied themselves running from stall-to-stall, over and through the slats in the stall gates.

Marjorie drove the Kawasaki four-wheeler into the field where she kept Jennings, her stallion, and she dropped a bale of hay from the cart onto the browning November grass. She checked on Gooch, Dawson, and Tank, the yearling she'd soon geld.

Ralph, the goat, was pregnant and would be giving birth to her billy any day.

Monday, November 6

With Election Day the next day, Marjorie did her chores early and then made arrangements with Wilson to care for her animals the next day. Vance Wilson was a late-fifties black man who worked in town at the Orange Body and Transmission Shop. A tall, laconic man with a receding hair line and an easy manner, he rented lodging from Marjorie and lived alone in one of the estate's out-buildings. Marjorie gave him a below-market rental rate in exchange for help with the animals and equipment maintenance. He walked her pastures and enclosures with her as she explained what she wanted done, given that she'd be away until Wednesday afternoon.

Marjorie packed her bags and prepared for her departure

the next morning to Roanoke.

Tuesday, November 7

Marjorie awoke early and carried her bags to the Mercedes in the pre-dawn darkness. She had already voted absentee, so she was free to leave well before the polls opened. The sun rose over her left shoulder as she ascended Afton Mountain driving Interstate 64 towards Staunton and Interstate 81. Coordinating with one of Sally's staffers, Marjorie met her twin sister at a precinct in Salem, a historically Republican stronghold adjacent to Roanoke. They worked all day together, calling on precincts in Christiansburg, Blacksburg, and Roanoke. It was a cold, clear day, and Marjorie was delighted by the beauty of her beloved home state. Her sister's energy seemed boundless, as she eagerly moved from voter-to-voter, volunteer-to-volunteer, asking for support.

By mid-afternoon, both women were exhausted, with hours still yet to go before the polls closed. Marjorie took a nap in the back seat of Sally's SUV in the parking lot of a Blacksburg polling location. Sally took a nap in the passenger seat as a staffer drove them back to Roanoke. The final hours until the election ended at 7:00 p.m. were spent at Roanoke polls.

By 7:45 p.m. the sisters were in the grand ballroom at the opulent Tudor-style Hotel Roanoke for the victory celebration. The crowd was large, festive, and optimistic. Results from some of the smaller precincts around the state were already trickling in.

Liza had driven down after work to join the celebration. Marjorie and Liza spent most of their time glued to one of the many big-screen televisions that were rapidly updating results. Sally, McGregor, and Willis all trailed in early returns, to be expected because Democrats were stronger in the urban areas and the early returns were typically from the rural areas. Nevertheless, Marjorie and Liza were still deeply troubled, and Marjorie felt anxious to the point of being mildly nauseous.

An hour later, momentum began to palpably shift towards the Democrats, but only mildly. Sally took a furtive look at the screen where Marjorie and Liza stood, but quickly brushed off any implications and returned to the crowd.

At 9:27 p.m. CNN reporter Maureen Gilmer came on-screen. "We are now ready to project that Miller McGregor, Jr., will be the next Governor of Virginia. With 78 percent of precincts reporting, Democratic candidate McGregor has received 52.3 percent of the vote. Because the remaining unreported precincts historically vote Democratic, we are projecting that McGregor will win with 53 to 55 percent of the vote over Republican Adam Westfall.

"We are now also ready to project that Republican candidate Brady Pasdon will be Virginia's next Attorney General. Pasdon currently has 55 percent of the vote. While the majority of the remaining votes will likely swing lightly to the Democrats, CNN's election experts expect Pasdon's lead to hold over Democrat Lawrence Willis."

"Darn! Pasdon's dumber than an ox," Liza voiced audibly.

"We still are not prepared to announce a winner in the race for Lt. Governor. Republican Ward Oates is currently leading with 51.3 percent of the vote. Challenger Sally Bradley, a state senator from Roanoke, is expected to close the gap, making this election extremely tight.

"We will now go to Bernard Reach, with the McGregor campaign at his celebration in Richmond. Bernard?"

"Maureen," Reach began, "Miller McGregor is getting ready to take the stage. The crowd is obviously buoyant here." Chants of "Miller, Miller" echoed in from the audience. "Here's McGregor…"

The camera switched to the lectern where a blue and purple sign said, "McGregor, Governor. Working for Virginia." A distinguished man in his fifties whom Marjorie had seen only three days earlier, wearing a dark suit, purple tie, and light-blue shirt, approached while his family, his wife, and his three teenage children, stood behind him. He had a lapel pin with the American and Virginia flags side-by-side. He waved and smiled grandly to the crowd. He said in a hoarse voice, "When we began this journey all those many months ago, it quickly became clear to me that I was never going to be successful in this campaign without you. The generous support from good Democrats and even from moderate Republicans was going to be essential to be victorious tonight. And here we are!"

The crowd erupted in applause. Behind Marjorie, more people gathered to watch. Marjorie saw a huge young man she knew to be Sally's campaign manager, Sam Sebrell, flitting around, with an iPad in his hand. Sebrell was a graduate of Virginia Tech where he'd played lineman on their football team. As large as he was, he resembled the actor who played Harry Potter in the movies, with his youngish looking face and round wire-rimmed eyeglasses.

McGregor continued, "So I thank you all. First, I want to thank my wife and best friend, Ronnie, without whom I'd never be successful. With this fine woman who is my life partner, and with my children who have worked as hard as I have, we have prevailed. I can't be happier to have taken this journey together.

"I am equally proud of the amazing group of campaign workers, paid and volunteer, that has refused to lose. You have called by telephone or knocked on almost three million doors of voters in this great commonwealth. I pledged when I began that nobody would out-work me, but it was your enthusiasm and energy that fueled my efforts. You are wonderful, spectacular."

Grand applause.

"To all of you here," McGregor looked at the camera, "and to all of you watching from around the state, my victory is your victory. Your tireless work has made this possible. I owe you an enormous debt of gratitude. Let me applaud you," he clapped, echoing painfully in the microphone. "From the green mountains of Cumberland Gap to the orchard fields of Winchester to the farms around Danville to the breaking waves at Assateague, thank you for what you've done.

"Finally, I thank our friends across the aisle. Thousands of Republicans across the state were willing to cross party lines and reject the hard-core, ideology-driven agenda of my opponent and embrace the 'Virginia Way,' of congeniality, honesty, and brotherhood. My opponent and I often disagreed, but I commend him for his service to the people of this state and for keeping this election clean and free of the mudslinging we all have come to abhor.

"My opponent, Mr. Westfall, called me a few minutes ago to concede. He was polite and gracious." He looked into the camera. "If you're watching, thank you for your principles and integrity, sir." Returning to his audience, "Mr. Westfall has sacrificed his time and energy to this race and I know how taxing it can be. He has made me a better candidate, and I am convinced he will make me a better Governor. Let us give him a round of applause!" he insisted.

The crowd responded as asked.

"It is humbling beyond words to join the esteemed Virginia Governors before me, an exclusive club that includes immortal leaders like the fiery orator Patrick Henry, James Monroe, James Madison, John Tyler, Edmund Randolph, and Benjamin Harrison. The second Governor of this commonwealth was Thomas Jefferson, perhaps the greatest visionary mind our nation has ever produced.

"We fight our partisan contests like every other state. But when the elections are over, we roll up our sleeves and get to work. Thomas Jefferson devoted much of his inaugural address reassuring Virginians that these differences are not in principle but merely in approach. It's the Virginia Way.

"We all want Virginia to be the best managed state in the nation. We want to be the best state to raise a child. We want to be exemplary for job growth and education. We want to be exemplary in inclusiveness regarding race, gender, or sexual orientation. We want to find innovative ways to protect our children and each other from violence, to reduce the proliferation of weapons of war among everyday citizens. We want to help our fellow citizens who suffer from PTSD and mental illness, and we recognize the vital role of government in that effort. We want everybody in our state to have clean air, clean water, and access to affordable health care. We want to lead, not follow. And we will.

"Before I turn over the microphone to Lawrence Willis, our candidate for Attorney General, I want to shout-out to

Sally Bradley, our candidate for Lt. Governor. Sally is with her supporters over in Roanoke. She has run an amazing campaign, and her vote tally is still too close to call. But if you're listening, Sally, I want you to know that all of us are with you, and we're confident you will prevail."

The audience applauded once again.

"Again, thank you to everyone here, for all of you listening at celebrations across the state, and for all Virginians who voted today and made democracy work.

"Here, I give you Larry Willis."

A young, handsome black lawyer took the stage. Like McGregor behind him, he thanked his wife and his campaign staff. As the loser in the race to be Virginia's Attorney General, he spoke about his gratitude and informed the attendees that he had called the winner, his opponent Brady Pasdon, to congratulate him.

Marjorie glanced at Sally, who had an expression of uncertainty painted on her face. Thinking as always as her sister's mirror, she wondered if her own expression was the same. Sally turned and walked towards the stage, gaining the Hotel Roanoke lectern. Someone switched off the televisions and Sally began to speak.

"Ladies… ladies and gentlemen. Please, may I have your attention? Thank you all for being here and for supporting me."

Applause.

"This has been a long, hard race. Never in my formative years did I envision running for such a lofty office. The good Lord has special plans for all of us, I'm convinced. When my husband died, I unwittingly became his surrogate. He was called to duty and with respect to him and his legacy, that calling inspired me. My candidacy is about him and about you, the voters, especially the women voters.

"You've been watching the election returns as I have. We don't know the outcome. I know it will be very close. In order for me to thank everyone personally, I will remain here as long as you do. But I feel deep inside," she padded her hand against her cancerous breast, "that we won't have a declared winner tonight.

"I have scheduled a press conference tomorrow on another matter. Please join me here at Hotel Roanoke in the Shenandoah Room at 10:00 a.m. as I have an announcement to make."

People in the audience looked at each other for clues, seemingly asking themselves if Sally thought the election would be decided by then. Why schedule a press conference the day after an election?

"Please join me in congratulating Governor-elect Miller McGregor, Jr. and Attorney General Elect Brady Pasdon."

Everyone applauded.

"Good night everyone!" She walked from the lectern and again joined supporters in the crowd.

Marjorie discreetly slipped a spare room key into Liza's hand. Even with such a progressive gathering, by habit Marjorie never showed any romantic connection with Liza or public displays of affection. "See you in a minute," Marjorie said, leaving the ballroom. She pecked her twin on the cheek on the way out and said, "I'm sorry we don't know yet. I'll see you at breakfast."

Marjorie had changed into her pajamas when Liza arrived, offering to massage her before sleep.

Wednesday, November 8

At 6:30 the next morning, three hours drive from Roanoke at the Patrick Henry Hotel in Richmond, Daniel Gold sat in the nude on the floor in the bathroom of Room 326, hugging the antique porcelain commode, vomiting vigorously and repeatedly. Kettledrums pounded in his head, the punishment from his intoxication from the prior evening, at his revelry at the Republican Victory Party. By the time he crashed at around 2:30 a.m., candidate for Governor Adam Westfall had already made his concession speech and candidate for Lt. Governor Ward Oates, was still locked in an undecided race against Democrat Sally Bradley. Gold had served as campaign assistant manager for Westfall in charge of messaging.

Gold's nightmare hangover from hell, his veisalgia, a word that once crossed his mind and stayed, was joined by pangs of aggravation and regret over Westfall's loss, and Westfall's utter failure to follow Gold's aggressive strategies. He retched again, painful bile pouring through his acid-scalded throat.

Finally regaining some semblance of composure, he struggled to his feet. He looked through the doorway towards his askew bed, trying fitfully to remember if when he reached it so few hours before he shared it with anyone, notably the buxom black woman draped in jewelry he'd dallied with earlier in the evening.

Seeing it vacant, his mind flashed back to his ex-wife, Tammy, and his first sexual encounter with her. It was nine years earlier, back when he was a competitive wrestler in the 85 kg (187 lb.) weight class at Penn State. He was in his senior year in Political Science and History, only two months before he was banned from the wrestling program for steroid use.

Tammy was a tall, thin girl, curly blond hair, and was the most passionate sexual animal he'd ever encountered. From that night they met at the Happy Valley Bar on College Avenue in State Park, they romped in his bed or hers almost every night thereafter. He'd always prided himself on his carnal energy, once tupping three different women in one night. But in Tammy, he met his match. She was insatiable.

They moved together to Alexandria, Virginia, the next year. He began his career as a congressional staffer, and she began hers in commercial real estate. Two years after their wedding, while she was scheduled for a conference in New York, he brought a young filly named Heather home with him. They were both lathered up in gin and tonics and the throes of coitus when Tammy arrived home. Much to his surprise, rather than being upset or angry, she quickly stripped and joined them.

Their troikas became regular, to the point where he often returned from work and found Tammy and Heather in bed together. Four months later, Tammy left him for Heather and filed for divorce.

For two years afterward, he took out his frustration by seeking every sex partner he could find. Finally, a scare with an angry ex-boyfriend of one of his lovers cooled his jets, so to speak, and his attention shifted to alcohol. And increasingly, politics. And the mealy-mouthed compromisers and conciliators in his party.

He staggered back to the bathroom, fell to his knees, and threw up again, and again.

Marjorie awoke and went outside for a smoke, watching the Norfolk Southern trains on the nearby track. She returned inside and was in the dining room reading the *Roanoke Star* when Sally arrived. "Good morning," Sally said cheerily. "How'd you sleep?"

"Not that well. Troubled. How about you?"

"Fine," Sally boasted. "I'm strangely elated. I just spent the greater part of a year running for office, and I don't know whether I won or lost. At least it's over. What does the paper say?"

"It says you're behind by 192 votes. There were over 2 million votes cast. That's less than one one-hundredth of a percent. It was a tie."

"So what does that mean?" Liza chimed right in, joining the twins and taking a chair for herself.

Sally said, "It means we have a recount. If the election is less than one percent, the loser can ask for a recount. I think maybe if it's more than a half-percent, the loser has to pay something for it. But I'm sure we'll learn more as this all unfolds."

"Are you down in the dumps?" Liza asked Sally.

"Not at all! As I was telling Marjorie, I'm on cloud nine. I have put a lot into this race, and now it's over. New challenges await, and a new chapter starts right now."

As breakfast was served, Marjorie read aloud. "Virginia voters have elected Democrat Miller McGregor, Jr. as their next Governor, defeating Republican Adam Westfall of Reston.

"Mr. McGregor is former mayor of Richmond and former chairman of the state Democratic Party. Educated at Columbia Law School, he is a founding director of Winston, Byrd, and McGregor. He is considered a moderate.

"Westfall is president of Carthage Industries in Reston. A

former General in the U.S. Army, Westfall had never before run for political office and was a tea party favorite. In the race for Lt. Governor, Republican Ward Oates contested Democrat Sally T. Bradley of Roanoke. As of press time, the race was too close to call, with Oates leading by a mere 192 votes. Any Virginia race closer than 0.5 percent qualifies for an automatic publicly funded recount.

"Mr. Oates is Chief Financial Officer for Freedom University in Lynchburg. He was born and raised in Dayton, Ohio. He earned a BS from the University of Cincinnati and an MBA from the Wharton College of Pennsylvania."

Marjorie took a sip of her steaming coffee, then continued, "Mrs. Bradley is a state Senator from Roanoke, currently principal in the law firm of Bradley, Bradley, and Rivers. She is a native of Orange, VA, and got her BS and JD degrees at the University of Virginia. Mrs. Bradley obtained her seat on the Virginia Senate after the death of her husband, Russell, and she was re-elected, gaining the seat in her own right two years later."

Marjorie smiled proudly at her.

"Brady Pasdon, retired rear-admiral of the Navy from Tappahannock was elected Attorney General with 53 percent of the vote over Lawrence Willis. Pasdon, 51, is from Indianapolis, Indiana. He attended Bob Jones University in South Carolina and the U. S. Naval Academy in Annapolis, Maryland. He worked in naval intelligence."

"He's got a screw loose," Liza quipped. "Does it say he's vehemently opposed to all abortions, even in the cases of rape or incest?" asking neither twin specifically. "Dang it! Does it say he Tweeted his support for a man who shot six bullets through an abortion clinic in Norfolk? Does it say how many of his own millions he poured into his own race? Not to mention the millions more he got from the Craig brothers! Bastard!"

"Settle down, love," Marjorie implored. "His win is no surprise; he was heavily favored."

Sebrell, Sally's campaign manager, entered the dining room, looking tired and worried. "Join us…" Sally offered.

"You're huge," Marjorie concluded, watching the young man approach and addressing him for the first time. "How tall are you?"

"I'm about six-feet, seven-inches tall and I weigh 280, plus or minus a few pounds, depending on what I had for break-fast." He chuckled as he pushed his eyeglasses up his nose. "I used to play football at Tech. Now I'm a competitive weight lifter." Interrupting himself, he turned to Sally and said, "I hate to be rude, but I've got to go. I got a call from mom. My grandma is in a hospital in Little Rock and in hospice care."

"Sam, I'm sorry."

"Thanks. She lived a long, productive life. Sally, it was an honor to serve you. You ran a clean race and you should be proud of yourself."

"You did a good job, too, Sam," Sally reassured. "I'm proud of you, too, and what we did. You go on now. I can introduce myself at my press conference."

"Ladies," Sebrell waved, "I'll be in touch with you in a few days, Sally. Good luck with your announcement."

By this time, back in Richmond, Daniel Gold was begin-ning to sober up. He showered and stood before the mirror with a white towel draped around his waist. In the mirror he saw a man aging ungracefully, with his formerly thick dark hair rapidly receding. His jaws were still chiseled, although less so than in his college days, with puffs of skin under his dark eyes and crows-feet wrinkles forming on the edges. He shaved the day's growth, nicking the unsightly mole growing just beneath his left nostril. It bled, and he stemmed the blood with a tissue, mopping up the spilled fluid on the sink with a white washcloth. He dressed, checked out, and headed for home in the Fan District.

An hour later, Sally stood behind a lectern in a small meeting room with large glass windows to the south, overlooking downtown and Mill Mountain, topped with its eponymous metal star, the world's largest freestanding illuminated man-made star and Roanoke's most prominent landmark. Her twin sister, Marjorie, stood by her side. There were 30 chairs in the room and half were occupied when the clock showed 10:00 a.m. Many in attendance held tiny digital voice recorders and notebooks. Marjorie recognized several as being primary benefactors of Sally's campaign.

"Good morning everyone and thank you for being here," Sally welcomed. "I plan to take just a few minutes of your time this morning. I know many of you worked late into the night, but I assure you you're not seeing double. This is my twin sister, Marjorie."

Marjorie nodded to the audience and did a perfunctory wave. She hated the limelight.

Sally continued, chuckling, "Does anybody know if I won yesterday?"

People giggled, nervously.

"As far as I know, my election against Mr. Oates was a tie. I don't think the State of Virginia wants us to share the seat.

I'm guessing Mr. Oates wouldn't approve."

More giggling.

"I'm sure we'll have a winner in due course. But that's not what I called this meeting for. I have some news to share with you, some unhappy news. I have recently learned I have cancer. Breast cancer. I found a lump a week ago."

Several people in the room raised their hand to their mouth. The fan in the room's ventilation system shut off, and it was quiet, save the outside rumble of a railroad under the gleaming glass pedestrian bridge linking the Hotel to Downtown Roanoke.

"Anyway, I didn't want it to be a distraction during the election. So I waited until today to announce it. If I have won this election, hopefully I'll be back at full strength soon and ready to assume my duties as Lt. Governor. If I have lost, I'll resume my Senate seat. Nothing will really change, I hope. I expect to beat this. I don't give up easily. That's all I had to say this morning. Are there any questions?"

"Arnie Roach, from the *Washington Daylight*," a short, balding man announced. "Did you consider withdrawing from this election?"

"No. The people of my party deserve a candidate. As I said, I hope everything will be back to normal in a couple of months."

"Karen Brislan, from the *Roanoke Star*," a heavy woman with dark, deep-set eyes spoke. "Ma'am, do you have a successor in mind?"

"Excuse me!" Sally snapped, angrily. She paused for a moment, apparently striving to regain her composure. "Again, I expect to beat this. The Virginia Constitution dictates the guidelines we must follow. If I'm not able to do my job, whichever it is, who will succeed me is not up to me."

"Ms. Bradley, I'm Perry McChesney from the *Staunton Daily News*," a bright, slim young man asserted, "Do you have any comment on where you are emotionally after the election?"

She sighed deeply. "Mr. McChesney, this has been an intense time in my life. It's hard for me to put on a happy face when my body is consuming itself from the inside. But that's not what you've asked about. I think we will prevail. I fear for what will happen if the other side wins. I am an optimistic person. But my guess is that my opponent is feeling much the same way. For the past 18 months, I have been consumed by trying to win. Starting right now, I am 100 percent focused on beating cancer.

"That said, I congratulate Governor-Elect McGregor and Attorney General-Elect Pasdon. The voters have spoken. Now, as Virginians, we must all rally behind our new officials and help them be successful."

McChesney followed up, "But if you do win and you're 100 percent focused on your disease, how can you serve the people?"

"Good question, and the people have a right to know. The only answer I have for you now is that I will do the best I can. There's no telling right now how debilitating my disease will be.

"Are there any other questions?"

"Karen Brislan again from the *Roanoke Star*. Ma'am, what happens now with your treatment?"

"I will undergo a mastectomy sometime during the next few weeks. My understanding is that once the healing is complete, I will have chemotherapy. I'm told the chemo is worse than the mastectomy, and unfortunately, it will happen during the next General Assembly session. I will do my best to maintain my commitments and do the job, either of the Lt. Governor or Senator that the voters have decided. I don't mean to be too graphic here, but I love my breasts." She looked downward towards them. "They make me feel like a woman. They nourished my child and they are a part of me. But they are diseased. I am ready to see them go."

The room got quiet as everyone absorbed the lugubrious news. Finally, Sally said, "I want to live my life like that bumper sticker that says, 'Ride it like you stole it.' I was put on earth to raise hell and I'm not done yet."

Sally's quip broke the grim mood and got everybody animated. The meeting ended and the reporters quietly filed out. Liza returned to Keswick but Marjorie decided to stay with Sally for a couple more days. They all checked out of the hotel and Marjorie in her Mercedes followed Sally's Ford back to her Grandin Village home.

Thursday, November 9

As Marjorie finished showering, Sally said she had gotten a call from a State Board of Elections official. "He's on his way here," Sally told Marjorie as she dried off her hair, a big blue towel wrapped around her.

"Now?"

"Yeah."

"What for?"

Sally said, "He wants to explain my situation, I suppose. Mr. Kinsey, he said. Will you sit in on our conversation? I'd like to have a second set of ears to what he says. Sam will want full details when he gets back."

Two hours later, a well-dressed man in a jacket and tie rang the doorbell. He drove a white Dodge Dart with "State of Virginia" tags on it, which he parked under the branches of the leaf-shorn white oak by the curb. Sally let him in, and Marjorie went into the kitchen to make coffee. When she returned, she found him and her sister sitting in the living room before a maple coffee table. He was already in mid-sentence.

"… have occurred before. Back in 2005, in our race for Attorney General, almost 2 million votes were cast and the winning margin was 360 votes. Then in 2013, again for Attorney General, the election had over 2 million votes and the difference was only 543. After a recount, the margin grew to 907 votes, but that's still amazingly close. Mathematically, it's almost impossible. But it happened, not once but twice. And now with your race, it's happened a third time."

"So what happens now?" Marjorie said, placing a coffee pot and three place-settings on the coffee table. "I hope you don't mind my asking. I don't mean to act ignorant, but it's not an act."

Sally laughed at her sister's joke, but Kinsey remained stone-faced.

"There are several phases of vote-counting in Virginia," Kinsey's lecture began. "The first vote count is comprised of the preliminary results on the night of the election. That's the part that has already happened. It is tallied by poll workers at every precinct, and then reported to the city or county voter registrar, who then reports it up to the chain to Richmond. These days, with all votes counted by machine, the early reports are generally accurate and, unless the vote count is close, we get clear winners statewide.

"This is the feed the news people get. Usually it's clear-cut enough to declare a winner. Often the loser calls the winner to concede." He pushed his thick-lens black-frame glasses up his ski-slope nose.

"By the way, if you decide you want a lawyer during this process," he interjected, "I will recite all this to him… or her, again."

Sally said, "My campaign manager went home for a few days. When he gets back, we'll strategize."

"Don't hesitate to ask me back," Kinsey continued, "It's my job. Anyway, the second phase is what is referred to as the 'canvass,' which is mandatory regardless of the initial outcome. It has begun already. The voter registrar and the three members of the electoral board in each locality meet, typically at a courthouse or government center to review the physical voter results tapes from each machine and to certify at the local level that the numbers their locality reported to Richmond were accurate. Both major parties may have an observer in the room for this process. Provisional votes in green envelopes are scrutinized and either counted or discarded. They generally were cast by people who failed to produce proper identification at the polls.

"Often in this phase, Richmond will receive new numbers from some localities. This is due to human error on election night. People have been working long hours and everybody is tired. With hundreds of precincts, these minor shifts can add up."

"Does this ever change outcomes?" Sally wanted to know.

"We had a situation in Henry County in the last presidential election," he recalled, "where an official left out a digit that cost a candidate 800 votes. So mistakes are rare, but of course they do happen.

"The third phase is the certification of results by the State Board of Elections. This is the point at which winning candidates are formally certified." He spooned in some sugar and took a sip of his coffee.

"The fourth phase is optional, the 'recount'. If the final results of an election are within 1 percent of each other, the losing candidate may ask for a recount within 10 days of certification of results. If the margin between the two candidates is between point-five percent and one percent, then the losing candidate must pay for the cost of the recount at a rate of $10 per precinct. If the margin between the two candidates is less than half a percent, then the state pays for it."

"So for my election," Sally interrupted, "a recount will be automatic."

"That's right," he reiterated. "Numbers in some localities can change, most often if they are relying on older optical scan ballots. The new touch-screen systems cannot ever really give a different answer than before. The only way we see discrepancies is in the event of a transcription error by the election official.

"Optical scan ballots can give a different result because sometimes the machine 'sees' differently than before. If so, the ballots can be visually inspected by the voter registrar and the electoral board to make individual assessments on the voters' intended candidate choice. So there can be small shifts in the totals here, too."

"Wow!" Marjorie exclaimed. "Complicated!"

"Yes, but there's even more," he persisted. "There is a little-known state law that allows a loser to ask the legislators to decide an election or to even call for a new one if voting irregularities can be substantively alleged."

"Again, I hate to be ignorant, but is there a Reader's Digest version?" Marjorie asked, again one-upping her sister, the candidate.

"Well, since we know the difference is within point-five percent there will be a recount. My office has set a tentative date of December 13 to begin. It takes some weeks to make arrangements. We'll know the winner within a week from that."

Sally asked, "What should I do in the meantime?"

He wiped his brow and said, "I understand you have some other issues to deal with. I read about your illness in the paper this morning. I cannot give you counsel, but if I were you, I would get a good doctor, have your campaign staff hire a good lawyer, and concentrate on getting healthy."

"Thank you, Mr. Kinsey. Thanks for driving all the way here to explain this."

"You're welcome. Best of luck."

As he put on his coat to prepare to depart, he complimented, "My job requires impartiality, but for what it's worth, you ran a great race."

"Thanks," Sally smiled.

Later that afternoon, Sally told Marjorie that she had an overdue obligation to a family member. Russ's sister, Selena Jewett, lived nearby in Fincastle. Jewett was also a widow and Sally had learned a few weeks earlier that she had been diagnosed with uterine cancer. "I haven't had the chance to visit with her, what with the election and all — I've barely had the chance to think about her. I'm going to drive up there. Do you want to go with me?"

The two women made the 20-minute drive together in Sally's Ford. Selena met them at the door where they exchanged hugs. "Please, come in!" Selena said excitedly.

Selena brought some herbal tea and peanut butter cookies. She began describing her ordeal in detail. Marjorie noticed how empathic Sally seemed, a quality that always impressed her, especially now that Sally was a politician. Marjorie knew, of course, that Sally was also likely to face many of the same challenges.

"I'm undergoing radiation now," Selena said. "They shoot at me with an x-ray machine."

"I thought they used implants these days," Sally offered.

"Sometimes they do, but for whatever reason my oncologist decided on external-beam treatment. I don't feel a thing, of course, when the treatments are happening. But I'm having nightmares about radioactivity shooting into my coochie garden."

The Taliaferro twins laughed at Selena's unexpected slang.

"Radiation is the strangest thing in the world. You can't see it. You can't smell or taste or feel it. The only way you know it's happening is that someone tells you. It's eerie how people scatter like I've got leprosy when they turn it on. Anyway, this goes on for a few more weeks. Then I'll do chemotherapy for awhile. I'm getting my treatments at UVA Medical Center."

"So will I!" Sally exclaimed. "Maybe we'll get our chemo treatments together!"

Marjorie added, "I live just up the road near Orange. It's about 45 minutes from UVA. Please call on me if you need anything."

Just then, the door opened and a small, well-built man in his early thirties entered. He wore a flannel shirt and jeans.

"John," Selena exclaimed, "Sweetie, come say hello."

"Hi Aunt Sally," he hugged her.

"Jack, do you remember my twin sister, Marjorie?"

"Yes, ma'am. It's been a long time, Marjorie." He extended his hand to shake hers, but she hugged him instead.

"How are things with you?" Sally asked.

"Hectic, as you can imagine."

Marjorie interrupted, "What do you do, Jack? Or is it John?"

"In the family, I'm 'John', but lots of friends call me 'Jack'. I'm a trooper; a state policeman. I'm the Governor's driver."

"Really?"

"Yeah, really. Somebody's gotta do it. After I left the Navy in '08, I joined the Virginia State Police. I was driving admirals around in the Navy so Uncle Russ helped me get the job as the Governor's chauffeur. It's a big, black Cadillac SUV."

"What do you think of the current Governor?" Marjorie asked, pryingly.

"Marjorie!" Sally snapped at her sister for her impertinence.

"It's okay," Jewett shrugged. "I'm really not allowed to have an opinion, or at least voice an opinion, on the man I work for. Let me just say that I have always been a Republican. Dad was an Eisenhower Republican, and I have always valued the ethic of responsibility and fiscal conservatism that General Eisenhower talked about."

Sally noted, "Eisenhower seemed to be the type of president everybody appreciated."

Selena agreed, "I think so, too. He was a war hero, but he never forgot his roots. He was a man of the people."

Jack continued, "He believed that government should not reward laziness or guarantee a free ride, but yet believed in the expansion of social security, improved housing, and health protection for everybody.

"I really feel like the party has become a soup sandwich. It's been taken over by radicals," the young man continued. "Government needs to work for the people and provide reasonable regulations to protect people and the environment and make sure commerce is fair and competitive. I can't say who I voted for yesterday, but I'm glad Mr. McGregor won. I hope he'll keep me on as his driver. I hope you won, too, Aunt Sally. I think I can say I voted for you. Do we know yet?"

"No, Jack. There will be a recount; we'll know in a few weeks."

Selena wandered into the kitchen to prepare another cup of tea for John. While she was gone, he admitted to Sally and Marjorie that he was trying to spend more time with his mother, given her illness. He understood how serious her condition was.

When Selena returned, he cut off his thoughts in mid-sentence. Sally asked Selena a question that startled Marjorie with its directness. "What are your chances?" Marjorie knew by "chances" Sally meant "survival chances."

"I don't think I'll survive this," Selena admitted ruefully. "I think I brought on my cancer myself."

"Excuse me?" Marjorie couldn't believe her ears.

Selena took a sip of her tea. A chime echoed from the grandfather clock in the hallway. "My husband, Ralph, died three years ago. He was in an accident. He was associate pastor of our church. He and the pastor were driving eight kids in the church van to a meeting in Knoxville. They never even made it to the Interstate. A drunk driver ran a red light at Trinity Road. They had just filled the van with gas. The drunk driver's car ricocheted away, but their van was smashed into a power line pole where the gasoline exploded. It killed all ten of them, charring their bodies so badly that they had to be identified by dental records. The only survivor was the drunk driver, whose car bounced away. He served a year in jail for vehicular homicide and was released. I heard last month that he'd caused another accident."

The room was quiet for a moment before Selena continued, "God left me a few days after my Ralph died. I was sitting in church a week after the memorial service. I had always lived my life in Christ. My upbringing, my family life, my entire existence, has been about my faith in my Lord Jesus Christ. I had always identified myself as a faith-based person. I grew up with that identity, as a believer. I took comfort in the platitudes. 'God is always with you.' 'God will never give you more hardship than you can handle.' 'God loves you and will never forsake you.' Until that moment, I was a positive person, happy with my position in life, fixed on the rock.

"I sat on that pew that day and a river of tears flowed from my eyes. There was literally a puddle in my lap. I wept in sadness over the loss of my Ralph. But more than that, I wept in sadness of the loss of my faith. Why would a loving God do this to Ralph, to those children and their families, and to me?

"From that moment, those platitudes that had given me comfort before rang hollow and empty. God was not with me. God did not love me. God did indeed forsake me. My prayers were never again to be answered. I didn't know it then, but in hindsight it is clear to me now; I began the process of dying that moment. The person I had been died that day on that pew. The cells in my body, in the heart of my womanhood, began their pestilential quest to destroy my body. My uterus, which once had provided my greatest joy, the young man you see here," she winked at John, "at that moment began the process of devouring me.

"That drunk driver annihilated not only my fine and beloved husband, but the foundation of who I was. At that moment, I knew that God wasn't going to be with me or be there for me ever again. I didn't even know if God existed. I think many of the families of those killed were shaken as well. Many might be on their way back to Christ. But I knew there was no coming back for me." She took a small bite of a cookie and continued, with nobody else saying a word. "From my birth until that day, I had always been on the path of living. From that day forward, I began the path of dying. I was teaching English and composition at Hollins. It was mid-semester, but I went in the next day and resigned."

In Marjorie's mind, the woman was amazingly stoic, but Sally's eyes were teary.

"If my doctor doesn't tell me soon that the cancer cells are losing, I will stop my treatment and succumb."

Marjorie felt an empty place inside.

Selena continued, "There's another aspect of this that rocks me to the core. I always believed in heaven and hell. I believed that if I lived a good, righteous life, I'd go to heaven. Now I don't believe in either. Now I believe in nothing, that when I die there is no afterlife."

For many moments, the room was as quiet as a funeral home. Sally's right hand covered her eyes and she sighed. Marjorie sniffled and wiped a tear of depression from her cheek. John quietly left the room.

"I never thought I'd say this," Selena confided, "or even

think it. But strangely I'm okay with the notion that if this cancer kills me, there is nothing that follows."

The sisters stayed for another hour, consoling the stricken woman, and then drove back to Roanoke. Dark clouds loomed over Tinker Mountain, and it rained hard their last few miles down I-581 through downtown, hard enough to obscure their view of Mill Mountain Star. Marjorie's heart rested as heavily as an anvil, weighing Selena's admission of her abrogation of her spirituality. Marjorie glanced at her afflicted sister, unable to find the proper words to ask how Selena's conversion affected her.

Friday, November 10

Before noon the next morning, Marjorie was back on the road to Orange. It was a beautiful, cold, clear, crisp day. Clouds hung to the Blue Ridge Mountains paralleling Interstate 81 northward, distant in the view out her right-side window. Several red-tailed hawks sat placidly on telephone lines alongside the superhighway, waiting for animals to be rousted.

Radley and Boo were excited to see her, jumping at her and yapping. She sorted through her mail and went to feed the other animals. She filled the food dispenser for her barn cats, Hobbes, Cavendish, and Priestley, named for English philosophers Thomas Hobbes, Margaret Lucas Cavendish, and Joseph Priestley.

Like many of her neighbors, Marjorie kept what everybody called "barn cats" to keep the rodent population down. She balanced the benefit of having them kill mice, rats, moles, and other small mammals against the drawback of occasional bird kills. She never kept more than three at a time and always kept them neutered.

Hobbes and Cavendish were given to her as kittens. Hobbes was the largest of the three, and the only male, was a lovely gray stripped tabby. Cavendish was a petite predominately white calico with a sweet face and disposition. A standoffish feline, Priestley was a sleek, solid black cat, with haunting green eyes who took up at the barn and liked the accommodations, so stayed. When Priestley arrived, Marjorie thought she was a male, and named him appropriately, only to learn when she trapped him to take him to be spayed that she was a female.

Marjorie loved cats, but could not have them in the house, as she had become allergic in her adult years. Having them in her barn was the perfect way to have them in her life and enjoy them.

Her cats always greeted her with a chorus of meows and purrs, and showing their affection and appreciation by rubbing against her legs. Due to her allergy, she refrained from petting them.

The cats seemed to have a love/hate relationship with the corgi twins. They kept to the barn, seemingly knowing that the house was for the dogs and the barn was for them. Occasionally the dogs, especially Radley, would attempt to play with the cats, but only Hobbes would reciprocate, and only for fleeting moments.

Coyotes had increasingly made their way into the forests and farms of Virginia, so Marjorie was careful to ensure that the cats were safely inside each evening.

She was happy being home.

After fixing herself a hamburger and brown rice for dinner, she tidied up the kitchen. Sally called her to say that she had met with her doctor again as previously arranged, and reminded her the surgery was scheduled for a week from Monday, on November 20, in Charlottesville.

Marjorie sat down with a Marlboro and a glass of Merlot and read the *Richmond Reporter* article about Sally's cancer and wondered what lay ahead. She found similar articles in the other paper, *Charlottesville Guardian*, a semiweekly she subscribed to.

Saturday, November 11

Danny Gold drove his old black Hyundai westbound on Cary Street towards the exclusive Country Club of Virginia, on his way to a luncheon provided by Adam Westfall, his former boss and recently vanquished candidate for Governor of Virginia. He pulled into the circular driveway in front of the grand 6-story brick building and left his keys with the valet. He adjusted his tie while walking inside and sat at a table with Jorge Ortiz Gonzalez, Courtney Templeton, and several Republican campaign staffers he didn't know. A plate with rounded scoops of chicken salad, egg salad, and coleslaw awaited him.

Westfall introduced Clay Andrews, a preacher from nearby Chesterfield County, who gave a benediction. As the minister blessed the food and the people who prepared it and served it, Danny's mind smirked, wondering if the blessing would eventually encompass the chicken as well. The skin on his forearms prickled when Andrews extolled, "… in Jesus' name we pray. Amen."

Gold's table mates spoke of the weather and the recent big win by the local University of Richmond football team over cross-town Atlantic 10 conference rival Virginia Commonwealth University the week before. Some spoke of upcoming plans. It infuriated Gold, who seethed over the lost opportunity Westfall had, in his mind, squandered. Gold had fed Westfall plenty of dirt to use against McGregor. But instead of playing the no holds barred game that modern politics demanded, Westfall had played like he was on a girl's badminton team. Westfall rose to speak, but his words only infuriated Gold more. Conciliation. Compromise. Humility. "I want to thank all of you who worked so hard for me during my campaign," he mused. "We ran a campaign we can all be proud of."

Bullshit, Danny mumbled to himself, leaving hastily after the closing prayer, eager to hide his frustration from the others. The battle was just beginning, he convinced himself, unable to concede victory to the mealy Democrats. Republicans don't play to lose.

He drove off, contemplating his next move. With the campaign over and his boss a loser, he was technically unemployed. Campaigns were in his blood, but he didn't think he could stand to lose another one.

Sunday, November 12

Marjorie awoke to a steady rain, one of those cold November rains that makes every bone ache with chills. She threw her raincoat over her shoulder and walked the driveway to get her newspaper. Within seconds, she was shivering; she always felt that rain was colder than snow because rain could seemingly penetrate even waterproof materials.

The *Richmond Reporter*, with its typical conservative stance, always rankled her. But she had subscribed anyway once her brother-in-law and sister became politically active state-wide. Leaving her raincoat on a peg in the mud-room, Marjorie sat on a kitchen stool to drink her coffee. She removed the paper from its protective green plastic bag and turned to the opinion page, where what she found almost made her drop her coffee cup. It read in big letters.

Bradley must withdraw

Sally Taliaferro Bradley announced last week, the day after Election Day, that she has cancer. Clearly, she had known about her impairment before the election, and in not withdrawing has deliberately deceived the voters of Virginia.

The editorial went on to explain how the election result was still unknown and that election officials would be unable to prevent her from taking office if the results indeed proved her the winner over her opponent, Ward Oates.

Virginia clearly needs a full-time Lt. Governor, not somebody whose focus should rightfully be on herself. Win or lose the recount, she must concede the election to her opponent.

Marjorie could feel her blood boil. She speed-dialed Sally on her smart phone. "Did you see it?"

"What? The *Reporter* editorial. Yeah."

"Well?"

"Well what?"

"Are you going to concede?"

"No. Hell no," Sally ranted.

"Can they force you?"

"Well, the newspaper can't. But, there is a provision where the General Assembly can kick out a Governor or a Lt. Governor if they deem him or her unable to perform the duties of the office. But McGregor will cover my back," Sally reassured. "I spoke with him yesterday and he said so. Regardless, I might not win, in which case it's all a moot point, isn't it?"

"Sis?"

"Yeah?"

"Are you okay?" Marjorie sighed.

"I'm fine. Politics can be a vindictive game. But my expectation is that cancer will be a fiercer enemy than the Republicans."

Marjorie didn't know what to say. Sally broke the silence, "Margie, do you mind if I come to visit? Sam has turned me loose for a few days while they monitor the Electoral Board's work. I'm mentally exhausted. I'd just like to be on the farm for some R&R. Wednesday okay?"

Danny Gold's synagogue attendance had dropped off during the campaign, but he was resolved to get back on track. He sat in the pew at the Beth Shalom Synagogue of Richmond by himself, desperately trying to focus on the rabbi's exhortations, while constantly daydreaming.

His religious education never had a beginning. He was born in Woodmere, New York, on Long Island. When he was three and his sister was nine, the family was uprooted to the Upper Peninsula Michigan city of Houghton, on the Keweenaw Peninsula, where his father took a job with one of his uncles in a clothing store. There were no more than ten Jewish families in the entire city.

Hockey was king and frigid cold was the dominant theme. In being one of the coldest, snowiest places in the country due to its extreme northern location and the lake-effect moisture from Lake Superior, residents joked that Houghton had two seasons: winter and preparation for winter.

In Danny's sophomore year in high school, the store went out of business. His sister had left years earlier, at age 17, amidst allegations of sexual abuse at the hands of their father. After an extended unemployment, his father moved the family downstate to Ann Arbor where he took the only job he could find, a poorly paying stint at the University of Michigan library. His father died two years later. Danny finished high school in Ann Arbor, and when he left to attend college in Pennsylvania, his mother returned to Houghton.

Danny, owing to his rural Yooper upbringing, was constantly berated and taunted by the ubiquitous blue and gold clad local boys. He grew three inches and gained 40 pounds, and took up wrestling, shooting, drinking, and womanizing, the four areas where he found greatest personal satisfaction. He played a little tennis.

Rabbi Hershel Billet stood behind a large, wooden pulpit. He was in the midst of a sermon on justice and community service when a family of four entered, late, and sat one row ahead and to the left of Danny.

Danny's eye turned from the bald, white-robed rabbi with the red yarmulke seemingly glued to the back of his skull, to the family. The woman was a dark-haired beauty, tall and elegant, with a pale blue dress and high heels. Behind her followed two children. The girl was a mere late-teen, but she was striking! She sat beside her younger sister, nearest him. Danny's attention moved from mother to the elder daughter, where his gaze intensified.

He studied her libidinously, the peach-fuzz of vellus hair on the edge of her cheek, the gentle jut of her cheekbone, and the curving bobs of her jet-black hair draping over her white woolen vest. A pinkish gloss accentuated her lips. He was transfixed! Was she eighteen? – sixteen more likely; jail bait. Ah, but the purity of her young skin! He pictured her emerging muliebrity. Surely she was still a virgin. Had she ever climaxed or did she even know what an orgasm was? Were her breasts still developing and how might they feel under his fingertips? Would they feel sweaty? Would her nipples rise at his touch, at his gentle pinch? How would she smell if aroused? He sniffed at the air, sensing the smorgasbord of perfumes and colognes wafting from the people around him.

She felt his stare and turned her head slightly, drifting her eyes towards him and fashioning a modest smile. Gosh, she was bewitching! He became aroused and he shivered and squirmed in his pew. She looked away again, but his gaze continued, mesmerized.

"Where are we today?" Rabbi Billet implored. "According to a recent survey, only 30 percent of Jewish respondents acknowledged membership in a synagogue. Facts are facts. Locally and nationally, synagogue life is struggling…"

Danny's eye was drawn back to the girl and his imagination romped; he was mesmerized, spellbound. She was pure, taut, and velvety. Modest, undefiled, and lovely! Oh, what her nudity would look like!

Rabbi Billet continued, finishing his sermon and then saying, "Please rise. Let us turn to page 88 in our hymnal and sing together, JUDGE NOT.

All-seeing God, It is thine to know
The springs from where opinions flow
To judge from principles within
When frailty errs and when we sin.

As they sang, the girl's father, sitting beyond her, and her mother, felt Danny's stare as well. The father was a well-dressed, serious looking man with a fine, shaven face and thick tufts of dark hair. He stared back at Danny and scrunched his face angrily, disapprovingly. Danny's gaze returned to his hymnal. As the song concluded and the parishioners returned to their seats, Danny moved towards the distant aisle and walked briskly away and then outside to his car, his schlong annoyingly rubbing against his pant-legs.

Monday, November 13

Marjorie parked her Mercedes in a paid lot off the downtown mall in Charlottesville and walked the brick pedestrian-only Main Street past street vendors and late-season outdoor diners to the Mainly Curry restaurant entrance. She snubbed her Marlboro in a sand-bucket and walked inside where she found Liza, poking away at her iPad, waiting for her.

"Hey, sweetie," they hugged. They perused the menu and ordered from a young, disaffected woman who had a lower lip pin, a pierced nostril, a tattoo of a scorpion on her neck, and purple hair. The pierced woman brought them goblets filled with red wine.

"I'm stoked," Liza announced, bringing her lover up to date on her work at UVA. "One of our alumni recently gave us a substantial gift. We have a couple of professors who have written books that are being well-received by general audiences and the profession."

Marjorie watched Liza's long fingers draw sweeping arcs in the air, accentuating her excitement.

"…and I think McGregor will be a great Governor," Liza continued. "Just when I fear the imbeciles, the climate deniers, the fundamentalists, and the neo-Confederates are going to take over and send us back to the days of Reconstruction, the voters came through for me. Maybe we're on the right track after all."

"I saw a Confederate flag on my way here," Marjorie rued. "Whenever I do, which is pretty often since one of my neighbors insists on flying one all the time, I think how tragic it would be if the Confederacy had won."

"I think about it often, too," Liza agreed. "Criminy! What would have been the fate of my family? You can't replay history; what happened, happened. But you can't help but wonder."

"I know." Marjorie took a sip of wine and then returned her goblet to the table. "The crazy thing is that the Confederates never needed to win in order to win. They just needed not to lose, to convince the Federalists to give up. I had a conversation years ago with my grandfather who was from Illinois. He said, 'My great uncle was in the Civil War. He lost an arm at Shiloh.' I can't imagine what would have made him fight to what could have been his death just to keep the damn Southerners in the Union. 'Hell, let 'em go!' We might still be two countries today, and Virginia would be in the Confederate States of America."

As the waitress brought their steaming, redolent entrées, Marjorie was struck by the turn of events which had put her in the modern world of downtown Charlottesville opposite the part-African woman she loved, with a glowing iPad on the table alongside a battery-powered flickering light, while a mere few generations earlier, her countrymen were fighting and dying to ensure that Negroes would be forever enslaved and impoverished on the plantations in her beloved Virginia.

Tuesday, November 14

Marjorie woke in Liza's arms in her antique canopy bed at the Keswick estate. She had a quick breakfast of granola and yogurt before heading home to Runnymede. It was a windy, overcast day, and the rows of grape vines, bereft of leaves, strung from hidden wires, reminded her of mini-crucifixes, stretching across the gentle landscapes.

Her chores consumed the remainder of the day.

Wednesday, November 15

Danny Gold was already ruing his decision to travel back to Houghton to visit with his mother. It had been two years since he'd seen her, and his sister, now in Albuquerque, had informed him that she wasn't doing well. He never understood why his mother had returned to Houghton from Ann Arbor. It was almost as if she wished to punish herself… or separate herself from the unpleasant memory of his father's passing, downstate.

Flying between minor airports like Richmond and Green Bay was always inexplicably expensive, and had he not made the reservation six weeks earlier, he would never have gone. He emerged from the airplane in Green Bay into an Arctic blast of wind and blowing snow, the region's first storm of the year. It was already 4:30 p.m. when he secured his rental car and hit the road, with four-and-a-half-hours of dark, cold driving awaiting him.

It was nearing dinner time when Sally arrived during a sleet storm. Marjorie had invited Liza to join them for dinner. Marjorie made pesto noodles and sausage, Sally's favorite dinner. The pesto sauce came from the freezer, made from basil grown in the summer garden three months earlier.

"I love this dinner," Sally proclaimed, twisting green-stained noodles around her fork. "It has the four basic food groups."

"Yeah?" Liza asked.

"Yeah. Pesto, Parmesan, Merlot and 'filler'!"

"Filler?"

Marjorie interjected, "That would be everything else."

Everyone laughed. The women spoke not a word about either politics or cancer through dinner, and Sally went to bed early.

Marjorie and Liza fell asleep in the spoon position, their bodies close, warm, and damp from their lovemaking.

Thursday, November 16

Danny awoke to the fresh smell of coffee. He rose, stroked the crunchy deposits from the corners of his eyes, and shaved his two-day beard at his mother's bathroom sink he was sure she hadn't cleaned since the last time he visited. He made his way into the kitchen of his mother's small apartment. Any fantasies that his mother's infirmities, whatever they were, would soften her crusty personality were quickly dashed. Within minutes, her pretentiousness and affectations were grating on him, and he regretted the trouble and expense he'd made to visit.

Sally returned the cooking favor to her twin and her lover the next morning, making blueberry pancakes, served with soft crème cheese and Highland County maple syrup. Liza left to head back to work in Charlottesville and the sisters went to the barn to tack up two of the Lusitanos: Gooch, the mare, and Dawson, the gelding. She left Jennings, the stallion, and Tank behind.

They warmed the horses with a walk, then a trot, then alternating trot and canter. Marjorie deftly opened and closed gates while staying aboard. Marjorie was impressed by Sally's natural riding skills, especially knowing Sally's saddle time had been limited in recent years. It was cold. The rain had quit but icy tentacles still hung on the trees and shrubs. A white-tailed deer bounded away through the woods. Marjorie wondered about the intricacies of evolution, where a prey animal would have evolved with a waving flag on its rump.

The twins and their steeds slowed to a walk and dismounted to explore at the old slave cabin where they had spent so much time in their childhood.

The cabin was unheated, and it had no water supply. But during one of the many reconstructions, windows had been added and the wooden floor had been reinforced and stabilized. Even with no heat inside, it was much warmer than outside, and there was a pot-bellied stove in the center if additional warmth was ever desired. Marjorie made a mental note to return as soon as she could to repair the sagging door and to re-attach the wooden gate.

They re-mounted and continued their romp through the fields. They entered the woods and rode an old Indian trail where on several occasions they needed to bend over to clear low-hanging branches. The woods were wet and icy but beautiful in winter's browns. White-crowned sparrows flitted in the low shrubs, sporting the distinguishing black-and-white zebra stripes on their heads. The horses chuffed along willingly, twin vapor streams puffing from each steed's nostrils. Marjorie never grew tired of feeling equine power underneath her.

They emerged in their favorite childhood haunt, a fertile dell, near the River Thames, or factually the Rapidan River, but they liked to think of it as the Thames, for make-believe authenticity. They'd always known the place as Eghamshire at Runnymede Meadow. As teenagers, they realized with hilarity that the "mede" in "Runnymede" meant "meadow," thus the estate was "Runny meadow-meadow." They used the name Eghamshire for the dell because they thought it was a satirically comical, English-sounding place.

As children, and with the help of their father, they had built a tiny stage and audience area where they could play-act. There were still several poles planted into the ground where torches could be affixed for evening performances. There were a large, wooden, hand-hewed, weather-beaten table and several wooden chairs.

Even when friends came, they took them on a circuitous, purposefully confusing route so it could always remain their special hide-away. Marjorie had lost her virginity there at age 17, to a boy, the first and only heterosexual encounter of her life. In spite of the closeness she shared with her twin, she had never confessed. She decided to tell Sally about it, and Sally remembered the boy, and that she had never liked him. Both laughed heartily at the admission. Sally recounted her first sexual encounter in a dorm room at UVA the following year with a rugby player.

They stayed and ate the lunch they'd packed of pastrami on rye, sitting on the wooden chairs. The sun had broken through the clouds and the ice was melting rapidly. An osprey dove to catch a fish from the river, adjusting it in flight before returning to the branch of a large, barren, sycamore tree with a skeleton-white-trunk. A great blue heron walked the shoreline, fishing, seemingly oblivious to his competitor overhead. Marjorie smoked a Marlboro, and Sally scolded her for it.

Several times, Marjorie thought about her sister's affliction, feeling sympathetic. And guilty. Weren't twins supposed to share everything? Marjorie was the smoker, but Sally got cancer. What a cruel irony!

When Sally closed her eyes and pointed her face to the sun to catch all its warming rays, Marjorie was taken by how beautiful and youthful she looked. She wondered if Sally's disease would rob her of both. She felt a deep, visceral, permeating dread that while this day was perfect, the days to come would likely bring unprecedented pain and challenges for Sally and vicariously for herself.

Friday, November 17

By noon, Danny was on the road, headed back to Green Bay. He had planned to stay for five days, but an old high-school buddy had broken a date to go deer hunting and his mother was driving him crazy.

The airport in Green Bay was overwhelmed with green and gold-clad fans of the Packers, preparing for the drunken revelry that was officially a football game two days hence. He chuckled at the expression he'd often heard, that Green

Bay was a drinking town with a football problem. Green Bay was the NFL's least populated host city where the team was owned not by one or two millionaires but by 350,000 fans. Sports teams were often moving around: the Lakers moved from Minneapolis to Los Angeles where there are no lakes, the Cardinals moved to Phoenix where there are no cardinals, and the Jazz moved from New Orleans to Utah! But the Packers would never leave Green Bay because the fans there owned them.

He paid a premium to have his ticket changed and boarded two hours later. The 737 jet bounced harshly in the cross-wind leaving the runway, and Danny was sick the entire flight to his connection in Chicago. He wasn't in bed in Richmond until after 2:00 a.m.

Saturday, November 18

After finishing her chores, Marjorie drove westward to the nearby Shenandoah National Park for some hiking. Liza had planned to go with her, but cancelled at the last minute due to a sore foot. Marjorie decided to go anyway, even if alone.

Thronged in the summer, the Shenandoah Park, at the northern edge of the famous Blue Ridge, was a favorite off-season excursion for her. She walked the Rose River Loop Trail near Fishers Gap, falling in love again with the Virginia Blue Ridge Mountains. The area had a dusting of snow from the prior night, and the bright flakes sat softly on the piles of fallen, earth-toned leaves. The frozen ground crunched as she walked on it.

She saw a couple of young lovers sporting matching James Madison University sweatshirts, but nobody else. A mockingbird perched noisily in a tree near a sweeping overlook to the east, where she could easily see the entirety of the Southwest Mountains and the headwater area of the Rapidan River.

It was a sparkling day, and at a high point on the trail, she stopped to drink from her canteen and smoke a cigarette. The view was grand, and she could see the Washington Monument, some 100 miles away. She had never seen it before from that extreme distance, but understood it was often possible to see it in the early days of the park prior to the smog of industrialization.

The scene was of eternal beauty and hiking always restored her optimism. She was abundantly aware of Virginia's many warts, including her legacy of slavery, racism, civil strife, bigotry, and bloody battlefields. Nonetheless, Marjorie loved Virginia in the same deep, abiding, unconditional way a child loves her mother; she couldn't help herself.

Sunday, November 19

Mindful of her coming trials, Sally had asked Marjorie to join her at the church of their childhood, Orange's First Street Methodist Church. So after a mere two-day stay at her home in Roanoke, Sally returned early Sunday morning to Runnymede, making the 150-mile trip in two-and-a-half-hours.

Sally was a more regular church-goer than her twin. Marjorie had stopped going at all except special occasions like weddings and funerals, given the church's declaration that her homosexual practice was incompatible with Christian teaching. She went on this day solely to be supportive of her sister.

During the sermon about accepting fate without judgment, Marjorie's mind wandered and her eyes played with the colors streaming through the ornate stained glass windows. She still felt a faint presence of the Lord Jesus Christ in her life, but was flummoxed by the church's stand on homosexuality. She often heard words like "homosexual lifestyle" and "choice." How could anybody choose sexual attraction, or for that matter any attraction? The first openly gay woman she ever met was one of her professors. She had said, "As children grow up and their bodies develop hormones, sometimes little boys become sexually attracted to little girls and vice versa. Nobody knows why. Sometimes little girls become sexually aroused by other girls and boys by other boys. Nobody knows why that is, either." Why would any religion, especially one whose patron saint preached universal love, demonize people of the latter groups?

Marjorie thought about all the discrimination and abuse she and other gay people she knew had received. If being gay was a lifestyle, a "choice," surely nobody would ever choose it. Why did so many people vilify people they didn't understand? She could see no plausible way a woman would be sexually aroused by chest hair, bulging muscles, and penises – she thought penises were unspeakably ugly – but it never seemed right to frown on heterosexuals for it.

That afternoon, the twins took another horseback ride, shorter but as delightful as the earlier ride, romping through the Northern Piedmont fields near the banks of the Rapidan River. Marjorie watched her sister's cancer-laden breasts bouncing along underneath her blouse, knowing that by the next day they'd be gone. Marjorie's eyes teared up in the sorrowful realization, or simply in the wind.

Monday, November 20

The twins awoke early in preparation for their journey to the UVA Medical Center for Sally's surgery. Marjorie left a note for Vance Wilson on the kitchen peg-board with care-taking instructions. She fed the corgis, patted them on the head getting a quick lick in return, and both women walked outside. As Marjorie drove her sister to her fateful operation, she wondered what was done at modern hospitals with amputated body parts, recalling a Civil War book she'd read where the physicians, after cutting off an arm or a leg typically with a dirty saw, threw the parts into a pile that was raided by dogs or rats. What would a modern university medical center do to dispose of a cancerous breast? They couldn't very well send breasts to a land-fill, could they?

A cancerous tumor had only been detected in one of Sally's breasts, but she had decided, and then convinced Dr. Truesdell, that she wanted both to be removed, the other pro-phylactically. As the orderlies wheeled Sally away towards the surgery room, she cupped both breasts and muttered something largely unintelligible about thanking them for their service to her and seeing them again in the afterlife.

Marjorie was too nervous to wait in the hospital, so she walked to the UVA Law School where she called on Liza. Liza was busy with a proposal, so Marjorie sat quietly in her office, reading a novel from a local writer.

Marjorie was dozing in the same chair four hours later when her cell phone rang. An attendant in the surgical wing called to say Sally had emerged from surgery. Marjorie scurried back to the hospital. Within a few moments of her arrival, Sally began to wake, muttering phrases from her election campaign stump speech. Marjorie sat with her twin for several hours until a nurse suggested she leave. Marjorie departed, taking a last glance at her sister, wrapped in bandages and with multiple tubes attached. Marjorie spent the night at Liza's Keswick estate in order to be closer to UVA, but in spite of being in the arms of her lover, she slept fitfully.

Tuesday, November 21

When Marjorie arrived at the hospital the following morning, Sally was awake and chipper. Dr. Truesdell stopped to check on her, checking vital signs and looking over the incisions. "I want her to stay one more night. I did a lymph node dissection along with the double mastectomy, so things were a bit more complicated than I had hoped."

"Did you get everything?" Marjorie inquired.

"I don't know. We never know. I'm confident I got all the big, mean stuff. That's what the chemo is for, to clean up all the remaining little nasties. How are you feeling, Sally?"

"Optimistic. I'm ready to go!"

"Not so fast. Are you going back to Roanoke?"

Marjorie interjected, "She's going back to Orange with me."

"Good. I'll check on her again tomorrow morning. If everything is okay, you can take her home. I'll make an appointment to have her back in a week and I'll see how everything is healing."

While driving home to Orange, Marjorie heard on the radio that the Governor had called for a special election for the State Senate seat vacated by the Attorney General Elect Brady Pasdon. The commentator noted that if Sally won the Lt. Governorship, her vacated Senate seat would be contested in a special election, too, but nothing would be planned until that race was officially decided.

Marjorie fed the dogs and chickens and took four eggs from the chicken coop. She fell into an uneasy, sporadic sleep, dreaming about ancient battles with swords, torches, and trebuchets in Scotland.

Wednesday, November 22

Marjorie was back at the UVA Medical Center by 9:00 a.m. Sally was wheeled to the front door at 11:15 a.m. and released. By noon, they were back at Runnymede Meadow and Marjorie was fixing lunch. Sally slept most of the afternoon, but when awake that evening, the twins played chess, their favorite game, which Sally won. Marjorie cleared the dining room table and set out a large jigsaw puzzle with an image of an English manor house in a meadow to help Sally pass her recovery time.

In the time Marjorie spent not attending to her sister, she cooked for the following day's feast.

Thursday, November 23, Thanksgiving

On Thanksgiving morning while changing the dressings and bandages around the drain tubes, Marjorie noticed that the area of Sally's right breast incision was red and warm to the touch. She wasn't sure what to make of it, but resolved to keep an eye on it.

Sally spent most of the day dozing and reading her book about the culture along the Virginia and West Virginia border. The twins played another game of chess that afternoon. This time, Marjorie was victorious. Sally made a mistake that cost her rook that Marjorie thought might have been intentional.

That evening, Liza arrived and the three women enjoyed a typical Thanksgiving meal of turkey, dressing, gravy, sweet potatoes, and cranberry relish. Sally was still weak and sore, but enjoyed the evening. For the meal's prayer, Sally said, "We thank the Lord for all his blessings. It's been a tough, uncertain, demanding year. But we still have much to be thankful for."

Meanwhile, Danny Gold sat alone at an all-you-can-eat family restaurant in north Richmond, the only place he could find open on the holiday, thumbing through the current copy of *Guns and Ammo* magazine, spooning over-cooked turkey, stuffing, and flaccid green beans into his mouth. Three days before, Danny had run into Sol Horowitz, an acquaintance he'd met at the synagogue the prior summer, and subtly hinted that he'd appreciate an invitation to join Horowitz and his family for Thanksgiving. But Horowitz never took the bait. Gold had nobody else to ask, thus his solitary meal.

At a nearby table, two toddlers were screaming at each other. To Danny's great annoyance, their parents did nothing to restrain them and continued their raucous conversation unbothered. At another table, a man and woman who looked to be in their sixties sat across from each other and for the twenty minutes Danny watched them, they said absolutely nothing, as if mute in connubial boredom. He viewed them with contempt, wondering how any married couple could have lives so uninteresting as to have nothing to say to each other.

Looking around the room, he saw nobody seemingly older than 13 who wasn't overweight; many were morbidly obese. He finished his meal and left cash on the table for his tab, including an extra 10 percent for the tip.

Friday, November 24

Marjorie greeted Sam Sebrell who stopped by the next morning with some paperwork for Sally to study. Sally thanked him, noting that she didn't want to fall behind on the work of the upcoming session, whether she'd be presiding over the Senate as Lt. Governor or in the Senate in her held seat. Marjorie sat in to help Sally tell Sam more about the election official's visit weeks earlier.

"This is a strange place we're in. Technically, I'm out of a job," Sam announced. "The election is over."

"We have some money left in the campaign chest, don't we?" Sally implored.

"No. I made sure we spent every dime," Sebrell specified. "I was sure the election would be close. I didn't want anybody to think we'd held anything back, in case we lost."

Everyone was quiet, pondering the options.

"So right now, you're working for nothing," Sally maintained.

"Yeah, and my girlfriend back in Blacksburg isn't happy about it." Sebrell shrugged, "I believe in what we did, and I believe in you, Sally. I'll stay with you for a few more days, but I will need to get another job soon. And there will be some legal fees from the lawyers we need to watch over the election recount."

"I understand," Sally pleaded, clenching her jaw.

Late in the day, Sally complained to Marjorie that the incision was still painful, perhaps more so than she expected. She popped two pills she'd brought home from the hospital and went back to bed.

Saturday, November 25

As Marjorie was changing Sally's bandages, she could see that the affected area was still red and warm. Upon closer inspection, she saw some pus forming underneath a stitch. She decided to immediately hustle Sally back to the hospital. Marjorie placed Sally in the passenger seat of the Mercedes. On their way back to UVA, Marjorie called to tell Dr. Truesdell's nurse that they were coming in. They came through the emergency room and within an hour, Truesdell had been summoned from her day off, and Sally was under the knife again. Hours passed as Marjorie waited, overcome with anxiety.

"She developed a staph infection," Truesdell explained to Marjorie, returning from her post-surgery wash-up.

"How?" Marjorie asked, feeling guilty for not doing a better job.

"We can't know. You may have touched the area with a contaminated hand. You have a farm, right?"

"Yes," Marjorie admitted.

"There may have been microorganisms in the air. But sometimes patients develop staph infections right here at the hospital. Don't blame yourself. This happens from time-to-time. We'll treat this with antibiotics. But she'll need to stay here for awhile until the healing is well underway."

Marjorie entered the recovery room where Sally was just reviving from her anesthesia. Marjorie took a call on Sally's phone, walking back into the hall. "Hello, this is Marjorie."

"Hey Marjorie, it's Sam. May I please speak with Sally?"

"We're back at the hospital." She brought him up to speed on Sally's condition. "What's up?"

"I need you to tell her something for me." Sebrell explained the reason for his call and then hung up.

Marjorie walked back into Sally's room. As soon as Sally was fully cogent, she informed, "Sam called."

"What's on his mind?" Sally inquired, eagerly but groggily.

"He said the campaign just got a significant contribution, enough to keep him and the lawyers covered through the recount."

"Awesome! Where did it come from?"

"A woman named Anna Beth Murray. She's Tom Leathers' wife."

"Wow. Good for her! I wonder how she knew."

Marjorie departed for Runnymede Meadow within the hour.

Sunday, November 26

Liza had asked Marjorie to come over to Keswick to spend the afternoon with her. Liza loved collecting antiques and needed some help moving furniture around. She had bought a roll-top desk at a yard sale, and it was too heavy for her to move alone.

After moving the desk inside, the lovers spent much of the afternoon together, chatting, eating, and working. They went for a long walk alongside Chopping Bottom Branch. Wildlife was abundant, and they saw a fox, several deer, and a little green heron.

They were happy together. Marjorie found contentment knowing Liza was satisfied with her job, Sally was on the mend and the long election was over. And with the beauty and bounty of the Virginia Piedmont.

Monday, November 27

The weather turned decidedly colder and whispers of winter streamed through the rolling Rapidan River Valley as Marjorie fed the cats, horses and chickens. She went to the hen house where she collected three eggs, fewer than the usual four to six. Egg production was down as was typical for the colder months. While scooping feed from the bin, she noticed a snake skeleton behind it that she hadn't seen before. She moved a loose board to get a better look. Entwined within the vertebrae was a white golf ball.

The prior summer, she had problems with predation by snakes. So she decided to put golf balls in some of the nests, hoping to fool the snakes into swallowing them, preventing further digestion and ultimately killing them.

Marjorie's only phobia in life was snakes, and they terrified her. Sally often kidded her when they were growing up that Marjorie was unafraid of 1200-pound horses but petrified by 3-pound snakes. She felt guilty about killing snakes this way, but resigned herself to doing whatever it took to protect her chickens and keep them productive.

Marjorie carried the eggs inside and after removing her coat and boots, placed the eggs in the refrigerator.

Tuesday, November 28

Dr. Truesdell finally released Sally again, and Marjorie drove to UVA Medical Center to pick her up. Sally was surprisingly chipper, in spite of the cold, rainy day. "I'm tired of being in the hospital," she said three times on the way back to Runnymede Meadow Estate.

Marjorie felt awash in well-being, confident that better

times were ahead for her beloved sister.

Wednesday, November 29

Danny found himself at Chopper's Sports Bar near VCU, nursing a Jack Daniel's and pondering his future. A flat-chested coed of Asian descent seemed to be flirting with him, but he found himself uncharacteristically withdrawn. His mind returned to the sermon of the prior Sunday, to the girl he'd watched and lusted after.

It was unseasonably cold in Richmond, and the cold reminded him of Houghton and its interminable winters. Curiously, an early season National Hockey League game was on the big-screen. It was Tampa Bay against Anaheim. Why were there teams in Florida or California, places that never saw snow? How disingenuous and unnatural, watching hockey in a refrigerated arena, then walking outside to tropical breezes and palm trees! He tried to remember when he began his active dislike of hockey, a game he and all his classmates – at least the boys – were peer-required to play growing up.

He was never a good skater, but it was the messiness of it that repelled him. The bloody noses and the inevitable cuts and blood. The chipped and missing teeth, from the sharp skates and flying pucks. The fist-fights! The infernal malodorous smell, the eternal stench of sweat and dirty jock-straps in the locker room, of the pounds of padding!

Ah, but wrestling! He took a sip of his Jack Daniel's and grinned. Wrestling was pure. My body against my opponent's body, mano-a-mano. The take-down. The reversal. The escape. The pin, a helpless opponent. The victorious and the vanquished. Pure. Simple. Unequivocal.

Why was the world not purer?

A guy he knew, Noah Digges, walked past. Danny motioned him over to the bar. Digges had worked on the Overington campaign and was happy to have been successful. Digges was the only black at the upper levels of any of the campaigns, something that caused a fair amount of ribbing, given the Republican Party's increasingly smaller tent. They chatted for awhile, Digges mentioning that he'd taken a job working for a Republican Congressman in Texas who faced re-election and that he would be leaving Richmond and Virginia in a few days.

As Digges ordered a beer, Danny mentioned that he had an interest in Pasdon, perhaps working for him. Digges claimed, "I wouldn't give you a plug nickel for the guy. He says what tea party voters want to hear, but he's long been suspected of racism. 'Abortion' is in every sentence he utters; he's obsessed with it."

Danny countered, "Jorge Gonzales works for him. Would Pasdon hire a Hispanic if he was a racist?"

"Only if he wanted people to think he wasn't," Digges opined. "Careful, my friend. Between me and you, I think Pasdon has a fondness for teenage boys. But again, just a hunch."

"What do you know?" Gold prodded, always eager to know dirt on those around him.

"That's all I'm sayin', bro. I ain't fighting any Richmond battles any more. I'm outta here!" The black man walked away, leaving his tab behind for Danny.

As quickly as Digges left, Danny spotted Sol Horowitz walking inside. Danny motioned him over. Danny thought first about asking Horowitz about his Thanksgiving, but figured he'd be opening a can of worms. "What's shakin'?" came out of his mouth instead.

"Same *mishegas*, different day," the small, balding man quipped. "You?"

"Oh, all right I guess," Danny lied. "How's business?"

"*Feh*! Hell, the life of a private eye! Sketchy work. Customers who don't pay. It's a pile of crap, but somebody's got to do it. Cheating schmucks. Corrupt business partners. It could be worse; I could be in politics," he stabbed.

Danny chucked at the arrogant man's insult towards him. They small-talked for a while, mostly about the Redskins, their gridiron futility and the controversy over their name, until Horowitz's attention was diverted towards another friend. At that point, he summarily dismissed Danny and sidled briskly away.

Danny walked outside into the cool Richmond evening. Down the block, four white college kids were harassing a black street dweller. He thought for a moment about intervening, then turned and kept walking.

Thursday, November 30

At Sally's insistence, Marjorie drove the two of them to James Madison's home at Montpelier, four miles south of Orange. When the twins were growing up, the mansion and grounds were in private hands, owned by the duPont family. In 1984, the duPonts bequeathed Montpelier to the National Trust for Historic Preservation, which then had painstakingly restored the home, gardens, outbuildings, and cemeteries. Unable to visit as a child due to the private ownership, Sally repeatedly said that as an adult and a politician, she drew strength and inspiration from the brilliant Madison, feeling his presence there.

The mansion itself was designed and built by Madison's father as a two-story Georgian structure, constructed in brick fired on the grounds around 1760. Typical of the era, it had formal, symmetrical facades front and rear, with rooms stacked two-deep. On the main floor were a parlor, dining room, and two reception rooms with carved English red sandstone mantles. Meals were prepared in a separate kitchen and delivered by slaves to the dining room. In his final years, the aging former president stayed in a rear bedchamber on the main floor until his death. Other bedchambers were above, accessible through narrow staircases.

The original floor plan was expanded several times over the ensuing decades to reach the current grand size. As a public museum, the mansion was filled with interpretive displays and period paintings and furnishings.

The twins strolled leisurely as Sally was clearly still in pain, visiting the Annie duPont garden, the gazebo, and the slave quarters, several reconstructed wooden cabins. Trainers worked out with horses on a nearby oval track.

It was a clear, mild day and the view to the west and the Blue Ridge Mountains was superb and invigorating.

Two

"The tree of liberty must be refreshed from time to time with the blood of patriots and tyrants."
— THOMAS JEFFERSON, 2ND GOVERNOR OF VIRGINIA

Friday, December 1

Now unemployed, Danny had time on his hands. He sorted through various posts on GOP-Power, the website where Republican candidates and campaign workers found each other. There was nothing posted that interested him.

On his trip to Houghton, his mother had given him a box of family treasures, photo boxes and souvenirs. There was a picture of his dad, his older sister, Myra, and him, posing in front of Mount Rushmore on a trip they'd taken when he was six or seven. Danny stared at it for several minutes, overcome with emotion and regret. Seven faces: Washington, Jefferson, Teddy Roosevelt, Lincoln, his father, Myra, and him. His eyes darted from one to the next, over and over. Jefferson. Limited government. "The true foundation of republican government is the equal right of every citizen in his person and property and in their management," Jefferson had said, in a quote Danny thought he'd memorized during those formative years. His love of politics was nurtured then and had become an obsession.

The granite figures in the photo's background spoke to him boldly, but he drifted to the expressions on his father's face and his own. What was that boy, who would become the man he is now, thinking then? His father's expression was of joy but tinged with suspicion. He thought nothing of lashing Danny for minor provocations, punishment seldom meted out to Danny's sister. Myra was a happier child and her face showed a level of contentedness that Danny's didn't. Her happiness would be destroyed a few years later at puberty by their father's sexual advances towards her.

Danny was only able to come to grips with it in his twenties, but he hated his father. He hated him for his sternness and favoritism towards his sister. He hated him for his career failures and his submission to those in power around him. His father was weak and Danny abhorred weakness. Danny resolved to take what was his, to expect nothing from anyone, and to be an "alpha." He would dominate, never acquiesce.

His relationship with his father founded his political beliefs. People need to be strong and self-reliant. Government should leave people alone. Individuals have every right to do what they please, barring harm to others. The only legitimate purpose of government, and the only appropriate use of tax-generated dollars, was national defense. Those on welfare, food assistance, or any government hand-out, were weak, parasitic. Social Security should be voluntary and privately-based. Health care schemes like the Governor-elect's treasured Health-Net program were anathema. Nobody deserved a government-sponsored handout.

Saturday, December 2

A few nights later, Danny was back in the same VCU neighborhood bar, Chopper's Sports Bar, where he'd spoken with Noah Digges. As he walked in, he recognized Jorge Gonzales hanging out with some friends, a mixed-racial group. Gonzales had been Brady Pasdon's campaign manager for Attorney General. Gonzales took leave from his friends to greet Danny, *"¿Que pasa, amigo?"*

"Hey, Jorge," Danny exclaimed graciously. They hadn't seen each other since the event at the Country Club of Virginia a few weeks earlier. They chatted about Westfall's loss.

"My guy didn't fight to win," Danny complained about his erstwhile boss. "Somehow he seemed to think McGregor would lie down and die, or somehow shame himself. I gave him the advice and tools to win, but he wimped out."

"You think?"

"Virginians hate the President. I told Westfall to pound on McGregor and his friendship with the President. Instead, he worked on the soft stuff. Jobs. The economy. Nobody's anti-job. We got no spacing. No traction. We could have won. We should have won. Makes me ill. Now your guy, he's a winner."

"Pasdon is a pain in the ass, but I suppose he told people what they wanted to hear," Gonzales admitted. "I also think we benefited from a weak opponent. To his credit, Pasdon didn't take his campaign lightly. In any event, we got the win."

"What are you doing now?" Danny inquired.

"Hey Jorge," one of his friends yelled. "Get over here."

"Listen Danny," Jorge said, "I gotta go. Let's get together again. You play tennis?"

"Poorly."

"Soon!" Gonzales drifted away.

Danny turned his attention to the women in the room. Four coeds were sitting together. One walked to the bar to get a bowl of popcorn. She wore a green sweatshirt with "William and Mary" and a cartoon griffin embroidered on it. She had dark, curly hair and deep-set brown eyes. Danny watched her walk, unrestrained breasts jiggling, and approached her. Forty-five minutes later, he was atop her in his bedroom.

Sunday, December 3

Danny, in an attempt to atone for his sins, went to synagogue again. This time he attended a new congregation, N'Vay Shalom on Forest Hill Avenue in south Richmond where he hoped not to be recognized. The rabbi, to his disgust, turned out to be a woman, and an unattractive one at that. There was no purity in a woman rabbi lecturing him about matters of faith. She had an overpowering New York accent which he found almost comical.

In the lobby afterwards, several people made friendly overtones towards him; they were far more affable than the other synagogue he attended. But he spurned their advances, unwilling to establish friendships, and he departed hastily after noshing free hors d'oeuvres.

Monday, December 4

Marjorie finished her chores and returned to the house to change Sally's bandages once again. Sally's healing process was ongoing, but Marjorie saw improvement from day to day, along with Sally's mood. Unspoken between the twins was the lengthy recovery still to follow.

Marjorie then drove to the University of Virginia Law

School and had a brown-bag lunch with Liza.

Tuesday, December 5

Marjorie made dinner at Runnymede Meadow Estate for Liza who was again to be guest speaker at Orange's Daughters of Dolley Society, the women's historical club where they had met years earlier. Marjorie and Liza drove to the Historical Society office on Caroline Street in downtown, where snowflake-replica Christmas tree ornaments with blinking orange lights had been in place for a week. Sally wasn't feeling well enough to attend, so she stayed behind.

As the members filed in, several spoke to Marjorie about Sally's condition, wishing her well. The president, Elaine Nash, welcomed the audience and introduced the speaker. "Ladies, we have again with us tonight Liza Randolph. Since she spoke with us a few years ago, she's taken the job as the Dean of the Law School at UVA and has moved to Keswick. Liza has a degree in history from Cambridge University in England. She also has a Law degree from William and Mary College. The title of her talk is, 'The progeny of James Madison'. Liza?"

"Thank you Elaine," she said, shaking her hand and advancing to the lectern, "and thanks to everyone for having me back. Tonight I'm going to talk about President Madison's family."

Marjorie was again struck by how elegant and attractive Liza was. Liza had lovely, soft eyes in a smooth face, with a ready smile. She was as shapely as a model.

"The title of my speech tonight is tongue-in-cheek. As far as we know, James Madison, 'Jemmy' to his friends, had no progeny. Jemmy was a sickly boy, small and thin. In fact, he was our smallest president, at only 5'5". His weight never exceeded 100 pounds. But what he lacked in size he more than made up for in brainpower. He may have had the highest IQ of anybody we've ever had in our highest office, although the folks down at Monticello might argue that."

A couple of smug chuckles emanated from the audience.

"As I mentioned, James Madison was reputedly known as 'Jemmy' or 'Little Jemmy'. He was a shy boy, and one editorial writer declared, 'His heart is petrified and hard as marble. His body is torpid, and he is without feeling.' I'm a bit less critical of him personally. He dealt with a lot in his long life, and he did so without emotional outbursts or melt-downs. I think he was a gem, so rather than calling him 'Jemmy' I call him 'Gem.'

"Our child prodigy left home at age 11 and was tutored by Donald Robertson, an instructor at the Innes Plantation in the Virginia Tidewater. Young Madison learned math, geology, geography and other life sciences, and languages. By age 16, Gem reputedly had learned six languages. He credited his aptitude to Robertson, who worked with the boys of many wealthier families in Virginia. I have a sneaking suspicion he knew even more languages.

"He returned to the family home here in Orange, Montpelier, to be tutored in preparation for college.

"While most of the college-bound boys of the area were sent to the College of William and Mary, which was already 75 years old, Jemmy chose the College of New Jersey, fearing the routine infestations of mosquito-borne diseases that afflicted the area around Williamsburg. It's not hard to understand his fear, as three of his siblings died in infancy and two more before reaching the age of eight due to a dysentery epidemic in 1775. The College of New Jersey is now Princeton University, and it was only five years old when Madison was born. While at Princeton, Madison mastered another language: Hebrew. Before Nobel Prize winner John Nash had 'a beautiful mind,' surely Madison's was equally beautiful. I often dream of time travel and the prospect of knowing him personally.

"Madison's roommate was Philip Freneau, a poet, newspaper editor, and nationalist. Madison was taken by Freneau's sister, Mary. Madison repeatedly proposed marriage to Mary who spurned him each time, choosing instead to remain single, something quite common for upper class women of the era.

"On September 15, 1794, Madison finally took marriage vows to Dolley Payne Todd, a 26-year old widow. By this time, Madison was 43, already past the typical life expectancy of a man of that era. That statistic is a bit misleading. The average life expectancy was around 40, but in truth, it was brought down by the extreme number of babies and children that died. Once you made it to adulthood, your chances for a long life were much better, although still not up to today's standards. Anyway, the lovebirds were introduced by mutual friend, Aaron Burr, in Philadelphia.

"Of course, you are all familiar with Dolley's special contributions. With her extraordinary social skills, she was the archetypal First Lady.

"Okay, now we get to the tongue-in-cheek part. Madison had no children! Dolley had two children by her first husband John Todd: William and John Payne, the latter who went by the name 'Payne'. Tragically, a yellow fever epidemic in 1793 killed William and John Todd, as well as her in-laws who lived nearby. After she married Jemmy, he adopted Payne.

"There is perhaps nobody in American history better named than Payne, because he was a drunkard and a lout, continually cooking his own goose. Never a productively employed man, 'Payne the drain' was a consistent source of disappointment to the Madisons, although Dolley always blithely doted on him anyway, perhaps wishing at some point he would straighten up and fly right. And he never married. Fortunately, he seems not to have cramped Gem's style.

"As far as we know, Gem never had the dalliances with any of his slaves that Jefferson is now known to have had with his mixed-race paramour, Sally Hemings, and perhaps others. Dolley had Payne, but he had no known, or proven, progeny, and if he did they had no bloodline to Madison. So other than Gem's siblings, we have no known bloodlines to Madison whatsoever."

Several women in the audience squirmed in their chairs uncomfortably.

"So the James Madison bloodline is a genetic cul-de-sac. All of the people who show up at meetings like these are mere admirers, rather than actual descendants. Some of us are descended from Madison's siblings and others from Madison's slaves, but his beautiful mind bloodline ended when he died at the ripe old age of 85 in June, 1836 while Dolley made one of her rare trips away from his bedside.

"Thanks for having me back to speak again. Are their any questions?"

After answering several queries from the audience, the formal presentation ended. Marjorie and Liza stayed around afterward and enjoyed cookies, brownies, orange punch, and conversation. As always, most of the women, maybe all of them, wore some piece of clothing with an orange color in it, typically either a blouse or a scarf. There was some talk about the recent election, and because of their association with Marjorie, their desire that Sally would win. There were some politically active women on both sides, but they were united in their beliefs about women's rights, especially for reproductive rights and equal pay.

Wednesday, December 6

It was Happy Hour at Chopper's Sports Bar, what had become Danny's favorite drinking hole and pickup joint. It was one of the few bars around that still had old-fashioned pinball machines. Danny had won his share of money at the pinball tables in his college days around State College, betting on games against his friends. He had become less successful in Richmond, both in making friends and in winning at pinball.

Jorge Gonzales approached and shoved Danny's machine, causing it to tilt and momentarily shut off, ruining Danny's score, just for spite. "Hey," Jorge boomed.

"Asshole," Danny retorted. He set another ball in motion.

"What's your candidate doing these days?"

The ball clanged noisily against the electronic bumpers, rolling rapidly across the playfield. Danny's fingers repeatedly activated the flippers. The backbox flashed lights and spiraling numbers. "Don't ask me. I think he's vanished. He certainly hasn't been in touch with me or any of his other staffers." The ball swept cleanly between the flippers and vanished. Danny set another in motion.

Jorge took another sip of his lager. "I'm guessing new

Governor McGregor is busy, formulating his agenda."

"Yeah," Danny said, punching both flippers repeatedly, "he'll be working on the legislature to get his Health-Net program passed. We can't let that happen." The ball ricocheted noisily, slapping the underside of the glass cover.

"What's your problem with it?"

"More government. Where does it end?" The ball slipped into the gutter. Danny looked at his friend. "Why should I be paying for somebody else's medical care? The Declaration of Independence declares our inalienable rights to life, liberty, and the pursuit of happiness. We're not granted happiness, only the pursuit of it. The founders never intended our government to take care of us. We're a nanny state now, only becoming more so."

"There seems to be a groundswell for legislation like this," Gonzales observed.

"Not if I can help it." The ball vanished between the flippers.

"I'm not saying I disagree with you, but the old system wasn't working very well."

"Bullshit!" Danny shrieked. "We have the best health care system in the world. The uninsured in this country are irresponsible. Go outside and walk Broad Street and tell me whether you think the schmucks smoking crack or fencing drugs deserve the insurance that you and I will be paying for. If some crack-head is addicted, do you think we should be paying for more crack to keep him from going nutzo in withdrawal? Besides, the uninsured go to emergency rooms. Health care is a commodity. It should be available to those that can afford it or care enough about themselves to get off their ass and work. Nobody should get it for free."

"Aren't you being…"

"Harsh?" Gold interrupted, sending the final silver ball in the set on its arch. "Socialized medicine is fundamentally anti-American. We're a capitalistic, individualistic society. It's just one more step towards socialism. Next thing you know, our government will dictate where we work, what companies are successful, and what products they can make. Besides, government can't seem to do anything right. Do you trust your medicine to a government-paid doctor? People will abuse the system, milk it just like they do the disability system. And it would ration health care, taking it from people who can afford it and are now insured." Danny slapped at the ball repeatedly with the flippers, shooting upwards across the play-field into the upper lanes against the spinners and bouncing bumpers.

"You're pretty passionate about this…" Gonzales concluded.

"Listen," Danny said, slapping the flipper actuators, "This would be the last straw. I can't let this happen."

"What do you intend to do about it? The election results are in."

"We don't know about the Lt. Governor's race yet. We have options." The final ball rolled into an escape lane and vanished as a shapely blonde woman crossed in front of Danny. "*Amigo*, I gotta go." He left in pursuit.

Thursday, December 7

Weeks had passed since Sally's infection had abated. Marjorie drove her back to the UVA Medical Center for a follow-up visit with her oncologist, Dr. Truesdell. Truesdell removed Sally's drain tube and again stitched her incision closed.

On the way back to Runnymede, Sally was perky, clearly relieved that another milestone in her healing had passed.

Friday, December 8

Danny Gold packed his bags and headed westward on I-64, headed to the venerable, opulent Homestead Resort in Bath County for the annual Republican Party of Virginia Strategy Summit conference. He wanted to carpool to save money on gas, but Jorge Gonzales begged out, saying he had another commitment afterwards and wouldn't be driving directly home. If the Republican Party hadn't rented Danny's room for him, he couldn't have gone at all.

Leaving Interstate 81 at Lexington and driving past the Virginia Horse Center and through Goshen Pass, Danny was struck by the beauty of the Virginia Appalachian Mountains, graceful and scenic even in leafless winter starkness. There was a frosting of snow on the higher peaks framing Warm Springs. Danny paid $12 admission, treating himself to a soak at the Jefferson Pools in Warm Springs. There were two adjacent pool houses, segregated by sexes, both octagonal in shape and open to the sky. The men's building was built in 1761, according to an informational plaque. With its multiple rotting boards, it looked to Danny as if it hadn't been maintained since.

The waters in the men's building were 98°F, luxurious, pure, and deep. Danny and the other bathers were nude. They used polystyrene flotation devices to stay afloat in the 9' depth.

Danny then motored the short distance to Hot Springs and the Homestead, parking in a satellite parking lot and getting a ride to the hotel from a courtesy bus. He ate alone in the bar, not seeing anyone he knew. He was about to move on a woman sitting nearby until her man, larger than he, arrived.

Saturday, December 9

"Let us bow our heads," Delegate White from Pulaski said, "Dear Lord, as we gather here at this meeting of your servants, we are mindful of your blessings as they are so graciously bestowed upon us. We give thanks to you for providing this day, this stunning venue at the Homestead Resort, for this food and the people who prepare and serve it. In Jesus' name. Amen."

"Amen," echoed around the room.

Danny Gold sniffled and then wiped his nose on the bottom of his tie, then returned to his chair. He always hated these perfunctory public devotionals, especially those ending with pleas to Jesus. It had become a thorn in his side, but thus far a tolerable thorn, that his Republican Party had so closely hung its collective hat on Christianity to the exclusion of his Judaism and the religious convictions of an increasing number of citizens.

A tall, grey-haired man approached the lectern at the lunchtime gathering, "Ladies and gentlemen, my name is Hamilton Graham, and I am Chairman of the Virginia Republican Party. Thank you for being here at our annual Strategy Summit. This afternoon and through the day tomorrow, we will be discussing tactics for regaining the critical control of the legislature we need to move our conservative message forward."

Gold's mind drifted as he waffled down his roast duckling

and butter-spiced potato slices. As befitting the duckling, he too was in a foul mood. He had come to grips with the election, where Democrat Miller McGregor had decisively beaten Adam Westfall, the candidate Gold had worked for as special strategy assistant. Critically, Republican Ward Oates was still in a challenged election with Democrat Sally Bradley for Lt. Governor. Oates was the chief financial officer of Liberty University, founded in Lynchburg by televangelist Jerry Falwell.

Republican Brady Pasdon's defeat of Democrat Lawrence Willis for the State Attorney General was critical to the Party's cause.

So the balance of power was split. The Democrats had the Governor's office along with half the seats in the 40-member State Senate. The Republicans had the Attorney General, the other half of the Senate, and a clear majority in the House of Delegates. It was absolutely critical that Oates win the Lt. Governor seat over Bradley, as the Lt. Governor casts the tie-breaker votes in the Senate, which would occur on every party-line vote.

Danny again began to stew over Westfall's loss. In Danny's view, Westfall had made a critical mistake in supporting the President's plan to more adequately fund health care for veterans returning from the Middle East wars. Westfall was a solid conservative in most ways, including gun rights, fiscal matters, and the rights of the unborn. But as the son of a World War II general, Westfall explained his support as a patriotism issue, against fiscal conservative values. Danny felt like it cost him the election. And as he had told Gonzales a week earlier, Westfall's failure to link McGregor with the President was fatal.

Chairman Graham spoke about the various factions

within the Party, the tea partiers, the evangelicals, and the traditional fiscal conservatives, and the overriding need to maintain solidarity.

At one of the break-out sessions that afternoon, Gold heard about changes and improvements in the Voter Vault, the system the Republicans used to track voter trends down to an individual, household, and neighborhood basis that their computer geeks were working on for the next election cycle. It was reputedly closing the gap on the superior microtargeting program, the WAN system, of the Democrats.

Strolling the hallway afterward on his way to the final plenary session, Gold ran into Gonzales, who was talking with Courtney Templeton, who had been Brady Pasdon's successful campaign manager. Templeton said, "Which way do you think the Lt. Governor's going to go?"

Gonzales claimed, "Oates will win. But I'm basing that on nothing more than pure optimism."

Danny gave Templeton the once-over. She was tall and stately, with a conservative white blouse under a dark jacket and curly auburn hair. "I've been analyzing the votes across the board," Danny boasted. "Like always, people are pretty consistent in voting for the party line. I think we'll win."

"Why? What did you find?" Templeton prompted.

"Great Falls district. Solidly Republican. Westfall got 68 percent, higher than might be expected because it's near his home district. Overington got 64 percent, as did their state delegate, Tom Linkous. I figure there's no reason why Oates shouldn't have polled similarly. But he got 57 percent. I'm thinking there are some miscounted votes there that will swing our way in the recount."

"We did pretty well under the circumstances," Templeton

contended. She brushed back her hair, showing above her wrist what Danny thought was a tattoo.

"Bullshit!" Gold could no longer contain his frustration and contempt for the weakness of the woman opposite him. "Westfall should have won. If he hadn't listened to his wimp-ass campaign manager, Paul Murray, he'd have won. We're making too many concessions. We're getting too soft."

Templeton shrugged impertinently as if what he'd said she found offensive and walked away, shadowed by Danny's licentious stare. He deduced that she might not be as straight-laced as she appeared. He lusted over her, yet felt she might someday present a challenge to him.

Sunday, December 10

Danny Gold sat on a plush upholstered chair in the opulent lobby of the Homestead, reading the latest news from the *National Review Online*. Behind him, a woman and two men sat down in the midst of a conversation. One was Brady Pasdon, the new Attorney General. He was railing about abortion. The woman spoke first, "... had one when I was eighteen. I was out drinking and the next thing I knew, I was pregnant. My parents forced me to abort it. I've regretted it ever since."

"It's always been pretty clear-cut for me," Pasdon said. "It's murder, pure and simple. The people who elected me expect me to fight it. More than a few voters told me it was the only issue that they considered."

Danny was ambivalent about it. But he knew it was a strong motivator for Republican voters. So he accepted the fact and used the evangelical crowd as foot soldiers for the issues he championed.

"After I'm inaugurated," Pasdon gloated, "I will be Planned Parenthood's worst nightmare."

Danny left the Homestead just before 3:00 p.m. in a cold rain. The drive over the mountains was perilous, with the rain freezing on the roadway surface. Several cars were in the ditch and an accident blocked his progress for 45 minutes near Millboro Springs. The trip back to Richmond, normally less than three hours, took over four.

Monday, December 11

Early Monday afternoon, an unseasonably mild day in Orange, Marjorie got a call from her veterinarian, Dr. Angela Endres, confirming her appointment for the following day to assist Marjorie in gelding Tank, the Lusitano. The two women discussed the yearling's vaccinations and worming treatments and ensured he was ready for surgery.

Marjorie had earned a BS degree from UVA in Biology with a minor in Philosophy, intending to go to veterinary school before switching to Business and getting her MBA at Williams College at Xavier University in Cincinnati. So she was well-versed in the veterinary, and was happy to have a local veterinarian like Endres who honored her expertise and let her do most of the work while merely supervising.

Tuesday, December 12

Veterinarian Endres, who Marjorie thought looked young enough to be still in high school, arrived promptly at 9:00 a.m. Marjorie enticed Tank into a small fenced enclosure near the north barn by dangling a carrot over her head. He came trotting in and grabbed it from her outstretched hand while Andres plunged a hypodermic needle into his upper rump. He flinched slightly, but kept chewing the carrot. "Easy, boy," Marjorie said as she walked him slowly around the paddock by his bridle until the tranquilizer chemical kicked in, as the young horse slumped to the ground. They maneuvered him onto his back, his back legs splayed and airborne. She placed a soft blanket, triple wrapped, under his head.

The two women worked quickly, businesslike, without conversation or instructions.

Marjorie put on her rubber gloves and washed his scrotal area with water from a hose. She took the short scalpel from Angela's hand. She made two 4" long slits, one in each testicular sack. She grabbed the left testicle first, and stretched it by the epididymis, the tube connecting the testicle with the vas deferens. The testicle was slightly smaller than her fist. She took a metal clamp, an emasculator, about the size of regular pliers and attached it to the tube to crush it and break the blood supply. She left it in place for sixty seconds, checking with her digital watch. Then she slit the tube and pitched the testicle to the corgis, which they played with, wrestling it from each other, until it split and they ate it.

Marjorie then moved to the other testicle, repeated the procedure. She pitched the other testicle to the dogs which they fought over again. "Be sure to slice off that hanging skin," Endres pointed. Marjorie did as instructed, completed the job, and then brushed some disinfectant on the scrotal skin and some Vaseline on the inside of the legs to prevent any dripping blood from scalding the skin.

The two wounds were kept open to allow for healing, as stitching them might have allowed bacteria inside. Marjorie's mind wandered to her sister as she and the vet were washing the surgical tools. She thought of Sally's incisions and how they had become infected.

Doctor Endres departed just over an hour from her arrival, and Marjorie stayed by Tank's side until he shook off the anesthetic and struggled to his feet. She walked him around the paddock where she left him for the day until she took him inside the barn overnight. By the time she finished her other chores, fixed supper for herself and Sally, and checked some of her investments, she was dead-tired.

Wednesday, December 13

On Wednesday, December 13 the statewide recount began in the Bradley v. Oates race for the Virginia Lt. Governor. Sally was still at Marjorie's house recuperating. Still on antibiotics and pain medication, her days were spent mostly in her bed or nearby in the upholstered chair, reading her way through legislative homework, interspersed with Marjorie's collection of detective novels set in the American Southwest. With the influx of money they'd received, Sam Sebrell had stayed on with the campaign and spoke with Sally by phone a couple of times each day, often funneling information to her about upcoming legislation likely to arrive at the General Assembly once they returned to session.

Thursday, December 14

At the meeting at the Homestead the previous weekend, Danny had agreed to play tennis with Jorge Gonzales, which they did on Thursday. Gonzales was the more skilled player, overcoming Danny's greater size and strength. Danny was behind in the second set when he felt like he pulled a muscle in his left calf and promptly withdrew.

They made their way to the clubhouse of the indoor tennis facility where they ordered beers. Jorge told Danny that with the election over and Pasdon's new job as the state Attorney General, Jorge was obviously no longer campaign manager, but Pasdon had kept him on as a personal, special assistant, at least for the time being. Still, he was in the process of looking for a national campaign somewhere else in the country to join. He had feelers for senate races in Colorado and Connecticut, but no firm offers. Danny admitted that his future was uncertain as well.

In passing, Jorge mentioned that Courtney Templeton, who had been Brady Pasdon's successful campaign manager, had been retained as official spokesperson, in Pasdon's new role as Attorney General.

Friday, December 15

At Runnymede, Marjorie began her farm chores on a brisk, clear day, finding that Ralph the goat had given birth to a female kid. Marjorie gave her a close look and saw that both mother and offspring were in good shape. She named the baby goat Fairfax. She took several photos of the kid with her phone to show Sally.

The cycle of life on the farm was always constant and reassuring to Marjorie. She loved being immersed in the sights, smells, and tastes of the farm.

Tank was healing nicely from his surgery, already returned to what Marjorie jokingly called his "equine hyperspace."

Saturday, December 16

Marjorie awoke to the first snowfall of the year, about four inches of the pristine white stuff, covering her lawn and farm fields. She found an old pair of rubber boots for Sally and the newer pair for herself and they walked around the yard. Blue jays, chickadees, and northern cardinals feasted at her feeder, splashing snow and sunflower seed husks from the feeder base. The sun was beginning to break through the clouds and when it did the snow illuminated in a blaze of pellucid white.

Sally reminisced about a particularly memorable snowfall during their childhood when their long-departed father hitched up one of the horses to an antique sled he kept in the barn. Neither sister remembered its fate. Both were saddened that it had long since vanished.

It was a happy time and Marjorie savored the joy she and her sister felt.

Sunday, December 17

Much of the snow had melted by the next day when Liza came over for a visit. They watched football on television at Liza's insistence, as one of her high school friend's son played for the Seattle Seahawks, and she wanted to see how well he played. The Seahawks beat the host Atlanta Falcons by 14 points. The threesome had a nice meal of veal and rice before Liza returned home to Keswick.

Monday, December 18

Danny spent the better part of his day researching the

career of Courtney Templeton, exploring the Internet with key word searches. Minneapolis born. San Francisco raised. Daughter of university professors, both Catholic. Stanford educated, International Studies and Political Science, Summa cum laude. Married at 23, divorced at 27. Now 33, one daughter, 7.

He was on a fishing expedition into her life, not knowing what to look for or really why. But he sensed that knowing more about her could help him in the future. He felt he could never know too much about somebody, friend or foe.

Tuesday, December 19

"Good news!" yelled Sam Sebrell over the speaker phone to Sally, as she and Marjorie were having a late breakfast together. "Mr. Kinsey from the elections bureau just called. You won!"

"Yeah-boy howdee!" Marjorie shrieked, rushing to hug Sally. "Awesomesauce!"

"Well, well," Sally confirmed, with a decidedly subdued pleasure. "We did it. Thank you, Sam."

"Congratulate yourself, Sally. You're the candidate. It's about you."

"Wow," Sally agreed, letting her excitement wash over her. "Virginia's next Lt. Governor, little ole me."

Marjorie's face flushed with pride and joy, and she laughed. Boo barked twice, loudly.

"What now?" Sally inquired.

"Kinsey said you'd be getting a certified letter in the mail tomorrow with the official results, saying you are the winner. Do you feel like you'd like to make a public statement?"

"Nobody needs to see me like this," she complained, brushing her hair from the edge of her face. "I'm guessing they'll deliver the letter to my house, right?"

"Yes, they will."

"I'm still in Orange with Marjorie," Sally assessed her current situation.

"We were planning to get you back to Roanoke on Thursday anyway," Marjorie offered. "Doc Truesdell has released you to be home and on your own again. Let's just go tomorrow."

Sebrell said, "Does that work for you, Sally?"

"I suppose so." Sally thought for a moment, staring down at her chest where her breasts once were. "I'll prepare a written statement for you Sam, and I'll e-mail it within the hour. You can share it with the media or whoever calls."

Sally finished breakfast and adjourned to her laptop, typing the following statement:

> The election results have been recounted and the people of Virginia have spoken. I am gratified to be the new Lt. Governor-elect of this great, historic Commonwealth. My election is one of the closest in history, meaning that almost half the voters would have preferred my opponent. As I prepare to take office, I will be constantly reminded that once sworn in, I will be morally, legally, and ethically bound to represent all Virginians, whether they supported me or not. I thank my campaign manager, Sam Sebrell, my staff, and everyone who honored me by their vote, and I look forward to continuing my service to my fellow Virginians.

She purposefully said nothing about her illness, knowing the questions would arrive in due course. After having Marjorie buddy-check it for grammar and content, she fired it off to Sebrell for distribution to the press.

Wednesday, December 20

At breakfast, Sally assured Marjorie she felt well enough to drive. She and Marjorie packed their things and both departed for Roanoke. Marjorie planned to stay with her twin through Christmas to help her settle in and enjoy the holiday together. Sally got a 15-minute head start and was already on the way towards Charlottesville when Marjorie herded the corgis into the Mercedes and hit the road herself, leaving instructions for Wilson to care for the farm animals while she was gone, including Ralph, the momma goat, and kid, Fairfax.

Two hours after their arrival at Sally's Grandin Village home in Roanoke, it began snowing. Before it ended, it left six inches of white powder snow on the outside world. Marjorie had brought some flour and shortening from home, and the twins spent the evening joyously wrapping presents and baking cookies.

Thursday, December 21

The next morning, Sally drove alone to Fincastle to call on Selena Jewett, her sister-in-law. Upon her return just after noon, Sally reported to Marjorie that Selena's cancer was not yet in remission and her outcome was still in doubt.

Later that afternoon, after hearing Sally's Westminster Chime doorbell, Marjorie answered the door to find a tall, distinguished man she recognized right away. "Senator Leathers!"

"You're Marjorie, right?"

"Yes, sir!"

"This is my wife, Anna Beth," he gestured at the equally tall woman, dressed in a stylish fur coat, standing beside him.

"Please, come in," Marjorie raved.

"I told him we should call first…" Anna Beth smiled.

"Nonsense!" Leathers insisted, unwrapping his scarf. "I wanted to surprise…"

"Tom Leathers!" Sally shouted, joining the troika. "To what do we owe this pleasure?"

"We…" Anna Beth blurted.

"We wanted to congratulate you personally," Tom blurted even louder, in his distinctive baritone.

"Thanks," Sally accepted.

"We are so happy for you!" Anna Beth extolled.

"I'll make some tea," Marjorie offered. "Anna Beth, come with me, would you?" The two women walked into the kitchen while Sally and U. S. Senator Tom Leathers made their way into the living room. "What a delight to meet you!" Marjorie exclaimed. "I've long been a fan of your husband."

"That's nice of you to say," the distinguished woman confirmed. "When my husband finished his term as Governor, he had the highest approval rating in the history of polling. He's sure made a lot of friends," she implored, continuing to unwrap her scarf. "When we were in college, I fell in love with his sincerity and sense of righteousness. But he was lacking in direction. My daddy was never sure Tom would make anything of himself. But he has! And even now, it astounds me as we travel the state together how many people really adore him."

Marjorie put a kettle on the stove and set four cups and saucers on a tray. "Did you just come by to see Sally?"

"Well," Anna Beth confessed, "we were on our way

through anyway. Our daughter, Taylor, graduated from Virginia Tech and the commencement was last week. So we've been in the area. Tom was always so fond of your brother-in-law and your sister. When he heard she'd won, he insisted we stop by. I would have called…"

"Not to worry!" Marjorie affirmed. "It's a thrill for me to meet you both and I'm sure Sally is grateful."

The tea water, still hot from breakfast, was quickly reheated. The two women joined the politicians in the other room. The senator was in mid-sentence when they reunited. "…not telling you anything you don't know already, but they play hardball these days. Any congeniality that existed when I began in politics is gone. There is no such word as compromise any more."

"But you got so much done in a bipartisan way when you were Governor," Sally noted. "Russ used to tell me how deftly you moved the General Assembly to act."

"I was proud of what I – we – got done, true," Leathers admitted. "But I almost believe the other guys got together afterward and said, 'It was a mistake, giving this Governor what he wanted. It helped him leave office with high approval ratings and then go on to the U. S. Senate.' Since then they've been determined not to ever help the other side again."

"Even if it means hurting the state?" Marjorie queried.

"Even if it means hurting the state," the Senator echoed. "Yup. Sad, isn't it?"

The foursome talked for over an hour, mostly about Leathers' efforts to bring bipartisanship and statesmanship back to Washington. He explained how the U. S. Senate was categorically unfair, giving each state regardless of population two senators. California, with its 35 million people had two senators, the same as Wyoming with its 600,000. "This really benefits the Republicans, because most of the more sparsely populated states tend to vote for them, and they are disproportionately represented." He explained that in the state and federal houses of the people, the U. S. House of Representatives and the Virginia House of Delegates, the winner-take-all system was unnaturally benefiting incumbents and impeding the ability of third-party or independent candidates to win. When Sally chided him about his success, he said sheepishly, "I have done well in the current system, but there are lots of good people out there that would be great legislators that don't even run because they're in the wrong district and will never win."

"And, if you don't mind me saying so," Marjorie interposed, "lots of piss-poor legislators that will never lose because of the make-up of their district."

"Isn't gerrymandering a big part of the problem?" Anna Beth asked.

"Sure," her husband agreed. "But let's not be fooled into thinking it is the entire problem. Look at a region of the state like Southwest Virginia where we are now. It leans about 60 percent Republican. It may have ten delegate districts. Even without any craven or malevolent districting, it could still produce ten Republican winners. The opposite is true in some Northern Virginia areas. What this means is that 40 percent of the people in Southwest Virginia who are not Republicans never get proper representation. It also means that you may have a great candidate who is a Democrat who can never win unless she moves to Northern Virginia or somewhere else where there is a more level playing field."

"What are you getting at? What would be a better

solution?" Marjorie voiced what she thought the other women were thinking.

"In a Republican district, most of the representatives should be Republicans, but not all. John Adams said, about our representative assemblies, they should 'be in miniature an exact portrait of the people at large.' So to my example, Southwest Virginia should ideally have 6 Republican and 4 Democratic Delegates."

"How can we fix that?" Marjorie inquired.

"There are a number of proportional election systems that have been devised. For example, there is Instant Runoff Voting. Another is Ranked Choice Voting. The best for legislative elections is probably Proportional Representation Voting.

"Almost universally, when a new democracy emerges around the world, they use one of those systems. Invariably they produce better results and more active voter participation. We're pretty proud of our democracy here in America, but it is an anachronism based upon only formerly relevant compromises. And huge, disgraceful percentages of people don't even bother to vote. They think the game is rigged and their vote doesn't count. Sadly, they're largely right."

"I wish these things could get fixed," Sally shrugged.

"Me too," the tall, thick-haired man said, "But let's face it; government is not about fixing society's vexing problems. I'm not sure it ever was, but it's worse now. Now it's about protecting turf and the status of the wealthy, the people in our society who need protection the least."

"Honey," Anna Beth interrupted.

"Yeah, we gotta go. We need to be back in Arlington by dark."

"Thank you so much for stopping by," the twins harmonized.

"It's always a pleasure to see you," Leathers said to Sally, returning his tea cup to its saucer. "What's the prognosis?"

"I'm still recovering from the staph infection. Then the real hell starts, the chemotherapy. I'm going to go to the inauguration and then start my treatments. Hopefully I'll be able to fulfill my duties during the upcoming session. At some point, they'll want to do the reconstructive surgery and give me a boob-boost…"

The distinguished man chuckled under his breath, glancing at Sally's erstwhile bustline.

"… but that will wait until I'm stronger. I am determined to beat this thing. Anna Beth," Sally continued, "I can't tell you how much I appreciate your contribution to my campaign. It has allowed me to keep Sam Sebrell on staff and keep the lawyers who are working on the recount paid. It was a godsend."

"You're welcome. Happy solstice!"

"Happy solstice to you, too. And Merry Christmas!"

Friday, December 22

Marjorie drove Sally to Tanglewood Mall where a vendor was selling the last remaining Christmas trees on the lot at half-price, due to the proximity to Christmas. He shook some snow that had fallen the night before off the branches of a small, slightly misshapen white pine and wrapped it for them, tying it to the bicycle rack on Sally's car.

On the way home, Marjorie said, "I'm not sure I understand what Senator Leathers was saying about elections and, you know, the anachronisms."

"This is something I've only learned since I entered politics," Sally confessed. "We've always had a system of one-man, one-vote. Actually, until women were allowed to vote, that was truer but not really. Prior to the Civil War, black men couldn't vote. After the War, black men could vote but returning white Confederate soldiers couldn't. You knew that couldn't last long. Anyway, we've always had elections where the winner gets at least one more vote than his or her challenger. If you have several candidates, the winner can win without even getting fifty percent. This was certainly a logical system, and it's easy enough for the voters to understand and the officials to count. But it isn't such a great system."

"Why not?"

"Well, to use an example similar to what the Senator talked about, let's talk about Congressmen in Virginia, our representatives to the U. S. House of Representatives. Right now, Virginia is a solid purple state, meaning it is pretty evenly split between the Republican and the Democrats. Yet the way our Congressional districts are made up, three have strong Democratic majorities and thus Democratic congressmen and eight have strong Republican majorities and thus Republican congressmen. There is almost no turnover because no matter what these guys do, and right now it is all men, they won't lose. Congress' approval ratings are an abysmal 12 percent or so, worse than such things as head lice and colonoscopies. Yet we re-elect them at rates over 90 percent. Most congressmen face stronger opposition from spin-off candidates from their own party than they do from the other party." Sally stopped at a red light. The road was wet in places from melting snow.

"So why…"

"So why is that a problem?" Sally interrupted, asking the question Marjorie was about to ask. "Lots of reasons. If congressmen don't face significant opposition, they are dis-incentivised to reach for compromise and conciliation. They don't even need to be civil or cooperative because they know they can't lose. Voters know they are disenfranchised and America now has among the lowest turn-out for its elections – particularly in non-presidential years – of all the world's democracies. The system is rigged and people know it. So they don't participate."

"Money is a problem, too, isn't it?" Marjorie suggested.

"Shit-absolutely! When the Supreme Court passed its Citizens United decision which opened the flood-gates to unlimited campaign contributions, I was convinced true democracy was over. Now I know I was right. What we see in our system today is the result of the deluge of money into the political process. Representatives have ceased doing the work of the people. They are in continuous election cycles, pleading from the wealthy for the funds they need to campaign."

"What can we do?" Marjorie wondered aloud, hinting frustration.

"You got me," Sally admitted with a shrug of her shoulders. "Seriously, in a few weeks I'll be the successor to the most powerful person in Virginia's government. And I'm nearly powerless to fix it."

Sally grew quiet. Still stopped at a traffic light, Marjorie had a chance to look at her twin sister who was again looking at her flat chest.

Sally lifted her head, took a deep breath, and said, "It's hard for me to even wrap my head around that right now. I just want to get well. But I have to tell you, and nobody should ever hear this coming from my lips, our system is benefiting only an infinitesimally small segment of our overall population. We're seeing unprecedented rates of income and wealth disparity in our country, not seen since the Gilded Age. Throughout history that has been a recipe for disaster. There's only so long that people will allow themselves to be tread upon."

"Are you suggesting there may be a revolution? Wow."

"I hope not," Sally ventured, as the light turned green and they began moving forward again. "Revolutions tend to be unruly things that hurt lots of people, often innocent people. But the masses can only take so much for so long. My political opponents for three decades have convinced hundreds of thousands of voters across Virginia to support them while doing nothing whatsoever to improve their lives that I can see. It's maddening."

The two spent the rest of the afternoon decorating the tree. Sally rested while Marjorie fixed salmon and rice with balsamic vinaigrette for dinner. After the meal, over a bottle of Riesling, Sally said, "One more thing about our discussion this afternoon… What makes me most pessimistic about the current system is that as broken as it is, it can only be fixed by our legislators, and they are the ones who most benefit from it being broken. I don't have a lot of hope."

"It seems our country is in a really bad state right now," Marjorie insisted.

"Lots of people think so. We've had worse times, of course. The Civil War. Reconstruction in the South. One hundred years of discrimination and segregation for blacks. It could be worse. It might soon be worse. But it's not good, for sure. We've got to count on cooler heads prevailing."

Saturday, December 23

Danny waited at Chopper's Sports Bar for Sol Horowitz to arrive. The smaller man entered with his typical scowl, asking impertinently, "What do you want, Danny? Bartender! Scotch on the rocks."

"Nice to see you, too. I've got some work for you," Danny announced.

Danny explained to the older man that his interest was in Courtney Templeton and told him what he'd learned. "Investigations are your business, not mine. I'm an amateur."

"What do you want to know?" Horowitz hoisted his Scotch to his mouth.

"I'm not sure. Dirt. Anything." Danny sipped his Pabst. "I'm just looking to find out anything she might not want other people to know."

"It's a hundred bucks an hour," Horowitz chirped. "Seventy-five for you, being in the tribe. Two-hundred and fifty dollars minimum. My guess is that if there is anything there, it won't take me long to find it. We're not talking about Al Capone here." He swallowed the remaining Scotch and turned to leave, placing a ten dollar bill on the bar.

"Happy Hanukkah," Danny yelled at him.

"Yeah."

Sunday, December 24

On Sunday morning, Sally left Marjorie while she visited the cemetery where her late husband, Russ, was buried. Upon her return, the twins went downtown to the Center in the Square, where they enjoyed the new butterfly habitat. They ventured to the roof which afforded a splendid view of the

Roanoke Valley, rimmed by low, snow-frosted mountains, including the nearest, Mill Mountain, to the south.

Their mood was celebratory and it was the perfect Christmas Eve.

Monday, December 25

On Christmas Day, Sally attended the Grandin Methodist Church in the morning, leaving Marjorie at home. During the afternoon, they took the corgis on a walk on a portion of the new Roanoke River Greenway from Wasena Park to Piedmont Park in light, falling snow. Several people recognized Sally and did a double-take on the likeness of the twins. Many congratulated Sally on her election and wished her well with overcoming her disease. Several of Sally's neighbors stopped by to visit and share the season's good cheer.

Marjorie realized how proud she was of her sister, impressed by her public persona and her resolve in the face of daunting challenges. She saw in her sister, still a mirror of herself, a strong, brave, and courageous woman.

Tuesday, December 26

The next day, under cold, blustery skies, Marjorie loaded up the Mercedes and with the corgis returned to Runnymede Meadow. Wilson had done his typical good job managing her farm in her absence. She checked first on Tank and saw that his scrotal wounds were healing. Ralph's kid, Fairfax, was hobbling around on infant legs, sporting a fubsy, appealing face.

Everything was in good order. Flurries of snow were falling and the air was crisp. Returning to the house, Marjorie was eager to put the election anxieties behind her and return to her normal life on her beloved estate.

Wednesday, December 27

Marjorie began her morning chores, feeding the cats and horses first, Boo and Radley in tow. On her way to the chicken coop, she caught a flash of movement from the corners of her eyes. Against the backdrop of a dusting of snow and the white painted fence slats, she saw a beautiful red fox. It had a long, expansive bushy tail, almost equal to its body in length. The fox stood immobile, staring at her as she stared at it. Boo and Radley, sensing her awareness, saw the fox as well. Strangely, they seemed fixed in their stares equally intently. The four of them stood there for a long moment, transfixed, the vulpine, two canines, and the human, until the fox turned and with an agile, nimble movement, slunk through the slats and vanished.

Marjorie looked down at Boo and Radley. The dogs looked up at her, tongues wagging, as if saying, "Was there something we were supposed to do?"

Thursday, December 28

"I'll send it to you on an e-mail attachment," Liza called to tell Marjorie. Liza had composed some notes to the Albemarle Democratic Party regarding the upcoming session, and she'd asked Marjorie to read and comment on it before it was submitted.

Marjorie downloaded it onto her desktop computer. She went outside and sat on the covered patio to smoke a cigarette before returning to steep a cup of tea. She situated herself in her favorite chair, put some Mozart on the stereo, and began her work.

Liza's tone was decidedly optimistic. It recognized Virginia's ongoing shift from its history as a largely rural, southern-leaning, often racist and conservative state to becoming more urbanized, multi-cultural, and progressive. Issues that would likely hit the General Assembly would be foremost like the passage of the Health-Net program, new funding for secondary education, particularly regarding music, dance, and the arts, new transportation infrastructure including pedestrian and rail, particularly extension of the Acela high-speed line from Washington down to Richmond, and the expansion of women's health care facilities throughout the state, especially in rural areas. Virginia was the nation's first state to have a black Governor, and Liza suggested that the dark days of insularity, supremacy and narrow-mindedness might finally be fading to the past. Virginia's population, and her voters, were becoming better educated, more urban and suburban, and more colorful – primarily Hispanic and Asian – all demographic shifts that helped level the playing field in many areas where conservatives had long dominated.

Marjorie made a few grammatical corrections and some minor word suggestions, but left the gist intact. She went to bed feeling contented and optimistic over prospects for the New Year, now only three days away.

Friday, December 29

While mucking the stalls, Marjorie heard on the radio that the Governor had called for a special election to replace Sally's vacated state senate seat. The special election for Pasdon was the following Tuesday, and by all reports it had been one of the most expensive albeit short, campaigns, in the state's history. Sally's replacement special election would surely be no different.

Saturday, December 30

Never the city person, Marjorie only begrudgingly agreed to go with Liza to Washington, DC, to celebrate the New Year. They visited the Smithsonian's Natural History museum, Marjorie's favorite.

On Liza's insistence, they visited the Holocaust Museum. Marjorie had always resisted opportunities to go, rationalizing that she never needed to see it to feel the despair that systematic mass murder could produce. Exhibit after exhibit wore on her psyche until she was forced to leave. She went outside and sat on a bench while her lover finished her tour. When Liza emerged, they walked towards the White House, quietly. Liza spoke first, "You know, when the Nazis came to power in the early 1930s, Germany was one of the most advanced, affluent, and educated countries in the world."

"It pains me to see how the world stood aside while the Nazis killed so many," Marjorie noted.

"There was a quote I heard once," Liza recalled, "about how they came for the Jews and I didn't speak out because I wasn't a Jew and they came for the socialists and I didn't speak out because I wasn't a socialist and when they came for me, there was nobody left to speak for me. We can't let the fight for justice be waged only by others."

Sunday, December 31

Marjorie and Liza toured the National Zoo most of New

Year's Eve. Marjorie was spellbound by the little penguins, darting around like jets in their pool. Liza was transfixed by the Sumatran tiger, which, much to her surprise, spent much of its time in the frigid water of its enclosure. The guide said that the tiger was the only species of cat, big or small, that enjoyed being in the water and had exceptional swimming capabilities.

They had a nice dinner together at one of Liza's old favorite restaurants in Georgetown and then made their way to the mall for the fireworks, which were amazing.

Danny Gold drove aimlessly the streets of Richmond on New Year's Eve, sulking over not being invited to any celebrations. There were some cars clustered at some houses, indicating parties inside. But otherwise, it seemed like any other winter evening. He drove down the famed Monument Avenue and around the traffic circles hosting statues of Virginian Confederate participants of the Civil War, including Robert E. Lee, J.E.B. Stuart, Jefferson Davis, and Stonewall Jackson.

How bland, he thought, was this mid-sized Southern city on this day of international celebration. He finally parked near the James River and walked the small bridge to the Great Ship Lock Park, where he watched some fireworks to the south at Rocketts Landing.

Three

Monday, January 1

Marjorie and Liza returned to their respective estates in Orange and Keswick, and to their household chores. Marjorie prepared for departure again the next day to Roanoke, where she was to help Sally pack for the inauguration in Richmond the following Saturday.

Tuesday, January 2

Marjorie left before dawn towards Roanoke, leaving the corgis behind in the care of Vance Wilson. She and Sally spent much of the day assembling Sally's various dresses, gowns, and jewelry. Sally sent her into town to an alteration shop where she retrieved a gown that had been re-fitted to Sally's new, surgically-altered bustline. The inauguration was on Saturday, and Sally was nervous and excited. Sam Sebrell came over to discuss the day's scheduled events.

After his departure, Marjorie had too much to drink and both twins laughed raucously like schoolgirls as they sorted through the dresses and jewelry they'd wear for the special event.

Wednesday January 3

Marjorie returned home early to Runnymede Meadow Estate, learning on the radio that Republican Rance Stevenson had won the special election for the senate seat vacated by Republican Brady Pasdon when he won his race for Attorney General. It was imperative for the Democrats to maintain parity in the state senate by holding Sally's seat in her replacement special election, two weeks away.

Washing dinner dishes at the kitchen sink, Marjorie saw outside that a nearly full moon had risen over the eastern horizon. She finished rinsing and dried her hands. Calling the dogs to accompany her, she donned her heaviest down jacket and walked outside into the yard. It was a cold, sparkling evening, with nary a wisp of wind. She sensed a faint smell of wood smoke. She sat on one of her Adirondack chairs, looking to the northeast, the moon to her right. Radley jumped to her lap and Boo huddled around her boots. She cradled her hands inside Radley's fur to keep them warm. Her moonshadow stretched across the yard.

Marjorie heard the hooting of an owl coming from the big pine on her left. "Who, who, who cooks for you!" it hooted. She saw it, a plump barred owl, perched comfortably on a branch, illuminated by the moon. Its banded chest heaved with each hoot and its head swung nearly completely around, first one way and then the other. The moonlight was intense enough to highlight the bird's features, including its thin, yellow beak. But its eyes, deeply set inside its double-oval face, set were darker than outer space. "Who, who cooks for you? Who, who, who, WHOOOO?" it accused. She watched it for several moments before it spread its expansive wings and glided silently away.

She stayed outside for several more moments before the cold drove her back to the warmth of her home.

Thursday, January 4

Danny met Jorge again for a tennis match. Having been playing more regularly, Danny's skills were improving as was his stamina. Still, he lost the first set. The game score was even in the second set when he went to pick up a ball in the back netting where his eyes caught a woman playing in the neighboring court. He stopped to assess her for a moment. She was tall, stately, with curly red hair. She wore a tight, low-cut tennis dress and cute white shoes and socks. She sensed his gaze and gave him a perfunctory smile before returning to her serve. She would be his next conquest, he decided.

Concluding his game with Jorge which he lost 6-4, 7-6, Danny wandered to the registration desk. He waited for the attendant to become distracted by another customer and while his attention was removed, Danny surreptitiously looked at the reservation book on the counter and found the names of the players beside him: Rhonda McCarty and Alison Partlow. The red-head would be Alison, he guessed.

He also noticed their name for the same time and court a week later. He'd be back.

Friday, January 5

On the day before Inauguration Day, Marjorie packed her bag and drove to Keswick to pick up Liza. They met Sally who was driving from Roanoke at the Interstate 64 Exit 129 Park and Ride and the three drove into Richmond to their hotel in Marjorie's Mercedes. They had dinner with a joyous crowd of supporters at Winston's Bistro in the Fan district. The mood was festive in spite of the frigid temperature the night was producing.

Saturday, January 6

Early on Inauguration Day, the three women had breakfast together in the hotel restaurant much as they had done the day after the election. They had a surprise visit from Miller McGregor, the Governor-Elect, who said to Sally playfully, "I have a surprise for you later today."

The three women looked at each other with puzzled expressions.

McGregor smiled, "Nope, it wouldn't be a surprise if I told you now. Gotta run and get ready! Dress warm! It's cold outside."

Sally, Marjorie, and Liza met Sam Sebrell in the lobby and the foursome walked the five blocks to the Virginia State Capitol, home of the oldest continuous law-making body in the Americas. In spite of the Arctic air, it was a sterling, sunny day with little wind. As they passed some less than reputable looking street people, Marjorie wondered if Sally would be getting police protection as the state's Lt. Governor, knowing that the Governor himself would always have an assigned escort, likely Sally's nephew John Jewett.

After being sworn in by the Chief Justice of the Virginia Supreme Court, the new Lt. Governor Sally Taliaferro Bradley and the new Attorney General Brady Alexander Pasdon took their seats on the front row of the stage with Marjorie being Sally's special guest beside her and Pasdon's wife beside him. The new Governor, Miller McGregor, Jr., was then sworn in. He began his inauguration speech at a lectern decorated with the seal of the Commonwealth of Virginia, showing the Roman goddess Virtus standing tall over a vanquished foe. She had an exposed left breast, a spear in her right hand and a sword in her left. Her left foot was placed on the chest of a fallen man, his crown fallen from his head and a broken chain in his left hand and a scourge in his right.

"Mr. Speaker, Lt. Governor Bradley, Attorney General Overington, Members of the General Assembly, Justices of the Supreme Court, guests and friends from across our Commonwealth and nation, my fellow Virginians: It is the greatest and most humbling honor of my life to have received the trust you have placed in me. It is a breathtaking position for anyone to stand here before you as the Governor of this great Commonwealth, a state that has produced such impressive leaders as George Washington, Patrick Henry, Thomas Jefferson, James Madison, James Monroe, Robert E. Lee, Woodrow Wilson, and so many others. Patrick Henry himself was our first Governor, followed by Thomas Jefferson, two men who have inspired countless people not just here in Virginia or the United States of America, but in all the nations of the world.

"Before I continue with my remarks this glorious afternoon, I want to ask our new Lt. Governor, Sally Bradley, to stand, and for us all to show her the support she'll need over the next few weeks and months as she faces her battle with cancer. Sally?"

He turned and looked towards her, motioning her to stand. When she did, the audience rose to their feet as well and applauded her heartily. She waved and smiled, pumped her fist against her heart and pointed to them, and smiled again. She walked to the lectern and hugged the Governor, hugged his wife Ronnie, returned to her place and hugged Marjorie, and sat down, as did the crowd.

McGregor continued, "Sally lost her husband, Senator Russell Bradley, a few years ago. She took the torch he held so high and has continued to lead, inspire, and motivate thousands of Virginians, especially girls and women, to achieve greatness. She's a strong woman, a fighter, and I'm sure she'll prevail. But I'm equally sure our support, your support, will be welcomed." Everyone applauded again.

McGregor returned to his speech, evoking themes of perseverance and sacrifice, of mutual interest and shared responsibility. But his primary theme was courage. "We have faced many tests as a state. Our recent commemoration of the sesquicentennial of the great War Between the States reminds us that we share a common destiny. There are those among us who look to divide and sow the seeds of discontentment and disillusion. But we as Virginians understand that to move our society and our economy forward, we must work together. While industry and commerce must be allowed to move forward, the state has an active roll to play in commonsense regulation and guidelines.

"The challenges presented to Patrick Henry and Thomas Jefferson during our nation's founding and the challenges presented to John Letcher during the Civil War are different from the challenges we face now, but the values and common purpose are the same. When any Virginian goes to bed hungry, we all suffer. When any Virginian lacks access to a world-class education, we all suffer. When any Virginian has only contaminated water to drink or polluted air to breathe, we all suffer. Ours is a shared destiny and a shared purpose.

"Virginia and Virginians have always led the world. We are not a people who accept mediocrity or mere competence. We always have and must continue to set a high bar for ourselves and reach for excellence, always knowing that there is more to be done.

"We must have the courage to fight what has long been conventional wisdom, that austerity is the path to prosperity, because it has never been borne by facts. The free enterprise system has long been the engine of job and wealth creation, but only upon a foundation of well-maintained roads, modern ports, efficient airports, rapid train and transit services, can commerce move and flourish. Only with well-educated and well-trained young people can we stay at the forefront of new technologies and lead the world in innovation and creativity. And only with strict, commonsense regulation can we keep our environment safe and healthy, because when our rivers and air are polluted, we seal our fate in poverty forever.

"There are those among us who say we should cut back, trim our budgets, eliminate programs like music, dance, and art in our schools, let hungry children fend for themselves, let mentally ill people go untreated, and let our utilities and corporations pollute our rivers and our air. Those people are wrong! My mother, a high school teacher at Thomas Jefferson High School here in Richmond, instilled in me and my siblings the essential value of an education. I got that great education because the visionary men who stood before me as governors of Virginia and the men and women in the Legislatures over which they served recognized that to compete and thrive, our citizens must be educated as well or better than any in the world. Great schools, great teachers, and great administrators don't come cheaply, and we must be willing to pay for them."

Marjorie noticed that as applause interrupted the speech, there were those who were heartily in approval and those who seemed to vehemently disagree. What a challenge it would be to govern such a diverse state with such acrimony and divisiveness!

McGregor continued by speaking about energy, indicating his desire to have Virginia lead the way in new technologies and the urgency of diversification. He spoke about the recent earthquake in Algeria and urged Virginians to help that badly stricken, impoverished north-African nation and of the typhoon that had devastated parts of the Philippines and their need for assistance. And he spoke about the corrosive influence of big money in the government, saying, "Virginia works best when its government works for the people."

He closed with, "Thank you all and let us move forward, working for the good of the people of the Commonwealth of Virginia."

Sunday, January 7

After an exhausting weekend, Marjorie, Sally and Liza returned home. Marjorie dropped Sally at the park and ride to get her car, and then Liza at Keswick. Sally followed Marjorie to Runnymede Meadow. Marjorie fed the corgis and Sally went to sleep early, anticipating her scheduled visit to the UVA medical center the next day.

Monday, January 8

The next morning, Marjorie and Sally drove separate cars from Orange to Charlottesville for Sally's first appointment with her radiation oncologist, Maneesha Anaokar. The small, dark-haired woman spoke to the sisters about Sally's upcoming treatment. "We are not going to start chemotherapy just yet. Today we're going to do what's called a MUGA scan. That's a Multigated Acquisition Scan, which is a test to determine the ejection capability of your heart. We inject you with a rapidly degrading radioactive tracer. Then we watch your chest with a gamma camera to see how your heart moves blood. Then a week from today, assuming all goes well, we'll begin your chemotherapy."

Sally was asked to strip from the waist up and lay on a padded table. Anaokar placed electrodes on her chest. She then injected a clear fluid containing a radioactive tracer into Sally's arm. Then with a special camera, Anaokar photographed the movement of the tracer. She had Sally stand up and do several jumping jacks and then return to the table so the movement of blood during exercise could be seen. The whole procedure took just over two hours.

Marjorie stayed to support her sister. By early afternoon, they had gone back to their separate homes. Sally would only be staying in Roanoke for two nights, as she was due back in Richmond for the start of the General Assembly term on Wednesday.

Tuesday, January 9

The mailman seldom had good news for Danny Gold, so his solution was to check his mailbox with decreasing frequency. But the three invoices from his credit card companies were getting harder to ignore. He remembered something he'd once heard from a wrestling coach, that one of the definitions of bad news is that it doesn't get better the longer you ignore it. The overdue charges were beginning to add up and he desperately needed a job. He wrote and mailed three checks, all insufficient to cover his overall debts.

He typed the URL for the website GOP-Power on his laptop and searched for jobs. A congressman running for reelection in Massachusetts – Danny couldn't stomach that liberal environment. A state senator running in Alaska – a shiver went up his spine just thinking about it. A congressional election in red state South Carolina caught his eye until he noticed that it was in the bluest district in the state and he was tired of losing. Nothing appealed to him. He was adamant that he'd not stoop so low as to take an entry-level job, at least unless his desperation level rose.

Wednesday January 10

"Hey," Sally's voice said in Marjorie's speaker phone.

"Hey back. How's it going?"

It was 7:20 p.m. on the first full day of the General Assembly.

"Not bad. It's the typical confusion of the first day back. All the rookies are scratching their heads, trying to figure out why they bothered to run for office in the first place. All the veterans are like rabid wolves, staking out their turf. Usual insanity; it's madness."

"Where's your office?" Marjorie asked.

"It's in the Governor's office building, just southeast of the Capital. Pretty nice digs, really. Nobody will let me carry anything heavier than this smart-phone. I'm feeling pretty pampered."

They talked more about expectations for the session and for Sally's return the following Monday for her chemo treatment.

"I've kept Sam Sebrell on as my Chief of Staff. He'll be working overtime with all the time I'll be gone for treatments."

Sally mentioned before they hung up that John Jewett had indeed been retained as the new Governor's personal police attendant and driver.

Thursday, January 11

Jorge wasn't able to play tennis the following week, but Danny went to the club anyway, hoping to meet the woman he'd coveted the week before. He sat in the clubhouse and watched the two women enter and sit together for a drink. When the smaller woman left, Danny ambled over.

"May I join you?" he asked, with insistence.

"I'm expecting someone," the redhead replied, curtly.

"Perhaps that someone is me," he retorted, taking a seat opposite her. "In case it is someone else, I'll make my stay brief."

"So what can I do for you?" she played along.

"Many wonderful things, I suspect. But it is my intention to do wonderful things unto you," he boasted, unflinchingly. He rubbed his tongue across his lips. "I'm Danny."

"Do tell," she retorted. She sipped her margarita.

"I do," he quipped, cockily, wiping his index finger across the rim of her drink and then transferring the salt to his lips. "It is among my greatest talents to bring pleasures to women they've never known before."

She smirked, choking on her drink. "Seriously?"

"Seriously."

"I'm Rhonda," she offered.

"Rhonda," he continued, "some men crave fancy cars. Some savor fine wines or smoke fat cigars. I am a connoisseur of fine women. The buoyancy of their hair. The curl of their eyebrows. The sparkling gaze of her eyes. The moisture of her skin and the smell of her sweat. The way your hips and buttocks move when you strike a tennis ball. The way your lips move when you laugh. Nothing about you escapes me."

She rested her glass back on the table, still clutching it. "Are you trying to seduce me?"

"Only if it be your pleasure." He reached out to her hand and ran his left index finger along the back of the knuckles of her right hand. "A woman must share her gifts carefully. She must know that the touch of a man's hand on hers is genuine. Seduction it is not. Lust must never be one-sided."

He saw through the glass-topped table her legs uncross and spread slightly. He continued to rub the back of her hand gently, softly, rotating the ring on her ring finger.

"Lust, eh? And?" she sighed.

"And if on your way here today, the thought crossed your mind that a tennis match with a girlfriend might only be a part of your day's pleasure, your opportunity is now."

She looked at his eyes, then at his hand rubbing the back of hers. Then she looked back at him. "My apartment is nearby," she smiled, taking a last sip of her margarita and licking the last tongue of salt from the rim. "Shall we go?" She got up abruptly, put a ten dollar bill on the table, and walked ahead of him outside to the parking lot. "I'll drive," she offered, reaching her Miata. "I'll bring you back later for your car."

Friday, January 12

Marjorie resolved to keep better abreast of the goings-on in the General Assembly, knowing that she'd be spending more time with her accomplished sister than in years past. She had to rub her eyes twice when in the morning edition of the *Richmond Reporter* she saw this headline,

**Virginia State Senator
Joan Brownlea, (D) Fairfax
introduces gay marriage
legalization legislation**

She called Sally to ask about it.

"Yeah," Sally exclaimed, "in the second day of the session, Joan went for a home run. The ball is headed for deep center-field. I don't think anybody saw it coming, but really we probably all should have. I don't know if the ball will clear the center-field wall. If a Republican wins my seat, this bill is toast. But if a Democrat wins and I cast the tie-breaker in the Senate, you'll know how I'll vote."

"I was hoping I didn't have to wonder about it."

"I know what you and Liza mean to each other. I know what so many other gay and lesbian couples mean to each other. You can count on me."

"Thanks," Marjorie said, appreciatively.

"You know what, sis? I love Virginia. I know you do too," Sally urged.

"Yeah," Marjorie concurred.

"But," Sally rolled on, "we've been on the wrong side of history before. We were on the wrong side of the slavery issue. We were on the wrong side of the civil rights issue. Do you know that our United States of America was the first country in the world to concertedly sterilize what it considered to be undesirable people, and Virginia was one of the leading states? We were on the wrong side of that. And we're still on the wrong side of gay rights. Martin Luther King said, 'Now is the time to make real the promises of democracy.' You don't need to worry how I'll vote."

Saturday, January 13

Sally left Richmond and drove to Runnymede Meadow Estate to spend the weekend with Marjorie, to relax and go over her homework away from the noise and bustle of the General Assembly and the city. At dinner that night of baked ham and seasoned potatoes, Marjorie ventured, "You mentioned something yesterday when we spoke about sterilizing undesirable people. I had no idea what you were talking about. So I looked it up."

"What did you find?" Sally coaxed.

"I was shocked. Virginia sterilized something like 8300 people against their will. This started in the 1920s and went on until the late 1970s. Awful!"

Sally took a sip of her pinot grigio and acknowledged, "Yeah. In the last term of the General Assembly, a lawyer from Lynchburg made a presentation, asking for reparations.

So I studied it. I was shocked, too."

"How do you think the state got away with that?" Marjorie spooned some gravy on her potatoes.

Sally put down her goblet and Marjorie instinctively refilled it for her. "There was a worldwide eugenics movement in the early 1900s. Eugenics is the science of improving the species by weeding out undesirable traits. We've been doing it with animals for centuries. Dogs in particular have been extensively bred for desirable traits, right Radley?"

Boo and Radley barked.

"Michigan had the first law in 1897 to allow sterilization. Many other states followed suit, in particular sterilizing prisoners in homes for mentally and physically disabled people. Astonishingly, in 1927, the Supreme Court in a case called Buck v. Bell, legitimized the sterilization of the intellectually disabled. The case was about a woman named Carrie Buck, who was sterilized against her volition, by a doctor named Priddy. Priddy died and his successor was a Dr. Bell, who became the accused. The ruling, favorable to sterilization, was written by Oliver Wendell Holmes. That really put things into high gear."

"How awful!"

"Yeah, and Virginia was one of the leading states."

"Damn."

Sally wiped a crumb from her lip. "After the war, seeing the insane brutality of the Nazis, the eugenics movement began to wane. But Virginia continued on for over thirty years, doing its last sterilization in 1979. So from 1924 until 1979, Virginia sterilized people against their will longer than any other state."

Marjorie was speechless. The piece of lamb she had on

her fork sat immobilized.

"You want to know something else?" Sally submitted. "As abhorrent as this is, the General Assembly never repealed the law allowing it."

"Really?"

"Really. It could happen again tomorrow, in the wrong set of circumstances."

"I don't know what to say," Marjorie said.

"Like I said yesterday, I love Virginia. We have so much to be proud of. I'm sure you've seen that old quote, 'To be a Virginian either by birth, marriage, adoption, or even on one's mother's side, is an introduction to any state in the Union, a Passport to any foreign country, and a benediction from above.' I don't think anybody knows who wrote it. We can be a pretty self-righteous people. But we owe it to ourselves and to others to be honest about our history."

Marjorie added, "We seem to have our share of warts."

Sunday, January 14

Sally returned to Richmond in the afternoon on a agonizingly cold day. As Marjorie helped with her bags and watched her drive away, swirls of snow tickled her nose. Sally called her two hours later to assure Marjorie of her safe arrival.

Monday, January 15

Marjorie was mucking the horse stalls when her smart phone ring tone of "Every little thin' gonna be all right," rang. "Hey."

"Bad news," Sally said in an ashen tone.

"What's wrong," Marjorie's chest tightened and her heart

skipped a beat.

"Barton Mullins has been in a traffic accident. It's serious."

"I'm sure I should recognize his name," Marjorie admitted, sheepishly.

"He was a good friend of Russ's. He was, ah *is*, a Democrat from Bristol. He and Russ often commuted to Richmond together. He was in the House in those days, but now he's in the Senate. Or he was until this morning. He was on his way to the capital. There was a backup on I-81 near Abingdon and when he slowed, a truck plowed into his car."

"Tragic!" Marjorie sympathized.

"He was alive when they got him to Johnston Memorial in Abingdon, but just barely."

The horror was sitting in with Marjorie when Sally informed, "He is the only Democrat in the Senate west of Roanoke. There is only one Democrat in the House of Delegates from the west."

Marjorie didn't know what to say. Sally continued, "Right now, he's in a coma. It's serious enough that he may never emerge from it."

Both women were quiet as they pondered the implications.

"What does this mean politically?" Marjorie quizzed.

"I'm not sure what happens now in the Senate. Right now, there is a twenty-nineteen split between the Republicans and the Democrats, with my old seat still open. If the Democratic candidate, my old friend Opal Witherspoon, wins, it'll be twenty-twenty. We'll know in a few days. If that happens, and if we have party line votes, I would cast the deciding vote. If Barton doesn't recover and can't serve, then there are eighteen Democrats and twenty Republicans."

Marjorie suggested, "Won't he be replaced? Won't there be another election?"

"I don't think so. I think the Governor will appoint someone, at least temporarily, to represent that district. But I suspect it will take a couple of weeks for him to make a decision."

"What happens in the meantime?" Marjorie inquired.

"I guess if there are strict party-line votes, the Republicans will win, twenty to eighteen now or twenty to nineteen if Opal is elected and sworn in. In any event, there won't be any ties. So no bills will come my way. Most bills take several weeks to wind their way through the legislative process, so I don't think it will matter much."

They talked about Sally's return to UVA on Monday and hung up. Marjorie spent most of the afternoon working with Tank, ensuring he was healing properly and continuing to exercise and move.

Tuesday, January 16

Danny played tennis again with Jorge. Danny was ahead 6-3, 4-3 when Jorge got a call on his cell phone and insisted he needed to leave. Rhonda wasn't at the club and Danny hadn't called her again. Although he was desirous of her, he convinced himself not to show too much eagerness.

Wednesday January 17

Marjorie was in Orange shopping for groceries when Sally called to tell her that her old friend Opal Witherspoon of Roanoke had won Sally's seat in the Senate. Sally wasn't sure how the injury to Barton Mullins had affected the voting, if at all. But she was relieved that the seat had remained in Democratic hands, although with Mullins' absence, the Senate would still be held by Republicans, twenty to nineteen. With the House of Delegates in Republican hands, the Governor would get few if any bills of his liking to sign.

Thursday, January 18

Sally called Marjorie briefly to tell her about her conversation with the new Senator-elect, Opal Witherspoon, telling Marjorie that she had told Witherspoon how happy she was and how important her victory was to maintaining a balance in the state government.

Friday, January 19

Danny waited at the same Chopper's Sports Bar for Sol Horowitz who had summoned him there, nursing another Pabst. Horowitz entered and with no fanfare, put two sheets of folded paper into Danny's shirt pocket. "Here's what you're looking for," Horowitz said perfunctorily and then just as quickly walked out.

Danny took out the sheets and unfolded them. One was an invoice for $250. The other only had a few words, but it brought a smile to his face. He finished his beer, paid his tab on a credit card that already had more debt than he could pay, and departed.

Saturday, January 20

As he drank his morning coffee, Danny again removed the sheets Horowitz gave him the day before. He read the report for the half-dozenth time, cocky and self-satisfied in his good fortune. Indeed, Courtney Templeton had an incident from her past, and Danny began to formulate a plan to take advantage of it.

He went for a jog on a cool, overcast but still morning, thinking about nothing but Courtney Templeton until he stepped on a curb awkwardly, painfully spraining his ankle. He limped home, feeling aged, embarrassed and defeated.

Sunday, January 21

Sally arrived at Runnymede Meadow from Richmond after dinner in preparation for her appointment at UVA Medical Center in the morning. It was already dark. The twins watched *Sleepless in Seattle* on the DVR before bedtime. It had always been one of Sally's favorite movies.

Monday, January 22

Sally's appointment wasn't until 1:15 p.m. so she convinced Marjorie they should go riding in the morning, bringing some joy before the beginning of what was sure to be an unrelentingly painful process. It was a cold but sunny day, with a azure sky of blue. "I'm not going to pass on opportunities for fun and joy," Sally said.

They rode Gooch and Dawson again. The corgis ran along, straining to keep up.

By afternoon, they were once again at UVA. Sally sat in the office of Maneesha Anaokar for briefing before the chemo session. Anaokar informed, "I'm going to give you an idea of what to expect. But I guarantee you; there will still be moments of fear and shock. I don't sugar-coat things."

The twins listened attentively as the health care professional continued.

"Chemotherapy is poison, specially formulated to stop the spread of rapidly reproducing cells, specifically cancerous cells. Your doctor waited until the healing from your surgery was over before getting started. I understand you had some infection."

"That's right," Sally provided. "A staph infection."

"That's why we've waited so long. I also understand the election had a part as well."

"Yes," Marjorie interjected. "Sally wanted to get through the inauguration."

"Chemo is the part of cancer treatment that everyone abhors. One of the chemicals we're going to use is called Adriamycin. People refer to it as the 'Red Devil' or 'Red Death'. It is bright, a rosy red color. It is a relative to mustard gas. We are going to pump it into your veins. I'll be wearing protective gloves, because if I get it on my skin, it will eat it alive. I inject it into your bigger veins for dilution effects.

"The side effects are miserable, frankly. In a week to ten days, your hair will begin falling out. Hair follicles are rapidly growing cells. You'll likely have diarrhea because the cells within your digestive tract are rapidly growing cells. Your mouth will feel like it's been infested by spoonfuls of stink bugs. Hopefully that will be the worst of it."

"Damn!" Marjorie fumed.

"There's more? What else?" Sally pried.

"Want the whole list?" the doctor clarified.

Sally nodded affirmatively. "Yes."

"You will be fatigued. You may have nausea and vomiting. Your skin will be extremely sensitive to the touch, and you may have bleeding problems like bloody noses. Your fingernails and toenails may become yellow, dark, or brittle and your fingertips will go numb. You may have memory problems. You'll want to be as careful as you can to write your appointments."

"I'm in a job that demands 110 percent."

"I know you are. The people of Virginia will need to be understanding of your situation. You may be there for them and you may not. That's the cold, hard truth."

Silence.

"Are you ready to get started?" Anaokar continued.

"Yes," Sally assured, with stoic determination.

They walked into the chemo room where Sally placed her left arm on an arm-rest. Anaokar scrubbed Sally's skin and inserted an IV. Anaokar set the red fluid drip and the red poison began its gravity-fed trip down the clear hose into Sally's bloodstream. Two hours later, Sally and Marjorie were on their way back to Runnymede Meadow.

Tuesday, January 23

The next morning at breakfast, Sally took a call on her cell phone, which she put on speaker. "Sally?" the familiar male voice said.

"Yes?"

"It's Miller McGregor. How are you doing?"

"Hi Governor. I'm fine so far. I've got a bloodstream filled with poison, but it won't be doing its work for a few days. I'll be back in Richmond tomorrow, late morning."

"Good! Listen, I've got a favor to ask. Gretchen is e-mailing you right now with my main gubernatorial appointments.

I'd like your input. Would you mind looking them over?"

"Not at all. I'm flattered. You didn't need to do that."

"You're a good judge of character and you know lots of people. I value your feedback. If you see anybody you're skeptical about, let me know. Or if there is anyone whom I've left out who needs to be included, let me know that, too."

"I will, Governor," she promised.

"Miller. Please call me Miller."

"Yes, Miller. I'll get back to you by noon tomorrow."

"Thanks." He hung up.

"That was nice of him," Marjorie suggested.

"Yeah. He's a good guy. He'll be a great Governor. He's firm, decisive, intelligent, and sincere. He has a long future in politics. Virginia is considered an important swing state nationally, and ex-governors with national aspirations have lots of options when they're done. They only get one term. That's another Virginia anachronism. Do a lousy job and you get one term. Do a good job and you get one term. Do a great job and you get one term. Remember the song, *The Way It Is?* Some things will never change."

Wednesday January 24

Sally drove to Roanoke to put some household things in order. Per Marjorie's insistence, Sally planned to essentially move in with Marjorie at Runnymede Meadow during the period of her treatment. She reasoned it would be closer to UVA and closer to Richmond, two places she'd be spending most of her time. If she was indeed to become fatigued, it meant fewer of the longer trips to and from Roanoke.

As was her habit, Marjorie looked after the animals at the

estate. Tank was fully recovered from his castration, with no infections or problems. Ralph and her kid, Fairfax, were doing well and the newborn was growing rapidly.

A snowstorm was forecast for that evening, and Marjorie was glad that Sally had driven back to Roanoke before it began. It eventually began snowing around 4:00 p.m., and by early the next morning, Charlottesville had gotten fourteen inches and Roanoke twelve. It was the year's heaviest snowfall to date.

Thursday, January 25

Sally returned to Runnymede Meadow the following day with a carload of clothing and personal effects. The main roads had been cleared of snow, but there were lots of slick spots on Marjorie's driveway. Liza arrived after work and the women had a nice dinner together, eating one of Marjorie's chickens. The mood was bright and cheery, although it was clear to Marjorie that Sally was fatigued, evidenced as she was unloading her car. Nobody spoke a word about the chemotherapy sessions, past or upcoming.

Meanwhile, Danny Gold was driving northeasterly on US-360 from his home in Richmond to the mansion of Brady Pasdon in nearby Mechanicsville. Gold had called Pasdon the day before to ask for a face-to-face meeting, without revealing the nature of his call. To his relief, Pasdon accepted his request without undue inquiry and invited him over.

A black maid wearing a white apron met Danny at the door. She ushered him into Pasdon's office where Danny faced the new Attorney General who was sitting at a wide wooden banker's desk, staring at an oversized computer screen. Two televisions across the spacious, wood-shelved office were tuned to news channels, both muted.

"Danny, have a seat," the politician demanded. "What's up?"

"Good afternoon, Mr. Pasdon. How's your day?"

"I don't have time for pleasantries, Gold. State your business and let's move on."

"Yes, sir. I'll get right to it. I've learned of a situation that might be a serious embarrassment or worse to your tenure as Attorney General. It certainly would have derailed your campaign, had it been known."

Pasdon sniffled and said, "I'm listening."

"It's about Courtney Templeton."

"What about her?" Pasdon barked, defensively.

"You may not know about the, ah, abortion she had."

"Oh? When was that?" Pasdon reacted with incredulity. "She would have told me."

"Perhaps. Perhaps not. It was some time ago. I'm sure…"

"I've been fighting against that horrible act since the day…"

Danny jumped, "Yes, and that's why so many good people have supported you so enthusiastically!"

"How do you know?" Pasdon demanded.

"Let me just say I have my sources. It is incumbent on a professional political spokesperson like myself to stay abreast of the key players, both friends and foes. It is unbecoming of me to reveal the source of my intelligence."

As Danny pondered his use of the word "intelligence," Pasdon dropped his head in thought.

"I know you're busy," Danny assured. "I promised it would

be a brief meeting and I'll see myself out. If you decide to replace Templeton with someone who is, I'll say this with all due respect to her, more trustworthy and professional, now that Westfall's campaign is over I'm available." He dropped a business card with his phone number and e-mail, and turned to leave. "Good afternoon, sir, and congratulations again on your win." He turned and departed, feeling sanctimonious and self-satisfied.

Friday, January 26

Sally was resting through the afternoon on one of Marjorie's upholstered sofas. At 3:00 p.m., she switched on the television. Marjorie entered the room and brought her sister a glass of Coke with ice. Governor McGregor appeared on screen behind a lectern with the state's official seal with the familiar image of Virtus, as always standing over her vanquished opponent, representing tyranny. He spent several moments announcing his new cabinet, including two that Sally had suggested, for Secretary of Finance, Aubrey Brown, and Secretary of Education, Mollie Stoneman. When the conference ended Sally expressed deep satisfaction to Marjorie that the Governor had been so attentive to her recommendations.

Liza drove over late in the day with a casserole for dinner. She spent the night with Marjorie.

Saturday, January 27

Sally spent much of the day in bed with flu-like symptoms, including a runny nose, headache, and hacking cough. Marjorie and Liza nursed her, feeding her soup, and helping her with toilet functions. Sally was weak and clearly miserable. She spoke with a pronounced nasal tone. Marjorie had a runny nose as well.

Liza returned home to Keswick that afternoon, telling Marjorie that she was actively trying to avoid unnecessary exposure to any of the twins' germs, expressing her hope of staying healthy.

Sunday, January 28

"Marjorie!" Sally shrieked through the speaker of Marjorie's cell phone. "Come in the house!" Marjorie was in the barn shoveling manure. She knew from Sally's tone that something inside was terribly wrong. She dropped her mucking rake and sprinted back to the house, envisioning dreadful scenarios.

Marjorie burst through the back door and into the kitchen, mucking boots and all. "What's wrong?"

"He's dead," Sally coughed and sobbed. "Dead."

"Who's dead?"

"Miller," Sally wailed through tears. "Miller McGregor. The Governor is dead."

"Oh my God! What happened?"

Sally wiped her nose on a handkerchief. "I just got a call from the State Police. He was in a plane crash before dawn this morning. He was at a reception in Fairfax last night. He was being flown in his Governor's airplane to another meeting in the morning in Bristol. His airplane just vanished. There was a lot of fog overnight. The wreckage was found a half-hour ago on a ridgeline in Craig County, north of Roanoke. Miller, his pilot, and his chief of staff are all dead."

"Do you know the area?"

"Yeah, I know it well. Russ and I used to go hiking near

there on the Appalachian Trail."

Marjorie raised her hands to her face and then walked to hug her sister.

Sally sobbed and choked back her tears, "It's really crazy."

"What?"

"There was another airplane crash near there, back in 1971. It killed Audie Murphy. He was a war hero and an actor. There's a monument on the mountain; I've hiked by it."

"Wow."

"You know what else?" Sally observed. "This is really spooky. The area is called 'Millers Cove.'" She coughed violently, choking back tears.

Both women were silent for a moment, taking in the ramifications. Marjorie spoke next. "Are you thinking what I'm thinking?"

"Yeah. I'm going to be the new governor."

"Are you okay?"

Sally took a deep breath. "I feel like hell. I'm going back to bed."

"Sally?"

"Yeah?"

"Could this not have been an accident?"

Silence. "I don't know," Sally admitted. "I don't even want to think about it."

Three hours later, as Sally slept, Marjorie took a call on Sally's smart phone. "This is Marjorie Taliaferro."

"Hi Marjorie. This is Larry Kinsey. We met last month in Roanoke. May I please speak with Ms. Bradley?"

"Hi Mr. Kinsey. Sally isn't well."

"I understand she's being treated for her cancer."

"Yeah, she had her first chemo session a week or so ago.

Now she's got a cold or the flu. She's here at my house near Orange. She's sleeping right now. Do I need to wake her?"

"I suppose not," he said. "Do you know why I'm calling?"

"I think so. It's about the Governor… I mean the late Governor."

"Yes. I need to speak with her personally again. May I come there tomorrow afternoon? My boss needs to come, too. He's the head of elections in the state. I'm sure you know why."

"Yes, I think so."

"We need to discuss succession," he informed. "We're in uncharted territory with Sally being sick, but she'll need to take the oath of office very soon. We need to talk with her about it."

"I understand. I'll let her know when she wakes." Marjorie gave him directions to her estate. "We'll see you tomorrow. Goodbye."

Marjorie hung up the phone. She went into Sally's bedroom and found her still asleep, her breathing labored and uneven. Marjorie put her hand near Sally's forehead and could tell even without touching that Sally had a fever. She walked outside and called Shaunica Sarver, her general practitioner who lived just north, near Culpeper. Dr. Sarver said, "I'm in Washington right now. I'll be home after midnight. I'll swing by first thing in the morning and have a look."

Marjorie found an old mercury thermometer and took Sally's temperature. 103°F.

Before she went to bed, Marjorie checked Sally's cell phone again for any messages. There were a couple of messages including one from Sam, which she'd deal with in the morning. Otherwise, on the state political news-board was an announcement that public relations director for Attorney General Brady Pasdon, Courtney Templeton, had resigned effective immediately. No reason was given and no replacement was mentioned.

Monday, January 29

A large, friendly black woman appeared at Marjorie's door at 7:45 a.m. the next morning, carrying a black leather bag. Shaunica Sarver smiled at Marjorie and asked, "Where's my patient?" Within ten minutes of examining Sally, Sarver said, "I think she has pneumonia. Her heart rate is high, her blood pressure is low, and her respiratory rate is elevated. She still has a fever. When I auscultate, I hear blocked passageways in her lungs. This isn't too clinical, but she's pretty sick. We need to get her back to UVA."

Sally, who was barely awake, coughed out, "What's wrong with me?"

"Pneumonia," Sarver repeated. "We need to get you to the hospital."

"We can't, at least not now," Marjorie blurted. "We have election officials coming this afternoon to discuss getting Sally sworn in as governor."

"You'll need to go afterwards, then. I'll have my staff call and make an appointment for you. Who is her primary care doctor?"

"Her doctor is in Roanoke, so I'm not sure," Marjorie resigned.

"Who is her oncologist at UVA?"

Marjorie exchanged contact information with Sarver who departed shortly thereafter. Handing Marjorie a half-dozen surgical masks, Sarver said, "You've probably already been exposed to whatever germs Sally has. But when you have guests, put one on each of them to protect them. Put one on Sally, too. After her meeting, get her to UVA."

Three hours later, Larry Kinsey arrived from Richmond in the same car he'd used for the visit in Roanoke. With him was a man he introduced as Charles Baynes, Virginia's Head of Elections. Marjorie explained Sally's condition and put surgical masks on both men. Bringing them into Sally's room, Marjorie woke Sally, lifted her head gently off the pillow, and put one on her as well.

Kinsey spoke first. "Mrs. Bradley, do you remember me? Larry Kinsey. I'm an election official."

Sally opened her eyes languidly and nodded her head.

"This is Charles Baynes. He's the head of Elections."

Baynes began speaking through his mask, "We're sorry to bother you, given your illness, Mrs. Bradley. But time is of the essence. As you know, Governor McGregor passed away over the weekend. You will become our next governor as soon as you're sworn in."

Marjorie's mind's eye pictured a devastated Lyndon Johnson, being administered the oath of office on Air Force One on the tarmac in Dallas, his right hand raised beside his face and Lady Bird and Jackie Kennedy flanking him, on that awful day from her childhood.

Kinsey added, "The Chief Justice of the Supreme Court of Virginia will do the swearing in. He wants it done at the State Capital in Richmond. Our instructions are to ensure that you be there as soon as possible."

Baynes interjected, his mask pulsating as he spoke, "You should be there this evening, but under the circumstances, that seems impossible." Turning to Marjorie, "When do you think she can travel to Richmond?"

"She was examined by a doctor this morning," Marjorie explained. "We're going to UVA Medical Center as soon as we're done here. She thinks its pneumonia. We'll know by then."

Baynes turned back to Sally. "Madam, Lt. Governor?"

Sally nodded again, her eyes shut.

"Ma'am, this is a risky time. It is critical that our state have a governor. If you can't take the oath, the Chief Justice may appoint someone else. Next in line is the Attorney General. Nobody is quite sure what will happen."

Everyone looked at Sally who was deathlike in her stillness. She opened her eyes again and mumbled, "Okay." Her eyes closed again.

"Madam Lt. Governor," Kinsey noted, "There are powerful people in Richmond who are your political enemies. They will not want you to become governor."

"That's enough, gentlemen," Marjorie insisted, "I think my sister has heard what she needs to hear. Let's go, please." The two men looked at each other with resignation and then acquiescence. She escorted them outside to the parlor. "What's next?"

"Nobody knows," Baynes insisted ruefully. "As I said, we're in uncharted territory. The Governor is dead. The next in line is your sister. She is incapacitated, surely in the near term and possibly in the long term. There won't be another election. The succession path is clear, from the governor to the Lt. Governor to the Attorney General. But the General Assembly has some power to influence the process. The House is solidly Republican. The Senate is now Republican controlled twenty to eighteen, twenty to nineteen when Ms. Bradley's replacement is sworn in. Anything could happen, but I suspect it will happen quickly."

"When's Governor McGregor's funeral? Sally was very fond of the Governor."

"Wednesday, I think," Kinsey stated.

"If Sally can't go and she's not still in the hospital, I'll find a nurse to be with her and I'll go," Marjorie concluded.

The men drove away through a light, blowing snow.

Moments later, Marjorie helped Sally get dressed and then drove her to the UVA Medical Center once more. Within hours, the prognosis of pneumonia was confirmed, and Sally was admitted so she could be constantly monitored and treated with antibiotics.

Marjorie returned home and had dinner accompanied by the corgis. Radley chomped loudly on a leather chewy toy, occasionally fighting Boo over it. Marjorie called Liza to bring her up to speed on the day's news before going to bed.

Tuesday, January 30

The next morning, Marjorie called UVA and learned that Sally's vital signs were unchanged. Sally's doctor would give Marjorie no estimate of Sally's release date.

That afternoon, Marjorie got an alert on her smart phone about a press conference being held at 4:30 p.m. by the Republican delegation in the General Assembly. She went inside to watch it on WIOH television in Charlottesville, the NBC affiliate.

The commentator said, "We are now going live where Rupert B. Overington, Republican Delegate from Harrisonburg, will make an announcement. Overington is currently the Speaker of the Virginia House of Delegates. Mr. Overington is a graduate of Bob Johnson University and Trinity Law School."

A handsome man with stylishly long blond hair and a goatee sat in a wheelchair, holding a microphone. He began, "Good afternoon, ladies and gentlemen. I am Rupe Overington, the Speaker of the Virginia House of Delegates. We all have heavy hearts today as we have lost a great Virginian in Miller McGregor, who died in a terrible airplane accident on Sunday. Our thoughts and prayers are with Mrs. McGregor and her family.

"Although there is no reason to expect foul-play, a full investigation is underway, ordered by the Virginia Secretary of Public Safety, Trevor Cameron. All of us need to know why that airplane went down at a cost of three lives.

"I assume most Virginians have lowered their flags to half-staff in reverence to the deceased Governor. A call like this would normally be made by the Governor, but sadly at this moment, our great Commonwealth does not have one. In the line of succession, the Lt. Governor is first. Currently, our Lt. Governor, Sally Taliaferro Bradley, is stricken with a potentially fatal disease which she knew about but only disclosed after the election, which she won by the narrowest of margins. As I speak, Mrs. Bradley is currently hospitalized at the University of Virginia Medical Center with an uncertain prognosis.

"It goes without saying that our great Commonwealth cannot and should not be unrepresented by not having a governor. Therefore, as Speaker of the House of Delegates, the people's chamber, I call on Lt. Governor Bradley to immediately appear at the State Capital in Richmond if she is indeed functional, of sound mind and body, and able to execute the duties of the governor. Otherwise, she risks losing the position to the second in successional line, the Attorney General, who is the newly elected and installed, Brady Pasdon."

Overington pointed behind him where Pasdon stood.

"That's all I have. We will entertain a question or two."

"Arnie Roach, from the *Washington Daylight*." Marjorie recognized him from the press conference in Roanoke. "According to the Virginia Constitution, whose call is this?"

"It is up to the legislature. The Constitution allows for the next in line to be bypassed if the General Assembly deems that that person is incapable of performing the duties of the job."

"Sir, I am Jose Cepeda, *Norfolk Daily Mail*. Can Mrs. Bradley be sworn in at the hospital?"

Overington stroked his chin and said, "The oath of office can be performed anywhere, but Mrs. Bradley will only be elevated to the Governorship if the legislature deems her fit to serve."

Cepeda continued, "Would Mr. Pasdon care to comment?"

Overington looked over his shoulder where Pasdon stood silently. Pasdon walked slowly to stand beside Overington and took the microphone. He was about seventy years old, tall and bald, with a self-righteous smirk. He said merely, "We all wish Mrs. Bradley the best for a speedy recovery." He handed the mic back to Overington and walked back to his prior place.

"Karen Brislan, from the *Roanoke Star*. Mr. Speaker, do you know the extent of Mrs. Bradley's illness and her prognosis?"

"Not fully. I'm told she has cancer, which may be terminal."

Brislan, clearly perturbed, proposed petulantly, "Mr. Speaker, is it likely that she might recover?"

"We can't know. Her life is in the hands of the good Lord above."

Brislan snapped back, "Would you care to admit that all of us have an expiration date?"

Overington sniffled and wrinkled his nose in a condescending way, and said, "There will be no further questions."

Wednesday January 31

Marjorie stopped by UVA to see Sally before heading to Richmond for the McGregor funeral. Sally was running a high fever and was inattentive. Marjorie decided not to mention anything about the prior day's press conference or the machinations going on in Richmond as Sally convalesced.

Shortly before noon, Marjorie continued to Richmond for the 2:30 p.m. memorial service for Miller McGregor, Jr., the Governor of Virginia. McGregor was the first Governor of Virginia since George William Smith over 200 years earlier to die in office. So it was national news and was attended by throngs of black-clad mourners. There was a heavy State Police presence, with uniformed and armed troopers surrounding the church and adjacent cemetery. The casket was closed and murmurs of a charred body circulated through the crowd. The deceased Governor's five children were in attendance, ages 14 through 28, and the youngest, a boy, wept uncontrollably during the entire service. A murder of crows roosted in the tall pines nearby, cawing loudly and distractingly, preventing many mourners from hearing the minister's prayers.

With neither Liza nor Sally able to attend with her, Marjorie was alone. After the graveside service, mourners were welcomed to pay respects to the deceased's family. Marjorie queued up with over three hundred other people. It began to rain lightly.

Standing in line and lost in thought, Marjorie sensed that the young, dark-haired man with dark sunglasses and the unsightly mole over his lip behind her was about to speak to her. She turned towards him.

"How's your cancer?" he blurted.

"Who the hell are you?" Marjorie accused, facing him, taking his inquiry as if spoken invidiously.

Danny Gold immediately regretted speaking at all, much less saying what he said. "Listen, I'm sorry. I just wanted to sound sympathetic." Damn, he scolded himself!

"What?!? Sound sympathetic?" Marjorie fired back.

"Again, I'm sorry Ms. Bradley. I was just surprised to see you here, given your illness."

"First of all, I'm not Ms. Bradley. I'm Marjorie Taliaferro. Sally Bradley is my twin sister. Second, her condition is none of your business. Who are you, anyway? Now I'm asking twice." She sensed a deep disingenuousness and was immediately suspicious.

"I'm Daniel Gold. I work in elections. I knew the Governor. And I know of Ms. Bradley."

"If you know so much, why are you asking me questions?" Marjorie snapped back. She was flummoxed by her own distrust and suspicion toward a stranger who appeared to have done nothing outwardly unfriendly or threatening. He had a portentous air and she had a bad feeling. "I'll tell her you asked about her." She turned and faced frontward again.

So unnerved by Gold's impertinence and his continuing looming presence behind her, moments later she left the line and queued up again at the back. She waited for over an hour, and the line, while noticeably smaller, seemed still uncomfortably long. She was wet and getting increasingly cold. The funeral home people had covered the casket with dirt and were dismantling the canopy. She abandoned the line and walked to her car.

Before hitting the road for home, Marjorie called Sally to check on her condition. The call was intercepted by a floor nurse who told Marjorie that Sally's fever was still high and the hospital was taking steps to control it. Marjorie took the old road, US-33, the "Spotswood Trail," back to Gordonsville and then home to Orange, finishing off three cigarettes on her way.

Liza called Marjorie that evening, asking about Sally. Marjorie told her about the fever and her overall weakness. She also mentioned that Sally's hair was beginning to fall out in awful, grotesque chunks. "One of the nurses said she'd bring a razor and cut it all off before my visit tomorrow so I don't have to watch. Sally is so weak that she probably won't notice herself. She's in a terrible way. Oh, her fingernails are turning yellow, too."

"Did you watch the press conference yesterday?" Liza inquired.

"Yes."

"They're going to do it, aren't they?"

"It wouldn't surprise me," Marjorie admitted.

"Oh, my stars and garters. Those bastards! We can't let

this happen!" Liza screamed.

"I know, sweetie, but right now I just want to bring my sister home." Marjorie sobbed. Regaining her composure, she then told Liza about her encounter with the man named Gold at the funeral and her uneasiness about him. Marjorie decided not to tell Sally, at least yet.

Later that evening, Rhonda McCarty lifted her head from Danny Gold's pillow and sat upright, making no effort to cover her bare torso with a sheet or blanket. She reached over to his bed table where she'd left her wine goblet and took a sip. His bedroom was dim with a slender stream of light coming through his window around the curtain.

Danny opened his eyes, vainglorious in what he saw. He was apprehensive, wondering whether his lover would break the post-coital silence or would wait for him, further wondering what he'd say. "You were good," always sounded trite. "Thanks for putting out," seemed like an insult. With girls like Rhonda, it always seemed better to let his tool do the talking and let her initiate conversation.

"You said you were in politics," she ventured.

"Yeah. I was in communications for Adam Westfall's campaign for governor. He ignored me for the most part and lost."

"Now?"

"Technically unemployed. I'm hoping for a position with Brady Pasdon, the new Attorney General. He needs a communications specialist."

"Oh?" she wondered.

He sat up beside her. He took the wine goblet from her and took a sip. "The one he had resigned recently." He handed it back to her.

"Why?"

"Rumor has it she once had an abortion. He's vehemently anti-abortion."

"You ever had an abortion?" she prodded.

He laughed contemptuously. He ran his finger up and down her thigh, still clammy with perspiration. He said nothing.

She prodded again, "You ever impregnated anybody?"

"Damn, woman, not that I know of."

"You're a bastard, Danny Gold," she claimed.

"That's what I'm told," he smirked.

She smiled a wry smile, "I've got to go. I'll see you around." She emerged from his bed, clothed herself, and left.

Four

"I think if you run away from who you are, that you're a Democrat and you're proud to be a Democrat, it's foolish. And the reason it's foolish is you've got a lot to be proud of."
– TIM KAINE, 70TH GOVERNOR OF VIRGINIA

Thursday, February 1

The next morning's headline in the *Richmond Reporter* was bold and large.

Brady Pasdon is the new Governor

Then in a smaller headline,

General Assembly agrees to bypass Lt. Governor Sally Bradley in party line vote

Holy guacamole, Marjorie murmured to herself. She was reading that the General Assembly had already appointed Hampton judge Wiley Isner to be the interim Attorney General when the phone rang.

"I'm not going to take this," Liza screamed. "We need to fight back!"

"Good morning to you, too," Marjorie interjected some

sarcastic levity.

"I'm sorry. Good morning. I love you. I'm as mad as a wet hen, just broiling!"

Marjorie's left eyebrow raised involuntarily. "I'm sure we'll all be doing some screaming. Other than that, what are your plans?"

"Fuck, I don't know! None yet, but I'm meeting with some friends in Charlottesville tonight to talk about it. Please come."

"I'll drive to UVA to check on Sally later this afternoon. I'll come if I can. It all depends on how Sally's doing."

"Okay, keep me posted."

Marjorie finished her chores and drove once again to the UVA Medical Center to see her twin. The nurse intercepted her in the hallway. "She's better today. I think the antibiotics have kicked in. She's still weak, but the fever is down."

Marjorie entered Sally's room and found her sitting upright in her bed, alert and talkative. She was as hairless as Disney's Shrek.

"What's shakin', sis?" Sally ran her hand over what used to be her hair.

"I can't even remember what you know and what you don't know," Marjorie shrugged. "Do you know that Miller McGregor was killed in a plane crash?"

"Yes. I assume I'll be sworn in as the new Governor."

"Well, not exactly. You better sit down."

Both women laughed sardonically, as Sally was already sitting, laughter they hadn't shared in many days. Marjorie explained the situation and the take-over by the Republicans.

"That means they hold the Governor's office, the Attorney General, and until Senator Mullins is replaced, and then only if he's replaced by another Democrat, both houses of the General Assembly," Sally concluded, talking more to herself. "I bet those guys are wetting their pants with excitement."

"Are you okay? With the situation, I mean."

"Well, I'm certainly not happy about it. Am I still the Lt. Governor?" Sally prodded.

"I'm not sure I've heard anybody say," Marjorie pondered.

"It doesn't make a hill of beans difference, anyway."

"Why's that?"

"The Lt. Governor is the surrogate for the Governor, when he needs her. But Pasdon won't call on me to do anything. The other job is to cast the tiebreaker vote in the Senate, but with an uneven number of Senators, there won't be any ties unless someone abstains. So I'm impotent."

Both women were quiet for a moment before Sally spoke again. "I need to beat this pneumonia first. Then I'll beat the cancer. Then we can deal with the goddamn Republicans."

Marjorie was elated that her sister's spunk was back. Then, unexpectedly, a shiver consumed her body and her skin prickled. "Can you walk?"

"Yes."

"Let's get you out of here."

Sally opened up her hands. "Now?"

"Yeah, if you can walk and your fever is down, I'm taking you home. Something tells me it's time to leave here." Marjorie walked to the hallway and summoned a nurse.

"I can't release her without Doctor Anaokar's approval," the nurse insisted.

"Please get her on the phone for me."

An hour later, Marjorie and Sally were halfway home to Orange. A car with high, blue-white headlights followed them most of the way, only turning off when they reached the driveway to Runnymede Meadow Estate. Boo and Radley jumped all over Sally when she came inside, licking her face, then Marjorie's. Marjorie gave Sally a bright pink bandanna to cover her pate. Then Sally went to bed.

Friday, February 2

Marjorie was feeding the chickens when she got a call from Liza. "Hey sweetie."

"How's Sally?" Liza inquired.

"Not sure. She was asleep when I left the house to do my chores."

Liza began, "Please, do you mind going inside and putting me on the speaker phone?"

"Why? What's up?"

"I've got some information on Danny Gold. Did you tell her about him and his being at the funeral?"

"Not yet. Let me go inside. I'll call you back."

Marjorie finished her work at the coop and returned to the house. She walked into Sally's room and found her sitting upright on her bed, checking messages on her tablet. Marjorie told Sally about the funeral and the creepy guy, Daniel Gold, who asked about her. Then Marjorie called Liza back as promised.

Liza enumerated to the twins, "I have a friend who worked on the McGregor campaign. She was his communications director, the same position Danny Gold had for Adam Westfall. She hired a watcher to go to Westfall's campaign stops to film him, record his speeches, and watch for misstatements or gaffes. It is a common thing to do; Gold hired someone to follow McGregor around, too. Remember a few years ago when that candidate for U. S. Senate called somebody a macaca? The target of his slur was the watcher. Anyway, Gold is as admired as he is loathed and feared."

Marjorie processed words she heard Liza use like "conniving," "manipulative," and "cunning." Liza said he kept extensive records on friends and foes alike. He was a real ladies' man and he did tennis, shooting, and womanizing for fun.

"Nobody seems to know what he's up to these days," Liza continued. "With Westfall's loss, he is unemployed, I suppose. But at least as of last week when you saw him he was still in Richmond. I suspect we haven't seen the end of him."

Saturday, February 3

Marjorie was returning to the house with the *Richmond Reporter* when she noticed the headline that said,

Three dead, scores ill in food poisoning at UVA Medical Center.
Authorities are investigating potential foul-play

Yesterday, in an incident that has raised suspicions by Charlottesville Police, a food-borne pathogen was detected in meals served the prior evening. An investigation is underway for the identity of a man seen on security cameras and pictured below. Most of those afflicted were in a bronchial wing where patients were being treated for bronchitis, pneumonia, and other lung ailments.

Marjorie read the column quickly and was overwhelmed

with angst and anxiety. If at all possible, she would not leave Sally unescorted again.

On the bottom of the same page Marjorie found this:

Pasdon announces new staffer

Governor Brady Pasdon has announced that Daniel Gold of Richmond will be his new Communications Director. Gold replaces Courtney Templeton who resigned without explanation a week ago from that position. Previously, she had served as Communications Director for Pasdon's campaign.

The article mentioned Gold's qualifications and bio. Pasdon's only quote was, "I will be making staff decisions as quickly as possible to ensure that Virginia's citizens have accountable, responsible representation in the executive office in Richmond."

Marjorie was filled with torment by the memory of her encounter with Gold and his new position of power.

Sunday, February 4

The next morning's *Richmond Reporter* ran an editorial provocatively entitled,

Virginia Republicans execute coup d'état

The paper's opinion writer was scathing in his criticism of the take-over by the Republican Party in the General Assembly and the "utter failure" to fully give Lt. Governor Bradley the opportunity for ascension to the Governor's seat. It called for the new Governor's immediate resignation and the restoration of the prior balance of power. It said, "Until two weeks ago, the Democrats controlled the Governor's and Lt. Governor's office, and held the tie-breaking vote in the split Senate. Now, Republicans control all branches of government, in defiance of the will of the voters."

Monday, February 5

That Monday morning, Marjorie took a call from oncologist Maneesha Anaokar asking about Sally. When Anaokar asked about Sally's fever, Marjorie said, "It was down to 99°F when I checked late yesterday. I'll take it again today. She seems more alert and not as uncomfortable."

"This is the last thing you want to hear, but we need to stay on track as much as we can with the chemotherapy treatments. We should be administering it every two weeks. It was two weeks ago today with the first one."

"Damn" Marjorie muttered under her breath. Could it have been two weeks already?

Dr. Aaokar continued, "We won't do it as long as she still has her pneumonia symptoms. But I want you to call me whenever she seems ready again."

Marjorie's mind filled with dread. What a torturous dilemma: cancer or chemo. How true, she thought, that the cure could be more deadly than the disease. She hung up with the Doctor and took some juice to Sally who had just returned from the toilet to her bed.

"That was Dr. Anaokar."

"Let me guess. She wants to shoot me with more poison. Right?"

Sheepishly, "Yes."

Sally balled both her hands into fists. She wiped both hands over her bald head and cried, "So be it. But I can't do it yet."

"I understand," Marjorie reassured. "Anaokar understands, too."

Both were quiet for a moment before Marjorie offered, "Everybody would understand if you stopped doing the treatments."

"And then what?" Sally shot back, "I die? I'm just going to roll over and die? HELL WITH THAT! The Lord can have me when he wants me, but until then, I'm fighting this thing."

The room was quiet again, save the bright red northern cardinal that sang from the snow-covered tree branch by the window. "Tear, tear!"

"Fuck cancer," Sally screamed defiantly. "Fuck Red Devil! Fuck the fucking Republicans! Bring it on!!!" She put her hands over her face and rubbed the area where her eyebrows had been. Her eyes moistened and she sobbed.

"Tear, tear!" cried the cardinal.

Sally wiped moistness from her cheeks with a tissue. "But not yet. I can't do it again yet."

Marjorie sat beside her diseased sister and hugged her gently but meaningfully. Then without words she got up and went outside into a brisk, windy day to feed the animals. She wondered if she should tell Sally about the poisoning at the hospital, about the man, Gold, in Richmond, and about her sense of being followed.

An hour later, Sam arrived to go over some strategies and expected upcoming legislation with Sally. Marjorie felt sorry for her sister, impressed by her dedication and wondering if she'd be able to keep up with the intense demands, especially considering her limbo status. She wasn't governor, as she should be. Was she still Lt. Governor? If she had no official duties, should Sam keep her still so encumbered?

Concurrently in Richmond, Brady Pasdon had summoned Danny Gold into his office, where Danny was shown in by a short-skirted secretary. Cardboard boxes were strewn around the room as Pasdon was still unpacking his belongings. Gold had noticed several boxes in the hallway marked "McGregor," apparently awaiting delivery to the deceased Governor's widow.

"Well, Gold," Pasdon bellowed, "You got what you wanted."

"Yes sir. Thank you."

"Well?" The big man rose from his leather chair.

Well what?, Danny wondered. Did Pasdon want him to bow? To genuflect? Suck his dick? "Sir?"

"You are communications director. What direction would you like to see us taking?"

"You're the Governor, sir," Danny implored.

Pasdon snapped, "Don't lecture me, son. I'm asking all the people I appoint or hire to spell things out for me from their perspective. We control the Senate, the House, and the Executive branch. Now what?"

"Sir?"

"I want your input. How do you think we should proceed? We won't always dominate the government. While we have the power, what, in your view, should we do with it? I want your report on my desk by Wednesday, noon. Let's meet again on Thursday after I've had a chance to study it, and we can go over the details and do some strategizing."

"I'll have it to you then. Good afternoon." Danny walked away, feeling a bulge in his pants. On the way down the hall, he realized the new Governor was ostensibly handing him the reins to remake the laws of an entire state to his own desires.

Tuesday, February 6

Sally took a phone call later that afternoon from Sam Sebrell. When Marjorie asked about it, Sally told her that Sebrell had learned that the new Governor was not going to call for a special election for Barton Mullins, the stricken Senator, nor was he going to appoint a replacement, until after the current session of the General Assembly. What that meant is that the Senate, at least for that session, would have a 20-19 edge to the Republicans. On party line votes, as she expected, Sally would not have the opportunity to cast any votes as there would be no ties. If the Republicans chose to vote as a block, they could not be outvoted.

After dinner, Marjorie and Sally were playing chess, listening to the NPR affiliate station in Roanoke, when the evening jazz program was interrupted with news that a train had derailed near Norfolk while crossing a bridge. Thousands of gallons of crude oil and industrial chemicals had spilled into the rich estuary of the Elizabeth River and caught fire. Eight people were confirmed dead and an unknown number of others were injured. A toxic chemical plume was spreading northward towards the Hampton Roads area of the Chesapeake Bay. The Governor received the news while in New York, dining with four other Republican governors. He was currently en route to the scene.

Wednesday, February 7

"So did you hear?" Liza inquired angrily over the phone to Marjorie.

Marjorie was fixing lunch, a tuna noodle casserole with tomatoes and cucumbers. "What?"

"Governor Asshole has just issued his first Executive Order."

"Tell me," Marjorie implored. "Don't make me guess."

"We've instantly returned to the 1960s. The Governor has ordered that the Ten Commandments be posted in a prominent place in every public school in the state. We're back to having religion in the schools."

Marjorie put her cell phone on speaker and carried it into Sally's room. "I've put you on the speaker. I want Sally to hear this, too."

"Hi, Sally," Liza continued. "How are you feeling?"

"Weak, but I'm hanging in there." Sally put down the papers she was studying. "What's going on?"

"Our new esteemed Governor – or shall we call him King Pasdon – has just put religion back in the schools. Not only has he ordered that the Ten Commandments be posted prominently, but has ordered that every K-8th Grade classroom start each day with a prayer of not less than 30 seconds in length, and every child will attend a Bible study course for at least 45 minutes per week."

"Who will teach it?" Sally pondered aloud.

"The regular teacher, I suppose," Liza ventured, seemingly not really knowing.

"What if the teacher is Jewish, or Muslim, or atheist?" Marjorie pondered aloud.

"I suppose they'll bring in outside people, maybe preachers," Liza fumed. "Who knows? These courses will be Christian in nature, you can damn well bet."

Sally shrugged, "I'm sure this will be challenged in the

courts. This cannot stand."

"Maybe not," Liza's voice claimed, "but it has been put into effect immediately. Until it is overturned, *IF* it is overturned, it is now the law."

"Bastards," Sally grumbled.

"What happened to the separation of church and state?" Marjorie fumed.

"Where's Thomas Jefferson when we need him?" Sally quipped.

Liza's voice chimed, "I'm sure these Republicans would claim him as one of their own."

Sally continued, "Jefferson once wrote, 'Christianity neither is, nor ever was, a part of the common law.' He'd be turning over in his grave about now."

"You thinking what I'm thinking?" Sally suggested to Marjorie.

"I'm thinking that we've only seen the beginning," Marjorie predicted.

Thursday, February 8

Sally screamed over Marjorie's cell phone, "Marjorie. Come in here!"

Marjorie was out feeding her horses, but she stubbed out her cigarette and sprinted into the house. "What?" breathless and coughing.

"Look at this," Sally pointed at the television. The new Governor stood behind a lectern with the state seal and was already speaking.

"… because of the terrible nature of the crimes, and because of the urgency we all feel to be safe in our streets, in our schools, stores, and work places, it is imperative that convicted murderers be eliminated from our society. We currently have 22 inmates on Death Row. I have instructed our Corrections department to accelerate the executions of these heinous criminals. With my executive order, the next one will be carried out by electrocution tomorrow evening.

"Since the de facto moratorium by the Supreme Court in 1976, Virginia, along with Texas, leads the nation in executing these terrible people. Following our lead, I'm confident other states will free themselves to work their way through the backlog they have on their Death Rows, saving their citizens millions of dollars in incarceration fees. Many people erroneously believe that imprisoning a heinous criminal for life is cheaper than executing them. Admittedly, executions have high up-front costs, but over time, life without parole is significantly more expensive, according to the impartial Death Penalty Forum.

"Part of the reason it takes so long for executions to be carried out is the complex series of delays and appeals. I have instructed the new Attorney General, Wiley Isner, to submit to me a recommendation for accelerating the process.

"Furthermore, executing a brutal killer brings rapid closure to the victims' families, making it ultimately more humane.

"Thank you very much ladies and gentlemen for your time and attention."

Someone shouted, "I have a question, Governor Pasdon."

"I'm sorry, I won't be taking any questions now. Good day."

Sally turned off the set. "For pity's sake."

"We were right," Marjorie admitted. "When we said yesterday we've only seen the beginning, we were right. I should be hearing from Liza about now."

Sally agreed, "Well, the foxes are running the hen…"

The phone rang. As predicted, Liza's name appeared on the caller ID. Marjorie took it right to the speaker-phone.

"Egads, these fucking Republicans!" Liza exhorted, angrily. "They must be stopped."

"What do you have in mind?" Sally taunted. "I'd love to help, but I'm back under chemo tomorrow."

"Marjorie?" Liza implored her lover.

"Yes, sweetie."

"What are we going to do?"

Sadly, "I'm going to take care of my sister. Until she gets better, I'm afraid I can't be of much help. Be careful."

"Too late for that," Liza testified with a cynical chuckle. "I sent a commentary to the Richmond paper ten minutes ago. The new Governor isn't going to like it."

At that moment the new Governor was meeting with his director of communications, Daniel Gold, to go over Gold's position paper. Gold had laid out an agenda to eliminate the social safety net as quickly as possible and to eviscerate environmental and worker protections. Gold's paper had the words, "responsibility society" in nine places, emphasizing Gold's self-reliance, anti-government ethic. There was an active law-and-order component, with enhanced death penalties and mandatory sentencing. To make elections fairer and freer from fraud, Danny suggested several new voter requirements including valid photo identification cards. Pandering to Pasdon, Danny carefully included several hard-line abortion restrictions.

Danny was pleased that the budding Pasdon governorship

was eager to get underway and that Pasdon was so accepting of Danny's suggestions and direction, different from the cold shoulder he had felt so often from Westfall.

That evening as Marjorie was fixing dinner, Sally called her with an urgent voice into the living room. Marjorie arrived to see that Sally held the remote, having just adjusted the volume higher. "… reporting from the Lord Fairfax High School in Herndon." A yellow tape flapped in the wind behind the male reporter who wore a black blazer and red scarf. "Police have reported that the alleged perpetrator of this afternoon's horrific shooting has died in a nearby hospital. Sean Rutledge, 19, allegedly entered his former High School and shot to death biology teacher Wilson Stevens and eight students in Stevens' classroom. Another 13 were wounded, two critically. Rutledge wounded security officer, Reed Grant, in a shootout. Grant is expected to survive. Rutledge succumbed to wounds to the chest, arm, and abdomen, administered by Grant."

A small, young woman Marjorie assumed to be in her mid-twenties appeared in the picture as the cameraman scanned back. "We're now with Angie Gifford, who also teaches science here at Lord Fairfax. Ms. Gifford, can you tell us…"

Marjorie looked at the young woman, in tears and clearly deeply distressed. "I can't watch," Marjorie said, retreating to the security of her kitchen. She took a big onion from a wooden bowl and began slicing and then dicing it, letting the pungent mist whet the tears already forming in her eyes. When would the madness end?, she asked herself as she openly sobbed.

Friday, February 9

Sally returned to UVA for her second chemotherapy session with Marjorie by her side. The ruby fluid from the depths of hell was dripping into Sally's vein when they heard a familiar voice. "Aunt Sally!"

"Hi Jack. How are you doing? You remember Marjorie, don't you?"

"Yes, hi Marjorie. I…"

Sally interrupted, "Your mom must be here, right?"

"Yes, ma'am. She's in the next wing. Her cancer is back. Things are not looking good. I'm spending all my free time here. They don't expect her to live much longer."

Marjorie looked at the handsome young man in civilian clothes, the State Policeman who drove the Governor around. She realized that she hadn't thought about him since they met, but that it was entirely likely that he could have been killed in Miller McGregor's tragic accident.

"How's your treatment coming along?" he continued.

"I'm so sorry about your mother," Sally re-directed the conversation. "It was probably six weeks ago when I saw her last," she recalled.

"She's been here for a week," Jewett informed.

Returning to his question, Sally said, "I'm hanging in there. This is my second chemo session. I have one more to go."

"I'm sorry to be so blunt, Aunt Sally, but have they told you your chances?"

Sally shrugged, "I spoke with my doctor early on. She told me they can try to assess my percentage chance of full recovery. But they usually don't. If they say it is ninety-ten or fifty-fifty, it's really meaningless. These numbers apply to statistical groupings. As far as individual patients go, it's binary, either zero or one. If it's zero, I die. If it's one, I live. She said nobody with cancer is ever fully cured. The object of the game is to keep patients alive long enough to die of something else. But the Lord calls all of us home eventually."

"Yes, ma'am."

Marjorie admired his manners.

Sally continued, "I'll stop and see Selena before we go today. What room is she in?"

"2022," he replied, "but I'm not sure she'll know who you are. She's in constant pain and in and out of consciousness."

"I'd like to see her anyway."

"Yes, please do. Ma'am? I'm off on Monday, and I plan to come back here. I assume you're staying with Marjorie through all this."

"Yes," Marjorie nodded.

"If it's okay with you, I'd like to speak with you about Richmond."

The twins looked at each other quizzically. Then they both looked at Jewett. He nodded his head lightly, begging. "Marjorie, if you give me the address, I'll find you with my GPS. I'll see you around noon on Monday. I hope you get well soon." He bent down and kissed Sally on the cheek and then scurried away.

An hour later, the twins were on their way back to Runnymede. As was becoming habitual, Sally went to bed early and Marjorie sat up late, reading. She had just returned from filling the wood-stove for the night and taking a drag from her cigarette when her NPR station interrupted its broadcast of cosmic music to make an announcement.

"Tonight at 9:22 local time, convicted murderer Malcolm Dunlop was executed at the Greendale Correctional Facility in Sarratt by electrocution. Dunlop was convicted of the rape and murder of 73-year-old Mildred O'Brien of Petersburg in 2004. Ms. O'Brien was a widow who lived at home at the time of her murder. Her body was found two days later in the basement of her home. She had been disemboweled and beheaded.

"Mr. Dunlop was pronounced dead seven minutes after the first cycle of voltage. The electric chair, named 'Mr. Wattie', had not been used in 14 years. A grandson of Ms. O'Brien was a witness to the execution, however by state law, no relatives of the condemned man were allowed to be present.

"We now return you to our regularly scheduled programming, *Aural Starcases*."

Damn, Marjorie thought. This Governor wasn't wasting any time.

Saturday, February 10

That Saturday afternoon, Marjorie drove to Liza's estate in Keswick to attend a meeting. Liza was gathering a group of Charlottesville area women to discuss the emerging situation in Richmond, especially with regards to the fears of an assault on women's rights. Liza wore an orange shirt that said, *"I can't believe we still have to protest this shit."*

Marjorie recognized a few of the women, five of which were in her Daughters of Dolley Society in Orange. Until that time, she had not thought of the Society as being feminist. But apparently the new Governor's actions had radicalized several of them.

Liza spoke, rising from the upholstered antique chair in

her parlor, "Thank you all for coming. I think we're here for the same reason, that we have already seen an unprecedented, illegal, and radical overhaul of Virginia's government. The wackos have taken over, and they seem to be way worse than we ever dreamed in our worst nightmare.

"I recently wrote an editorial protesting what we're seeing and sent it to the Richmond paper. I have been given confirmation that it will be appearing in their Sunday edition, tomorrow. I think the proverbial excrement is poised to impact the spinning impeller."

Several people laughed at the reference.

"We are only now getting a sense of what is to come," Liza continued. "It's like a John Birch Society fairy tale. I am a professor of law, and what we've seen with the take-over is blatantly illegal. This is the kind of activity we haven't seen in this state since the onset of the Civil War."

Another woman, an attractive blond that Marjorie didn't know, stood up beside Liza. "The President is obviously apprised of our situation. But he's fighting his own battles. Virginia is a swing state and will be deeply contested in his re-election campaign. He doesn't want to do anything to turn off voters here."

"But," an elegant, grey-haired woman protested, "He'll turn me off if he doesn't act."

"My husband worked in several prior administrations," the blond woman continued. "He has contacts in the inner circle. The President is waiting for the situation to hopefully defuse itself."

"What should we do?" another woman asked to nobody in particular.

The blond woman commanded, "Raise a stink. Write your

state senator, regardless of his party. Write your newspaper. Overload social media. Raise hell."

Liza offered, "I've got another bee in my bonnet. Does anybody know the story of Lysistrada?" A couple of women nodded their heads affirmatively. Liza continued, "It was written in ancient Greece by Aristophanes. Lysistrada is the main character. The men of Greece are waging the seemingly interminable Peloponnesian War. Lysistrada convinces the women of Greece to withhold sexual privileges until they stop. We can stop having sex until this madness ends."

"We may be punishing the wrong people," the other woman suggested. "Democrats have sex, too. And I'm not sure we can convince the Republican women to stop having sex."

"Are there any Republican women left?" the blond joked. "If there are, I have no idea what they think the Party is doing for them."

The other woman intoned, "What if that doesn't work?"

Liza promised, "Then we'll take it to the streets. This will not stand. It must not stand."

Sunday, February 11

The *Richmond Reporter*'s lead editorial was entitled,

Republican Governor must resign

It was penned by Liza Randolph of Keswick. Her byline read, "Liza Randolph is the Thomas Jefferson Professor and Dean of the Law School at the University of Virginia in Charlottesville."

Liza's editorial was succinct and potent. It minced no words, calling Brady Pasdon's wresting of the Governorship as a blatant, illegal, in fact, treasonous act. Marjorie read it to Sally, propped in bed with her coffee, fearful of the implications of such a forceful, principled, public stand. Marjorie was certain the Governor's winged monkeys would soon be taking flight.

That afternoon, Danny was doing paperwork when he got a call from Rhonda, who he thought was out of town. "My trip got postponed. I'm at a friend's house in Windsor Farms. You should come over."

"Listen, that's nice of you, but I've got a lot…"

"Danny."

"Yeah."

"You're already an asshole. Don't be a fool, too." She gave him an address which he knew was in one of the swankier neighborhoods.

"Fine. Thanks." He rubbed on some deodorant, shaved, and put on some khaki slacks and a polo shirt.

Twenty minutes later he arrived at a huge Tudor style home where seven or eight cars, all premium models, lined the curving driveway. He plopped down the large knocker twice. A male voice bellowed from a speaker beside the door, "You are?"

"Gold. Danny Gold. Rhonda McCarty's friend."

The great wooden door opened and Danny was met by a trim, grey-haired man in a bathrobe. "Come on in," he said. "I'm Franklin," he held out his hand. "Good to meet you. Everybody's by the pool." Danny took his hand in his own and shook it. It was cold, apparently from being wet.

It being winter, Danny surmised the pool was indoors. He was led through the opulent house to a brightly lit room with a kidney-shaped pool, half inside and half outside beyond a sliding glass wall. The smell of marijuana mixed with chlorine wafted into his nostrils. None of the twenty or so people he saw were clothed. Two people were copulating on a sofa. He saw Rhonda across the room, reclining on an upholstered lounge chair, in the throes of orgasm, with the face of a large black man buried in her crotch.

"Change in that room," Franklin pointed to a closed door. Change to what?, Danny wondered.

Monday, February 12

As promised, John Jewett arrived just before noon on Monday, again wearing civilian clothes and driving a mile-weary Toyota hatchback, rusting on the rear quarter-panel. He explained that he had left the hospital after a short stay as his mother was unresponsive to him.

Marjorie placed before him a tuna sandwich and a soft drink.

"I have a lot on my mind," he began, with a nervous urgency. "I have a unique view of what goes on with the Governor. I don't typically fly with the Governor unless there is some compelling reason. So I wasn't on the flight. Otherwise, I'd be dead right now." He took a sip of root beer and continued. "When Governor McGregor died, I was just like everybody else, wondering what was going to happen. Then Mr. Pasdon took over. He called me into his office, and we had what I guess you would call a job interview. He asked me if I was a Democrat or a Republican, and I said I'd always been a Republican. He asked if there was any reason, given that I'd just been working for a Democratic Governor, that I couldn't faithfully work for him. I said no. So that was it."

Sally interjected, "So you stayed on as the Governor's personal driver."

"Right, yes ma'am."

A car pulled up the driveway, a blue Ford Escort. Jewett dropped his sandwich and jumped from his chair. "Who's that?" visibly shaken, nervous.

"It's Sam Sebrell," Sally said, reassuringly. "He's my top assistant. He was my campaign manager. I invited him to join us. Are you okay, John?"

"It's risky for me to be here," Jewett said. "I could lose my job. Or worse. Much worse."

"Sam's okay," Sally reassured. "I trust him implicitly."

The doorbell rang and Marjorie let Sebrell inside. Marjorie introduced the men.

"John was explaining the nature of his visit, Sam," Sally told her assistant.

"Yes, ma'am," Jewett continued. "As I was saying, it is risky for me to be here. I am betraying the Governor of the Commonwealth of Virginia just being here. But I hear things."

"What do you mean?" Sebrell inquired.

"You all know that Danny Gold is the new director of communications?"

"Yeah, we know of him," Marjorie said. "He approached me at the McGregor funeral. Creepy, big guy. Not as big as you, Sam," she looked at him, admiringly. "He was behind me in line. Sally, Liza, and I talked about him ten days or so ago."

"We hoped to be done with him," Sally shrugged.

"I know him, too," Sebrell said. "I mean I don't know him well. He has worked the other side of the aisle. But word on the street among the campaign operatives is that he's the

Darth Vader of the Grand Old Party. Even people who find complimentary things to say about him or admire him are fearful of him and don't like him."

"Anyway," Jewett continued, "They talk about things in the car as if I'm not even there. I keep the State Police radio on all the time so evidently they think I'm focused solely on that, but I multi-task. It is nothing for me to comprehend three or four conversations at the same time. I fought a war this way. People who couldn't multi-task came home in wooden boxes.

"Gold plays hardball. In my estimation, most of the things you're seeing now in the papers about Executive Orders and such originate from him."

"Not from Pasdon?" Sebrell wondered.

"Not from what I can tell," Jewett considered. "He gets really passionate about ending abortions in Virginia, but not much else. He almost seems manipulated."

Sally looked at her nephew-in-law with a stare of seriousness that unnerved Marjorie. Sally beseeched, "Why are you here, John?"

"Aunt Sally, these people have done you dirty. They have overstepped their bounds, and they know it. I took an oath when I joined the Navy. I took another when I joined the State Police. I take my oaths very seriously. What these people have done and are doing is wrong. They need to be stopped. When I was fifteen, my daddy said to me, 'Don't wait for somebody else to make what's wrong right again. Be part of the solution.'"

"You're offering to be an informant," Sam suggested.

"I hate the sound of it," Jewett admitted. "But yes, sir. I can't stop them myself," he admitted ruefully. "Somehow, I think you can. Mondays are my normal day off, so I can come and tell you what I know. I can't ever call you, any of you. You can't ever call me, no matter what. I can't be seen driving here. Is there a back way in? Private. Really private."

Marjorie affirmed, "We have a back driveway that also comes in off Spicers Mill Road."

"More private than that."

Sally said, "Off Tatums School Road, there is a tiny canoe launch on the other side of the Rapidan. It's shallow there and if you bring fishing waders, you can easily wade across. It's near our old play area, when Marjorie and I were children."

"Do you know how to ride a horse?" Marjorie asked.

"Yes."

"I can leave a horse for you to ride here and then back when we're done. Nobody will see you."

"That'll work. You must say nothing to anybody about me or my being here. Marjorie, I brought something along today for you. It is a tire trap. It will puncture the tire of anyone driving over it. I want you to bury it in your driveway. From now on, nobody should come here except the three of you, and you need to use the back driveway. Okay?"

"Wow," Sebrell intoned. "Do you think Governor McGregor's death was foul play?"

"I don't know," admitted the young trooper. "I'm hesitant to speculate. I will say that I think his enemies are capable of very bad things."

"Murder?" Sally asked.

"Like I said, I don't know. But my ears are always on. I'll see you all next week."

Marjorie gave him a candy bar, took his final instructions for placing the tire trap and protecting themselves, and sent

him on his way. When she got back, Sam and Sally were looking over some paperwork. Marjorie recapped, "You're sick,
Sally. Your political opponents have just stolen control of an
entire state. The Governor has died and a state senator is in a
coma, fighting for his life. Your campaign manager is working
for you for free."

"Yup," Sam hastened.

"Do you want out?" Sally questioned her right-hand man.

"I didn't take an oath," Sam confessed, "but I take my
obligations seriously. Like it or not, I'm in this, too."

The huge man rose from his chair, towering over Marjorie. He got quiet for a moment, and then he continued. "I
got a degree in Poly Sci at Virginia Tech, but most of what
I learned there came from football practice and during our
games at Lane Stadium. Coach B. at Tech is the finest man I've
ever known. He's generous, unpretentious, and kind. Everything he does he does with integrity. One of the reasons his
teams win so many games is that nobody ever wants to let
him down. He teaches loyalty, perseverance, and doing things
the right way. You're a lot like him, Sally. You're a winner, too,
a survivor, and I want to be on your team for as long as I can.
I don't ever want to let you down.

"So yeah, I'm still in."

Tuesday, February 13

"Today," began the new Governor at a hastily called press
conference that Sally was watching on television when Marjorie came into her bedroom carrying a pot of tea, "I have
asked the legislature to put forth new legislation to curb the
epidemic of voter fraud we've seen in recent elections here

in the Commonwealth and to make our voting process more consistent with the will of the people."

"Watch this," Sally insisted, as the Governor continued.

"First, we will no longer allow same-day voter registration. This system has been the source of more fraud problems than any other. We will no longer allow for paid voter registration drives. To reduce errors and save our taxpayers money, we will reduce the number of early-voting days from seventeen to five.

"We will insist on a valid identification card with two pieces of photo ID. Anyone who cannot produce two pieces of valid, approved identification will not be allowed to vote.

"I am also asking the Legislature to devise a simple civics test for any first-time voter to prove their worthiness to vote. I suggest it asks questions like, 'How many branches does the federal Government have?' and 'Who was our first President?' which will reassure other voters that all voting Virginians have a rudimentary knowledge of our American system and are thus capable of making good decisions as to who will govern us. We all need reassurance that our voters are intellectually and rationally equipped to cast their vital ballots.

"I ask the Legislature to move quickly. Our next election cycle is already underway and our devoted election officials across the state need time to prepare. I promise to sign a bill with these provisions the day it hits my desk."

Sally grabbed the remote and turned off the set. She wrinkled her mouth and blurted, "The good Governor is seemingly getting a bit desperate."

"What do you mean?"

"You know what he's trying to do, don't you?"

"I think so. Please enlighten me."

"He's trying to disenfranchise voters not inclined to vote for him and his mates," Sally asserted.

"How's that?" Marjorie poured the tea into the cups. It smelled of peppermint.

"Who votes for Republicans these days? Angry white guys. Republicans know they're on a demographic cul-de-sac. A Republican Senator from South Carolina a few years ago admitted the party wasn't generating enough angry white men to stay in business forever, or something similar. They know this."

"So?"

"So they have two main ways to stay relevant, and by staying relevant I mean winning elections. They can reach out to other groups, like women, Hispanics, blacks, and all the other minorities. And I don't mean just wafting out platitudes. I mean real, substantive actionable things that help these people. Or they can cheat. They're clearly choosing to cheat."

"What do you mean?" Marjorie took a sip. The tea was hot, and she blew across the top of the steaming liquid.

Sally took a sip and complained, "This tastes like rusty dishwater. No offense, sis. Everything else does, too.

"They have chosen to cheat in three ways. First, they're limiting access to voters who might vote against them. Second, they're finding and spending unfathomable amounts of money to spread their message. And third, and this one's been going on for some time, they're gerrymandering the districts to give them small majorities in many districts at the expense of huge majorities in a few. Democrats have done it too, but never with such accuracy and vengeance."

"So this action today is about the limiting of access?" Marjorie began to understand.

"Right. Angry white guys are more likely to be older, meaning they've voted before. Newer voters are typically immigrants or students. They may not have valid, or valid enough, identification cards. They may have committed a minor crime, something not serious enough to disqualify them, but something they don't want voting authorities to know. So they are more likely to be intimidated.

"I'll bet anything the new Governor won't allow a university student ID to be valid. That reference to some knowledge of civics is pure racism. Inner city kids have worse school systems and are more likely to drop out before the 12th Grade where Government classes are typically taught. Blacks are more likely to vote Democratic. It's just like the system in the Old South decades ago with poll taxes. We're re-entering the Jim Crow era, or at least will if this Governor gets his way." Sally took another sip. She took a deep breath and adjusted the knit stocking cap that covered her bald head.

Marjorie pleaded, "How do you feel?"

"Awful. Tired," Sally sighed. "My inner ears hurt. My fingertips and toes hurt. I feel like crawling into a cave and dying. But there's a silver lining with what the Governor is doing to destroy my state."

"What's that?"

"The bastard has given me a reason to live."

Wednesday, February 14

"Holy shit, what a clusterfuck!" Liza exclaimed over the phone. "I thought it couldn't get any worse," she told Marjorie, who was sorting through some tack in the barn. Marjorie put her on the speaker.

"What now?"

"There's a state Delegate from Strasburg who is proposing bills that will ban abortions, all of them, in Virginia, forever."

"How?"

"Let me read it to you. This is from the *Richmond Reporter*. 'Yesterday, Delegate Dick Deardan submitted legislation to the General Assembly called the Virginia Abortion Restriction and Abatement Act. Senator Deardan said, 'In order to protect Virginia's women, fetuses, the culture of life and our adherence to our Christian principles, I am submitting legislation that will reduce and ultimately eliminate the abhorrent practice of abortion of unborn persons.' His legislation calls for the following. First, all mention of the word 'fetus' will be struck from prior legislation in favor of the more accurate, 'unborn person,' indicating the legal definition of the unborn as a legitimate natural person. There will be an immediate cessation of all funding for state-supported abortion clinics throughout the Commonwealth. Any doctor who performs any abortion within the Commonwealth will have his license to practice medicine revoked and will be subject to criminal prosecution for murder. Pregnant women will heretofore be referred to as 'hosts' of the unborn persons. Because pregnancy is a natural state of female being, any birth control pharmaceuticals will be obtained only through the court order of a District Judge, and only in case of risk to the health of the host if she was to become pregnant.

"Any host who loses her unborn person to death without a doctor present will need to report her identity, that death, and the location of the remains, to an applicable medical examiner or sheriff within 24 hours or face prosecution.

"Mr. Deardan stated, 'Too many women have made the

fateful decision to terminate pregnancies and have ultimately regretted it, leaving them despondent and profoundly heartsick with regret and recrimination.'"

"My stars and garters," was all Marjorie could think to say.

"Assholes! Holy smokes! Every day brings a new torment, a new assault on the personal liberties of Virginians," Liza complained, agonizingly.

"It's ironic, too."

"How's that?"

"Aren't they the party that says we have too much government in our lives?" Marjorie spouted, acerbically.

Liza snapped, "They don't see it like that. They see that a fetus is a living human, and somebody needs to protect it. But it's an economic and racist thing, too."

"It is?"

"Yeah. Sure it is. The state's abortion clinics are mostly located in the inner cities. Their abortion clients are disproportionately black women. They think black women are promiscuous. So they want to punish them. Do you know why they think women have abortions?"

"I've never thought about it. Why?"

"I think most of them have no more an idea than the man in the moon. There are lots of reasons, of course. Women aren't prepared emotionally to be mothers. They don't have solid relationships with their sexual partners. They have health problems. Or because they have no access to contraception or their contraception fails. But often it's about money. These women simply don't think they have the money to give a child a good start in life. You'd think these good Christian men — and they're almost always men — would concentrate on finding ways these women could achieve more financial stability. But they don't do that. There's another irony with these guys."

"What's that?"

"They say they hate abortions. Frankly, everybody hates abortions. They're awful. They're intrusive, painful, and emotionally charged. Nobody should ever have to endure one. However, the best ways to prevent women who don't want to be pregnant from getting pregnant are education and contraception. The only source many of them have for education and contraception are state-supported clinics. So the solution for these pious, self-righteous bastards is to shut the clinics down. How hypocritical is that? I'm so mad I could spit."

"Any fallout from your article?" Marjorie implored.

"The rumor mill is churning. I haven't spoken with the President yet, but I'm sure he'll support me."

"You're sure?"

"Well, that's what academic freedom is supposed to be about. That's why they grant tenure. Universities are our last bastion of free thought and expression. What would be left of Mr. Jefferson's legacy if they throw me under the bus? I'll be okay. Somebody's got to speak up."

Liza asked about Sally's condition, and Marjorie told her about her weariness and fatigue. Liza gave a quick, "I've got to go; I love you," and hung up.

Danny Gold met with reporters in the press room of the Executive Office Building that afternoon. There were seventeen reporters present, all wearing press credentials. Danny began, "I'm sorry for the late notice, but the Governor has issued an executive order this morning to protect our state's children and teachers. I have a prepared statement for you. There are copies in the back of the room for each of you on the credenza.

"The Governor was devastated by the recent shooting at the Lord Fairfax High School in Herndon. Our classroom teachers in Virginia are unarmed and thus incapable of defending themselves and their students against deranged assailants. While the security officer at Lord Fairfax acted bravely, the loss of life was far greater than it needed to be. Therefore, the Governor has ordered the procurement of a hand-held semi-automatic, short-recoil pistol for every publicly employed teacher and administrator in the state. Working with an arms manufacturer in Hampton, shipments are already being staged for earliest delivery in two weeks.

"Funding is being provided by the Governor's Opportunity Fund. The Governor will ask the General Assembly next week for an appropriation to replace those funds so he can continue to use the currently designated funds for their original intent, which is attracting new companies and new jobs to the Commonwealth.

"Thanks everyone and that will be all."

"Mr. Gold!" two reporters shouted in unison.

"I'm sorry. I won't be taking any questions today." He turned and walked out.

Later that evening, Danny took Rhonda out to dinner at a restaurant in the Shockoe Bottom for St. Valentines Day. At her apartment, he gave her a revealing red negligee. He had folded it neatly and wrapped it in a silver Victoria's Secret box, hoping she'd think he bought it for her, when in reality it was pre-owned. An earlier paramour had left behind at his place.

Thursday, February 15

"Hey sweetie," Marjorie said, answering the phone with Liza's caller ID showing. It was 6:47 a.m. and darkness was giving way to morning light outside.

"They fired me," Liza admitted, bluntly and seemingly unemotionally.

"What?!?"

"Yeah, they fired me. Well, in fact, the University didn't fire me. The Governor fired me. Well, actually the Governor forced the University to fire me. There was this little thing about whether the University was ever interested in receiving another dime from the state government. So they caved."

"I thought UVA was one of the richest universities in the country, with the law school at the top of endowments."

"It is. But even the loss of a small amount of money was enough to send them into hysterics, from what I heard. Money talks these days. Everybody is in it for the money. The President of UVA makes almost three-quarters of a million dollars. He's not here to be buddies with the coeds. He's here to bring in the dough, from research money, from donors, and from the state. These days, everything we do is about the money. Higher education is no different from big business.

"The bastard was even too much of a chicken-shit to fire me in person. He had the provost send me an e-mail. 'Effective immediately, the University of Virginia has terminated your employment. You will have 24 hours to vacate your office. Please report to the campus security office upon your arrival on the Grounds this morning. They will escort you into your office to collect your belongings.' I'm on my way there now."

"I am so sorry. I love you."

"Bastards," Liza screamed. "Fuck-bastards! They don't know who they're tangling with. I'm as mad as a hornet in a field of lawn mowers. I'm not going away quietly."

Marjorie was devastated. Her sister had been jettisoned from the high office she'd rightfully and legally earned and was weak and fighting for her life. Her lover had been terminated from the job she'd always dreamed about. Her beloved state was being run by madmen. She felt demoralized, incapable of holding back the dam-break of misery. She walked into Sally's room where Sally had evidently just awoken. Sally's knit cap was lying on the pillow above her hairless scalp. In Marjorie's eyes, she had a strange, pallid, primordial beauty. Marjorie told her about Liza's misfortune, and Sally admitted she wasn't surprised.

Messaging him through his secretary, Governor Brady Pasdon had requested Danny Gold to sit in on the Governor's 2:00 p.m. appointment with Allison Donovan, Executive Director of the Charlottesville Planned Parenthood office. Donovan was surely there to protest the recent proposal of Senator Dick Deardan to defund her clinic, essentially shutting down all women's health services throughout the Commonwealth.

Danny was waiting in the Governor's secretary's office when Donovan arrived and told the secretary who she was and of her scheduled meeting with the Governor. Danny thought to introduce himself, but couldn't get himself to do so. "Hi, I'm Daniel Gold, representing the Governor in opposition to everything you do." "Hi, I'm Daniel Gold, the Governor's communications director, tasked with articulating the Governor's vehement pro-life positions to the state's citizens." Nothing he thought of sounded like something he'd want to say or she'd want to hear. Nor were they messages he thought might be conducive to follow-on small talk. So he sat silently.

In due course, they were escorted into the Governor's office. Donovan introduced herself to Pasdon and Pasdon introduced her to Danny. It was awkward to him and he was embarrassed but unapologetic about his prior poor manners towards her.

Danny tried to remain interested, or at least to seem like he was, putting on his best poker face. But his mind drifted away amidst the woman's protestations, and her words like "devastating" and "improper" and "demoralizing" vied for his attention as he savored his mind's eye image of Rhonda the prior evening in the red negligee he'd given her. Donovan was a dark-haired beauty herself, and her skirt inched enticingly up her thighs as she gesticulated to Pasdon, scooting forward in her chair in emphasis. Danny wondered what that same negligee might look like on her, reclining on a white bed sheet, probably still complaining about what his Party was doing to ruin the lives of Virginia women.

His mind drifted to a movie he'd seen a decade earlier where the main character saw every woman around him as naked, even though to others they were clothed. The memory amused him and he let out with an audible smirk, apparently at the same time Donovan had made a particularly impassioned plea to the Governor. She stared at him with a look of fiery contemptuousness.

"Ms. Donovan," Pasdon said, "I appreciate your passion."

Danny continued to stare lustily at the dark-haired woman's legs.

"But abortion is wrong," Pasdon continued. "It's not equivocal, and there is no room for debate. I see your work as murder and you as an accomplice to murder. Your continuing time here in my office is an affront to me and isn't fruitful for you. I wish you good day. Danny, will you please see Ms. Donovan out?"

"Never mind that, Governor," Donovan asserted, with a proper lack of emotion. "I know which door I came in. I can surely find my way out." She stormed out of the office, slamming the door.

Pasdon quipped Danny's way, "Boy, she was sure a turd in my punchbowl this morning."

Danny rubbed his nose, feeling a booger inside he wanted to pick out. "Do you want me to write a press release about this meeting?"

"What meeting? Nothing happened here. I assume you have work to do," Pasdon insisted, curtly. "That'll be all."

Danny followed Donovan's lead, slamming the door unintentionally as he closed it behind himself.

Friday, February 16

Governor Brady Pasdon issues executive order to cut all state budgets

By Steve Herning
Associated Press

Marjorie couldn't believe her eyes. It was front page news on the *Richmond Reporter* she read while carrying it back to the house. What insane news would each new day bring? She took the paper into Sally's bedroom. Sally was still dozing but Marjorie read it aloud anyway.

Governor Brady Pasdon today has asked all state departments to submit to him for his office's review a new budget proposal for cutting a minimum of 15% from their operating budgets in the next biennium. He also called for an immediate state income and sales tax reduction of 15%, indicating, "Our government's heavy hand is impeding commerce and job growth. I take these measures not lightly, understanding the potential pain it may bring to many already bloated budgets. However, we mustn't shirk from our responsibilities to make Virginia the nation's most vibrant economy and to devote ourselves to the cause of job creation."

The Governor asked that the revised budgets be submitted to his office in no more than two weeks. The cuts will apply to all state services including highway maintenance and construction, welfare, Medicaid, primary and secondary education, higher education, transportation, corrections, and public assistance.

"Devastating. Absolutely devastating," said Petersburg Public School System superintendent Vivian Isbell. "In the past ten years, we've cut after-school programs. Art programs. We discontinued band and choir. We sold our busses to a private company and all the children who use busses now must pay a mileage-based fee. What else can we cut? The Governor found the money to buy guns for all my teachers, but no money for their salaries."

Arnie Greer from the Virginia Chapter of the Sierra Club made this written comment, "The loss of funding to the state Department of Environmental Quality will most assuredly lead to more river contamination and more air pollution. Virginia in recent years has already seen its share of problems with some of the dirtiest rivers in the nation. This will only make things worse. Environmental protection is a universal, existential need. Our legislature in Richmond seems to see environmental protection instead as scourge hanging over commerce and 'progress.' Once you've ruined your environment, your future is doomed. What sort of Orwellian hell-world have we molded for ourselves where protection of our environment is so grandly denigrated?"

State Senator Cliven Westmoreland from Harrisonburg said, "Sure, there will be some pain. But my constituents are constantly harping on me, telling me that taxes are too high and are impeding investments and job growth. These are difficult times. Everybody's having to tighten their belts."

Fred Adkins from the Washington DC based, left-leaning think tank Center for Policy Research and the Economy said, "This is entirely misdirected thinking. Anybody who thinks we will achieve prosperity in America by slashing public spending budgets is sorely mistaken. How does Governor Pasdon think the United States pulled itself out of the Great Depression? By public works spending. In fact, the Great Depression was ended by the 'mother' of all public works projects, the build-up to World War II. I certainly don't advocate that we become embroiled in another war, but public works spending on infrastructure, arts, and public structures will build prosperity.

"During the height of the Great Depression in 1934, President Roosevelt signed into law the Public Works of Art Project. It hired almost 4000 artists who produced over 15,000 murals, prints, paintings, and sculptures for government buildings around the country. It's a small thing, but it illustrates the value of putting people to work to benefit everybody."

Superintendent Isbell also commented, "How will we have any hope of long-term economic prosperity tomorrow if we're not educating our children today? I just returned from a trip to Taiwan and Singapore. They're educating their children to be intellectual and economic leaders. How will we compete in the future?"

Asked to respond to Ms. Isbell's specific comments, spokesman Daniel Gold from the Governors' office said, "It is criminal that Superintendent Isbell is traveling to the other side of the world on taxpayer money. This is a typical example of the bloated budgets the Governor is addressing by this Executive Order."

The Governor had no other comment.

"Wow," Marjorie's different tone stirred Sally. "It's like there is a new abuse every day."

"Yeah," her sick sister sighed. "You know what's behind this, don't you?"

"I'm not sure," Marjorie admitted. "They hate taxes?"

"More than that. The state's biggest expense by far is

public schools. Virginia schools were integrated back in the 1960s, with some districts only allowing blacks when forced to do so. But the supremacists always resented it. So they're doing everything they can to make public schools fail. In this case, they're starving them of the funding they need to be successful. If they fail, there will be an outcry to shut them down. That will leave only private schools and only rich kids will get educated."

Sally rose from her reclining position and sat upright, bolstered against a pillow.

Marjorie handed her the glass of water on the bedside table and said, "It's like I don't even want to pick up the paper any more."

Saturday, February 17

As she was mucking the stalls on a cold February day, Marjorie's smart phone was abuzz with alerts. "Accident at North Anna Nuclear Power Station," her screen blazed. Details were sketchy, but a significant release of radioactive material from the power station into the North Anna reservoir had occurred overnight. The two reactor station, generating 1.8 gigawatts of power, had been operating smoothly from construction and licensing in the late 1970s with a good safety record. However, an earthquake in August 2010 was intense enough to cause damage to the core of one of the two reactors.

The hairs on Marjorie's neck bristled in the cold, fearing the effects. Although the power plant was to the east and downstream of her, it was only thirty miles away and the impact to her farm and her own safety was uncertain.

Governor Brady Pasdon was said to be on his way to assess the situation with engineers at the site. A news conference would be held later that afternoon.

Marjorie ran inside to tell Sally, who was propped in bed reading some paperwork. Sally wasn't surprised by the news. Sally explained that oversight of the public utilities had been continually weakened during recent years, as regulators were seen as impediments to the free action of commerce. "There has been an uptick in accidents like this nationally," Sally stated. "The foxes are guarding the hen-house."

Shifting from the current crisis, Sally informed her sister that the issue of uranium mining had come up in previous sessions of the legislature. "The General Assembly put a moratorium on mining of uranium in Virginia a couple of decades ago. There's a deposit in Pittsylvania County near the North Carolina border that is said to be the richest untapped reserve in the world. The pressure to open it up to mining is intense."

"Nuclear power is poison, pure and simple," Marjorie claimed.

"Not everybody thinks so," Sally countered. "The issue in Pittsylvania has centered on whether mining can be done safely in a wet climate, not whether nuclear power is safe. Most uranium is mined in arid places where the run-off can be contained. That site is upstream of Lake Gaston, which is the drinking water inlet for Virginia Beach. The people down there are mighty concerned. The General Assembly might rule on this in the current session."

"Which way do you expect it to go?"

Sally chuckled, "With the Republicans in charge, it seems increasingly likely that it will be approved. The energy and mining industries pour huge amounts of money into their campaigns. They've never seen a development project they didn't like, regardless of the environmental risks."

"What do you think we should do about the spill?"

"Hell," Sally shrugged, "How would I know? We can't very well evacuate your farm. I guess if it gets really bad, we can pack the corgis and head to Roanoke. But what about the horses?"

Marjorie's hand moved instinctively to cover her lower face. "I saw photos from Chernobyl in Russia years after that meltdown. The people had all left and the animals became feral. It was nightmarish."

"Let's see what Pasdon says and go from there," Sally fumed.

The news conference was scheduled for 1:00 p.m. Marjorie and Sally had taken calls from Liza and several other friends during the course of the morning, all expressing their concerns. Nobody knew quite what to do. At the appointed time, the twins were seated in front of Marjorie's television.

The Governor appeared on screen wearing a dark, fiber-pile jacket. The big, bald man was evidently in a conference room, standing in front of a map of the vast power station. Company officials and spokesman Daniel Gold stood behind him. He began, "There has been an unauthorized release of an as-yet unknown amount of radioactive water from the on-site cooling pools here at the North Anna Nuclear Power Plant. Most of the water was released from midnight last night until approximately 3:00 a.m. Radiographic technicians from the electrical utility and from the Nuclear Regulatory Commission in Washington are on-hand, assessing the extent of the spill.

"At this time, we don't believe the amount of material to be significant enough to warrant any evacuations from the area. We have placed a ban on all recreational boating on the Lake.

"While any spill of radioactive materials is serious and cause for concern, we do not believe at this time this spill warrants any remedial action. This power station has had an excellent safety record during its decades of operation, providing cost-effective power for the region. Nuclear power is safe, reliable, and affordable and as we work to understand why this has happened and to prevent it from happening again in the future, this will not derail our efforts to promote nuclear power in Virginia.

"I'll be happy to take questions now."

The camera stayed focused on the Governor, so it was impossible for television viewers to see who was asking the questions.

Pasdon echoed, "The question was about the safety of drinking water. Lake Anna was constructed specifically to serve as the cooling sink for the power plant. The outlet water from the plant is returned to the lake generally about 20 degrees warmer than it enters it, I'm told. The lake covers what was once farmland and timberland, but all that was cleared before the dam was built. There are no municipal water supplies that use the lake, so nobody's water should be affected. Next question?"

A moment later he continued, "No, there are no bans on fishing on the lake."

After another question was directed towards him, he said, "I'm not a big fan of eating fish anyway. My favorite meal is a good Virginia ham. To be honest with you, I'd probably wait awhile before I'd eat the fish. How long? I'm not willing to comment on that just yet until the scientists tell me more about the situation."

Answering another question he said, "The question was about the viability of the proposed uranium mine in Pittsylvania County. That deposit, if we begin mining it, could be a substantial revenue generator for that part of the state impacted by the outsourcing of jobs over the last few decades. I hope this little accident here won't poison the well, so to speak, on that worthwhile project. Even if the nation's utilities shift away from nuclear power, the Navy still runs all its submarines and aircraft carriers on nuclear power. As much as this frustrates the environmentalists, nuclear power is here to stay.

"That will be all for now," he concluded.

Marjorie shut off the TV. "So we really don't know."

"What?"

"How bad the spill was. Or what to do about it."

"I suspect it will take several days to fully access," Sally cautioned. "There's background radiation all the time. It's worse when you fly. Some areas of the country are worse than others. You get radiation in X-Rays. The effects of small amounts of radiation are not well known. Unless this spill is a lot worse than they're telling us, we are pretty well stuck."

Marjorie hastened, "It's frustrating. The Republicans are constantly telling us we have too much regulation. It's hard to call something an accident when the rules are so lax that things like this almost inevitably happen. The voters seldom seem to want to punish them."

The twins were quiet for a moment before Sally declared ruefully, "I need to get over cancer before I worry about what else might kill me."

Sunday, February 18

Early the following morning, Danny Gold was anxious as he and Governor Brady Pasdon were driven from their assessment visit at Lake Anna back to Richmond by State Policeman John Jewett.

The Governor was chatting on the cell phone with the Governor of Arkansas where a similar spill had happened months earlier, Danny overhearing words like "evacuation" and "ban" and "moratorium."

Pasdon hung up and began to detail his plan, "Until this crisis passes, we'll need to set up someone there in Mineral to do regular press conf…"

Danny interrupted, "With all due respect, sir, I think the less we say the better."

"How's that?" Pasdon interrogated.

"This isn't what we ever want to call a disaster. It's only an accident, a minor one. Radiation is something you can't touch, smell, or taste. The effects, if there are any, are minor, dispersed, and difficult to prove. And mostly years in the future"

"Yeah, but they're real."

"Yes, sir. But what's happened has happened. We can't let the utility's problem derail our agenda. We have lots to accomplish. We need to keep our eye on the ball."

"So we say little or nothing?"

"That would be my advice, sir. What you don't say can't hurt you."

Pasdon rubbed his chin thoughtfully for a moment, then called his wife to let her know when he'd be home. He didn't say anything for the rest of the trip.

Monday, February 19

Marjorie was walking back from the paddock with Radley and Boo nipping around her heels, when she saw the blue Ford Escort of Sam Sebrell coming up the back driveway. She had trotted out on Dawson leading Gooch, and left Gooch at the pre-arranged location for Jack Jewett's use. Liza had spent the night, wanting to become more involved with their meetings. Marjorie knew Jack wouldn't be happy having Liza there, but her lover was not to be denied. Marjorie would beg Jewett's forbearance.

Sam Sebrell arrived first and Marjorie invited the huge man inside. Liza was sitting in the parlor with Sally, who was noticeably in better health than recent days. Sally had put on an orange and blue lettered UVA sweatshirt, which clashed with the pink stocking cap that covered her baldness.

Sam was clearly exasperated. "I've hired two DC lawyers to see if we can contest the Governor's take-over. Nobody on the Governor's staff will return my calls or agree to see me. I'm not sure if there is any official word on your status, Sally, and whether there is anyone being installed or acting as Lt. Governor. I am contacting several members of the press and have put in a call with the U. S. Attorney General to see if the President will order some sort of intervention."

"I appreciate everything you're doing," Sally said.

"It's like they've gone crazy," Marjorie complained. "We need to do something."

A shave-and-a-haircut knock came from the back door. Marjorie strode there to let John Jewett inside. He was still wearing his wading boots, which he'd evidently worn on his ride on Gooch from his river crossing.

"Hello Jack…" Sally began.

"Who's she?" John accused, pointing at Liza.

"She's my partner," Marjorie admitted.

"I said I didn't want anyone else here," John complained.

"Listen," Liza asserted, "I was just fired from my job as Dean of the UVA Law School. I'm in this, too. Whatever is discussed here stays with me."

"Fair enough," John resigned after a long pause during which he gave Liza the once-over, "but if it ever becomes known that I've been here, I might as well get some butter and jam, 'cause I'm toast! And nobody else. Nobody!"

"Agreed," Sally stressed.

"Agreed," Liza echoed.

"Here's what's going on," Jack began. "On Saturday morning before we got the call to go to Lake Anna, I drove the Governor out to the Tidewater Gun Club near West Point so he could do some shooting. It's about an hour's drive. Danny Gold came along. He's become Pasdon's main policy adviser. Gold would make Grover Norquist seem like a weak-kneed liberal. Most of the actions you're seeing these days are Gold's suggestions. Yesterday he told the Governor that the less he said about the spill at North Anna the better off he'd be. It appears he's taken that advice to heart."

He went on to discuss how Pasdon was initially seemingly less reactionary and radical, but that Gold had convinced him that he should use his newly acquired power to transform the state to match his political convictions, in many instances over the objection of his Chief of Staff, Jorge Ortiz Gonzales.

"What are they up to next?" Liza inquired.

Jewett sniffled and then took a red bandanna out of his flannel shirt pocket and wiped his nose. "No telling. I think you can assume that things will get worse before they get better. If they get better…"

"How's your mom?" Sally changed the subject.

Radley chomped loudly on a leather chew toy on the tile floor. Boo barked loudly at her.

"Nothing new. She's on her death spiral."

Sally sniffled, "I feel badly. I wish I felt well enough to call on her. Hopefully by tomorrow or the next day – What day is it, Marjorie? – I'll be able to drive down there."

John replied, "It's Monday, but please save yourself a trip. She's unconscious anyway and she won't even know you're there. Please don't go there. You'd be best to remember her the way she was before."

Tuesday, February 20

Marjorie was feeding the chickens on a cold, blustery morning when she got a call from an old high school chum. Sylvia Lancaster, nee Cross, lived in Minneapolis, but she had heard through social media about Sally and called to inquire about her health. Marjorie put her cigarette on a low shelf while she continued to work. The corgis scurried around, pestering the chickens in their daily banter. The call, which Marjorie enjoyed, lasted twenty minutes. By that time, she had moved on to the barn where she was mucking the stalls and feeding the horses.

The corgis began barking furiously, running into and out of the barn. Their increased state of agitation puzzled Marjorie until she smelled smoke. She ran from the barn to the chicken coop where flames were licking the floorboard on the windward side.

"Free-falling hell," she shrieked in horror. She bolted to

the barn and yanked the fire extinguisher from the wall and sprinted back to the coop, yanking the pin as she ran. She pointed the nozzle but only a weak stream blew from it as she realized she hadn't recharged it for years. She sprinted back to the barn and grabbed a bucket, running past the water trough on her way to fill it, corgis noisily in tow. She poured the water against the burning building, extinguishing most but not all of the flame. She repeated the process two more times before the flame was fully doused. She collapsed to her knees, coughing and wincing from the exertion and adrenaline rush, chickens squawking angrily inside. She finally cleared her lungs and was able to stand up. She walked inside the coop and found three chickens dead inside, killed by the smoke or stress. She picked them up by their feet and walked outside, crying.

She buried the chickens near the garden and then took the eleven cigarettes still in her pack, wrenched them apart hoisting the tobacco bits to the wind, and stuffed the empty pack into her pocket. She vowed to never smoke again.

Wednesday, February 21

"Where's Sally?" Liza demanded. "Put me on the speaker phone."

"She's right here," Marjorie replied, and then hit the speaker button as told. The twins were cleaning up the kitchen after breakfast. Marjorie had just re-filled Sally's coffee cup.

"Good morning," Sally exclaimed. "How…"

"Nothing good about it," Liza interrupted. "Zounds! You'll never guess. Not in a million years. Guess!"

Sally turned to Marjorie, who turned her palms upwards.

"He's really done it now. He's started sterilizing people!"

Liza hastened.

Marjorie interrupted, "What are you talking about?"

"Involuntary sterilization. I'm as mad as a wet hen. I'm on my way to your place now. I am so angry I'm having trouble driving. I'll be there in a minute."

Fifteen minutes later, a hysterical, newly unemployed woman burst through the back door. She was still apoplectic. "Damn it! Goddamn it! Now he's sterilizing people! I can't… I can't believe it!"

"What are you trying to say?" Marjorie interjected, with hopeful re-assurance.

"Eugenics. Have you ever heard of the eugenics movement?"

Marjorie volunteered, "Yes. Sally and I talked about it a few weeks ago."

Sally added, "Yeah, Virginia was a leader in the movement for five decades. It was one of the darkest chapters in our state's history. Everyone should be glad it's over."

"*Au contraire ma cheri.*" Liza rued. "It's back." She explained that she'd heard from a friend of a friend that at the Waltons Ridge Correctional Center in Scott County in the far southwest corner of the state, two men had been sterilized against their will. One was in his late teens and the other was in his mid-twenties. Both were told they needed to be examined for venereal diseases, and they needed to be anesthetized for the evaluation. While they were under, they were given vasectomies. Both were deemed mentally deficient and had had a long history of minor robberies and burglaries. The younger man also had drug and assault charges. The superintendent at the facility was vying for a promotion, and he convinced himself that the Governor would be pleased by his actions, given the Governor's desire to reduce costs. The story was yet to hit the newspapers, but Liza was sure it would be national headlines the next day.

"I've had it up to here," Liza drew an imaginary line with her hand at about eye level. "This Governor must be stopped."

"What power do we have?" Marjorie mused. "What can we do?"

"I don't know," Liza fumed. "But I'm going to do something if it kills me. This cannot stand."

Thursday, February 22

Two headlines in the Virginia section of the *Washington Daylight* vied for Marjorie's attention as she walked back to the house on the long driveway from the mailbox at the highway, where she felt increasingly uncomfortable and vulnerable. The first read,

Governor Pasdon resumes involuntary sterilizations

and the second read,

Senator Ward Oates submits legislation to eliminate state minimum wage and overtime pay

She was half-way through reading the former when she reached the house, letting herself inside without even looking up from the paper.

Sally was wearing a blue muslin bath-robe and was sitting in the living room on the recliner where sunlight shone in through the large window, framed by stained glass. Marjorie sat on the couch nearby and read aloud to her sister. "Three days ago, Governor Brady Pasdon issued an executive order rescinding Virginia's ban on involuntary sterilizations of mentally and physically deficient people. Yesterday, two men at the Waltons Ridge Correctional Center in Scott County were sterilized against their will or knowledge. Spokesman Daniel Gold from the Governor's office issued a statement saying, 'Virginia spends millions of taxpayer dollars each year, hosting in its mental health and incarceration facilities people who have no business perpetuating their bloodlines. Governor Pasdon is at the forefront of what he believes will become a recurring national trend to cleanse and purify the gene pool. Virginia from the early twentieth century until the late 1970s, led the nation in its eugenics movement. We are now prepared to lead once again.'

"Geez, Pasdon is sounding more like Adolph Hitler every day," Marjorie peeked over the newspaper she was reading from.

Sally sighed, "Adolph Hitler was said to have modeled, or at least justified, his extermination rampage on the Jews and the Gypsies, on the eugenics movement in the United States. He began building his death camps and gassing 'undesirables'. Our own beloved Old Dominion sterilized more people than any other state."

Marjorie continued reading, "'Virginia's original policy was laid out in the 1924 Eugenical Sterilization Act. The Supreme Court in 1927 found it constitutional.

"Here's what you were talking about… 'Nazis cited the Virginia Act in their defense during the Nuremberg trials. An estimated 7000 Virginians underwent sterilization from 1924 until 1979, when the last one was performed. Over 65,000 people were sterilized nationally. Although the practice became less frequent after the Nuremberg Trials, the last Virginia sterilization was done on a sixteen-year-old girl named Angela Wegner, a run-away who was thought to be mentally deficient and promiscuous. The law was never officially rescinded.

""The Reverend Pat Krull of the Alexandria Unitarian Congregation of Alexandria said, 'As part of my ecumenical mission, I have been working for years to obtain restitution from the State Legislature to compensate past victims, many of whom are still alive. Never in my direst nightmares did I ever envision Virginia starting the program anew. I am shocked, horrified, and tormented.'

"Can you believe this?" Marjorie's hands balled into fists, clutching the newspaper.

"Never. Not in a million years," Sally railed. "When I took over Russ's seat, the General Assembly was still a congenial place. Virginia has always been conservative; don't get me wrong. But legislators had a sense of fairness and compromise and they got things done. The parties understood that the state's future was being restricted by its mortmain..."

"Its what?"

"Mortmain. It's the restrictive influence of the past on the present. Virginia would never be a viable state if it continued to focus on decisions made in the past. They knew balance was necessary and cooperation was expected by the voters."

"Not any more," Marjorie rued.

"So it would seem."

"There's more. Here's another article from our esteemed General Assembly," Marjorie cried. Reading aloud, first the headline, "Senator proposes bill to eliminate minimum wage. Virginia Senator and recently defeated candidate for Lt. Governor," Marjorie winked at her sister, "Ward Oates, Republican from Lynchburg, has submitted a bill to the General Assembly eliminating the state's minimum wage. Oates released a statement saying, 'A minimum wage is a drag on Virginia business, especially small businesses. Business owners in my district tell me that by paying market-based wages to their employees, they can hire more of them, helping to reduce our persistent unemployment. Virginia communities, especially here in Central and Southside, have been particularly hard hit. This proposal will benefit our communities immediately.

"Spokesman Daniel Gold from the Governor's office said, 'The Governor is pleased to have this needed and common-sense legislation coming to his office, and he will sign it into law immediately.'"

Marjorie looked at Sally. Her eyelashes and eyebrows were gone, victims of the chemo attack. But her hazel eyes were still strong. Marjorie ventured, "How are you doing today?"

"When's my next chemo?" Sally replied.

"Next Tuesday. It is the last one scheduled."

"First, I've got to beat cancer," Sally said with assurance. "Then I've got to find a way to beat these Republicans. How, I don't know yet."

"I suspect you'll have every woman and every low-wage worker in Virginia behind you," Marjorie hinted.

Friday, February 23

"Hey, love!" Liza yelled, as she approached her soul-mate.

Marjorie was mucking the barn stalls. She stopped, put down the muck rake, and embraced Liza, giving her a long, wet lips-to-lips kiss. "Good to see you. How are you doing?"

"I'm okay. I'm fine. But I needed a break. I've been working the phones, calling everybody I know to see what options we have for re-taking our state back from the lunatics." She bent down to pet the corgis who were jumping on the legs of her jeans.

"And?"

"And the Republicans are drowning in their own orgy of self-satisfying euphoric spittle. They are rapturous. All the Fox News' commentators are giddy. The rest of the nation's conservatives are watching Virginia like kids at Christmas. How's Sally?"

"Better. You haven't been inside yet?"

"No," Liza said. "I had a notion you'd be out here."

"Give me just a minute, and I'll be done. We can get some lunch."

Marjorie finished her chores and wiped some sanitizer on her hands. It was a cold, clear day and buzzards flew overhead. "I can see Sally getting her mojo back. She has one more chemo session next week. Hopefully, that will be her nadir."

The lovers walked inside, followed by the corgis, and Sally hugged Liza. Liza told Sally how good she looked. Liza began, "I've talked with hundreds of frustrated people in the last week. We're putting together ideas for what we can do to re-take the state."

"What kind of ideas?" Sally inquired.

"Nobody is sure yet," Liza begged. "Most ideas involve you."

"Makes sense," Marjorie agreed about her sister. "People will look to you for leadership, sis."

"I can't!" Sally implored. "One more session. One more! Once I recover from that, I'll rejoin my comrades on the front line."

Marjorie enjoyed and appreciated the warfare metaphors.

Liza shook her head. "We may not wait. Yesterday evening, four inmates at a women's jail in Fredericksburg were sterilized. One was fourteen. We have little time to waste. There was a rally last night in Jackson, Mississippi, in support of re-instituting their eugenics program. And Texas, emboldened by Virginia's recent executions, has developed an accelerated schedule for executing their death row prisoners. The cancer is spreading," Liza put her hand over mouth in apology over her ill-chosen image. "I'm sorry, Sally."

"Apology accepted."

"Anyway," Liza continued, "people across Virginia are furious. A man with a bullhorn was arrested in Virginia Beach for calling for a revolution. His audience had dozens of people openly brandishing assault weapons. And there were dozens of police around, dressed in riot gear like storm troopers. Things are getting tense."

"After Sally's last chemo session," Marjorie spoke in solidarity to her stricken sister, "hopefully we can re-engage."

Sally smiled in agreement.

"As I was sayin', people may not wait," Liza accented. "It is a nervous, volatile moment. The biggest upheaval our state has ever hosted was the Civil War. But I can see another one coming."

For the first time in weeks Sally put on a down coat and went outside for a stroll. Marjorie and Liza saw their rare chance and ran to the bedroom and made love. As they dressed, Marjorie said, "I want you to do something for me."

"What?"

Marjorie took her lover by the hand and walked together

into the bathroom. She picked up an electric shaver and handed it to Liza while pointing at her hair. "Cut it off," she demanded.

"No! Please no!" Liza insisted.

"Yes!" Marjorie insisted back. "You will or I will."

"I love your hair!"

"I love my hair, too, but I want you to cut it off. I have found an agency of the American Cancer Society that makes wigs for people who have lost their hair to cancer. There's a little girl out there somewhere that needs my hair more than I do. Besides, if Sally doesn't have any…"

Liza lovingly stroked her partner's hair, running her hands through it, massaging Marjorie's scalp. Then, with no further protest, Liza did what she was told. Marjorie sat on the closed toilet seat while locks of her auburn hair tumbled to the floor. When she finished, she turned to the mirror, wiped her hand over her pate, and nodded subtly.

"Well," Marjorie said.

"Well," Liza echoed. She pointed the shaver towards Marjorie, "Okay, get up. If you're making me do yours, I'm making you do mine," she insisted.

"I won't do it," Marjorie asserted.

Liza stared at her with a gaze to kill. She slapped the shaver into Marjorie's hand. Knowing her lover's will was as forceful as her own, Marjorie didn't bother to protest any further.

They had swept up the shorn hair and placed it into plastic bags, and were entering the parlor when Sally returned from her walk. Sally hung up her scarf on the pegboard by the door and then saw her sister. Then Liza appeared and Sally saw her, too. Sally brought her hand to her mouth, which was widening in surprise. "Oh, my," she whispered. "Don't that just take the cake?" Her eyes moistened and she began to sob. She ran to her twin and her twin's lover and embraced them.

Four hours later, Marjorie returned inside her house after feeding the chickens to the news from Sally that earlier that afternoon, a male student in Front Royal had killed a teacher and three other students. The alleged killer was a high school junior, six-feet, two-inches tall and 210 pounds, a linebacker on the football team. He had become abusive towards his biology teacher when he received a failing grade on a test. She was 25 years old, in her third year of teaching, and a recent graduate of Shenandoah University. She stood five-feet, one-inch tall and weighed 130-pounds. She had brandished her newly-acquired gun to defend herself, but he easily wrested it from her and shot her with it, and then proceeded to kill three other girls, reputedly one of which had spurned his affections two months earlier and two of her friends. Two other students, both males, were badly wounded. His shooting spree lasted until the clip was empty, with other students fleeing the building. Then he sat in a desk chair, put his smoking gun on the desktop surface, and waited for authorities to arrive, with the dead bodies surrounding him and blood-splatter on the walls and pools on the floor.

Saturday, February 24

It began snowing in the early morning and by daybreak, there was already ten inches on the ground with more coming. Marjorie and the corgis went to the barn and pulled some hay from the loft and drove it to the pasture. The Lusitanos were particularly frolicsome. Tank was fully healed from his castration and would soon be broken for the saddle in preparation for his sale.

That evening, as Marjorie was fixing dinner, her NPR station interrupted their programming to bring news of a coal mine explosion in Tazewell County in far southwest Virginia.

The coverage was detailed and horrific.

The Trump 2 mine was just outside of Jewell Ridge. Details were emerging from the disaster that occurred at 4:14 p.m. that afternoon, but as many as 25 to 30 miners were believed to be trapped inside where the explosion began at a depth of 1250 feet underground. The owner of the mine, Chester Natural Resources, Inc. had a long history of safety and environmental violations. Nineteen months earlier, a former superintendent, Brunswick McKeen, had written an editorial in the *Richmond Recorder* complaining about his company's insistence that he and other superintendents impede the regulatory efforts of the applicable safety and environmental agencies. McKeen's home was later destroyed in a fire of suspicious circumstances that killed his wife, grandson, and two dogs. McKeen was thought to have moved to Alaska in recent months. The President of Chester Natural Resources, DeWitt Chester, was one of the richest men in the Virginia coal fields and was a major contributor to Republican candidates.

Several tearful spouses were interviewed, all expressing their hope that their husbands would be found alive and their abiding faith in their Savior.

Snow continued falling in the darkness outside Marjorie's kitchen window, illuminated by the lamp post adjacent to her driveway.

Sunday, February 25

The new day dawned bright, clear, and extremely cold. There were twenty inches of snow on the ground, the most all winter. The thermometer read 11°F. A bright-red cardinal flashed to and from the feeder, screaming its familiar call, "Pret-ty, pret-ty. Cheer, Cheer." Marjorie had agreed on Friday to take Sally to church, but they checked the church's website and as expected found that it would not be opening due to the snow.

Marjorie was at a loss as to what to do with plowing their driveway, which she normally did herself with the Deere. Minding John Jewett's admonition and mindful of the tire trap, she decided not to plow the main driveway. But she didn't want to do the other driveway, either, fearing that if anyone was watching they'd know it was being accessed regularly. She walked the main driveway to get the newspaper. One lane of Woodberry Forest Road had been plowed and her paper was in the box as always. There were no cars whatsoever in sight on the road.

She walked back to the house where she found Sally sitting with a Bible. When Sally saw her, she said, "Well, we didn't have church today. I figured I'd do some devotional reading."

"You know," Marjorie affirmed, "I gave up on religion some time ago. When my own church said that my love for other women was an abomination to God, I figured it was time for me to go. Looks like you're still with it."

Sally brushed the blue stocking cap off her bald head and stroked the newly exposed skin. "I've been thinking a lot about what Selena Jewett said, about losing her faith. Let me read this. It's from Matthew, chapter 17. Jesus' disciples asked him about the power of faith. He said, 'I tell you the truth, if you have faith as small as a mustard seed, you can say to this mountain, 'Move from here to there' and it will move. Nothing will be impossible for you.' I think the savior has got a bit of hyperbole going there."

"True," Marjorie guffawed.

"If faith really moved mountains, we'd be using them instead of dynamite and drag-lines."

"What?" Marjorie quizzed.

"Mountaintop Removal Mining," Sally answered. "The accident in the coal mine the other day was a sub-surface mine. But coal mining in southwest Virginia and southern West Virginia is done mostly these days by destroying the mountains to get to the coal. Although it is safer from the miners' perspective, it is horrifically destructive to the landscape and the streams nearby. If we could use faith instead, it would save a lot of heartache. Somehow, I'm still compelled to seek whatever blessings worship might bring. But I don't for an instant believe that faith will cure my cancer or overturn the madness that has taken over our state government."

The sisters sat silently looking at each other. Marjorie ached for a cigarette. "Tear, tear," whistled the cardinal at the sunflower seed feeder.

"There's more, yes?" Marjorie hinted, detecting additional urgency in her twin. Twins have a bond that others can't replicate or even envision.

"You know me too well," Sally admitted. "Yeah, I keep thinking also about Selena, about her faith, and how she thought her loss of faith precipitated her cancer."

"Do you believe that?" Marjorie got up and put two more logs into the wood-stove.

"I don't know. What I do know is that stress can kill. When I have cancer already, I can't let the stress of what's now out of my control get the better of me."

"And?"

"And I have enough faith to know that we shall overcome. Deep in my heart, I do believe, we shall overcome some day. Isn't that how the old spiritual goes? It may take years to overcome what the Republicans are doing to our state right now, but Dr. King said, 'The arc of the moral universe is long, but it bends towards justice.' I'm not sure I believe in God any more, but I believe in that."

Marjorie said, "I do, too."

Sally looked at her Bible. "Something did change that day we spoke with Selena. I've thumbed through this old Bible four or five times since then. Each time, it has had less meaning. Cancer has been an epiphany for me. Let's be honest; Eve was not formed from one of Adam's ribs. The earth was not created in six days. Jonah wasn't swallowed by a whale. Noah didn't live to be 900 years old and he didn't sail the ark when he was 600. And he didn't take two of every species on earth onto the ark. What about the dolphins? Did he take two of them on the ark to save them from the flood?"

They both laughed.

"I'll tell you when I rejected the Bible," Marjorie concurred. "When I came to grips with my sexuality, I found the Bible had lots to say about it. The Old Testament says not to practice homosexuality, something like 'a man lying with another man as with a woman is a detestable sin.' But slavery, now, that's another story. There is nothing one human being has done to another that is more detestable than slavery, other than genocide. But the Bible not only doesn't condemn it, it gives fucking instructions! It says, 'When a man sells his daughter as a slave, she will not be freed at the end of six years as the men are. If she does not please the man who bought her, he may allow her to be bought back again.' Somehow, in a book millions of people revere and use as a guidebook for morality, it is moral to sell your own daughter as a sex slave. So much for family values!

"For almost two hundred and fifty years, pious white men here in my beloved Virginia justified bondage of blacks by quoting the Bible. Realizing that was the end for me."

Sally stood up gingerly, walked to the wood-stove, opened the door, and threw the Bible inside. Then she closed the door and latched it.

Marjorie thought to protest, but knew it was futile. And she really didn't understand why she would.

"Tear, tear," sang the cardinal at the window.

Monday, February 26

In anticipation of John Jewett's regular weekly visit, Marjorie tacked up Dawson and Gooch early and rode to the meeting spot, leaving Gooch, per usual, for John.

When she got back, Sally was awake and in the kitchen fixing pancakes for breakfast. The tart smell of peppermint tea filled the air. "Happy Birthday!" Sally exclaimed.

"Happy Birthday to you, too!" Marjorie echoed. "You're looking mighty chipper this morning."

"I'm feeling better than I have in weeks," Sally crowed, happily. "The day after tomorrow, I'm getting poisoned again, but today I'm going to be happy. Hey, I have something for you, a little birthday present..." She ran into her room, returning a moment later. "I have to laugh giving this to you."

Marjorie took the package, a small rectangular box with an orange bow. She unwrapped the ribbon and opened the box and the tissue inside. It was a curved, stainless silver comb. "Oops," she said, recognizing that she now had no need for it. She put it down on the kitchen counter. "I have something for you, too."

Marjorie retrieved a small cloth bag, tied with a string, and gave it to her sister. Sally untied the string and poured into her had a thin gold clip, engraved with two angels on it. Marjorie said, "It's a bookmark. It's for your Bible." Both women commenced laughing so hard Marjorie thought her side would split. Sally handed Marjorie a glass of orange juice, then clanked her own against it and said, "Well, happy birthday anyway!"

Neither Liza nor Sam arrived for their meeting, due to snow. But Jewett arrived on schedule, reliable as always.

Jewett said that it was unreported by the media, but the Governor had actually visited the prison where the capital punishment of the prior week had occurred. Jewett waited outside the prison, but Pasdon and Gold had gone inside to witness the execution. To Jewett's horror, neither man said anything about it on the drive back to Richmond, as if neither had a shred of conscience.

Instead, their conversation in the car was about Gold's plan to work with the FBI to obtain cell phone records for all Virginians without the imposition of a court order or court approved search warrant.

Marjorie's impression was that the assaults of the civil liberties of Virginia citizens were to be elemental to this Governor's tenure.

A half-hour after Jewett's departure, Marjorie rode to the river to retrieve Gooch.

Just before 4:00 p.m., Marjorie called the Cancer Clinic at the UVA Medical Center to confirm Sally's appointment for the following day. The snow was melting rapidly and she was assured that the roads in and around Charlottesville were fully cleared. The sun was out and with the day's high temperature approaching 40°F and forecast for 49°F the next day, Marjorie plowed both driveways on her Deere, carefully avoiding the area of the tire trap.

"Gold!" Danny Gold yelled at his cell phone several hours later, answering it while fumbling from bed and a deep sleep.

"Danny?"

"Yeah, what?"

"This is Brady Pasdon" claimed the voice on the other end. "Sorry to call you so late."

Danny looked at the bedside table. His illuminated digital clock said 1:45 a.m. He swung his legs from the sheets drunkenly and put his feet on the carpeted floor. "Good evening, Governor."

"Danny, I've got something on my mind I'd like to discuss with you. Can you come over to the mansion?"

"Now?"

"Yes, if you don't mind."

Doggone it all, Danny thought. The last thing he wanted to do was leave a warm bed in the middle of a cold night and go traipsing down to the Governor's Mansion. But you can't say no to the boss when he's the Chief Executive of the State.

"I'll be down as soon as I can," Danny grumbled quietly, shaking off a mild hangover. He turned on the bedside lamp. He brushed the sides of his head and tried to regain his senses. He stood up and noticed he was nude. His foot felt some clothing on the floor, and he realized he had shed his clothes in haste and left them. He turned to the bed and felt his pulse rate jump, seeing the head of a blonde-haired young woman on the other pillow.

He mumbled expletives to himself, assessing his predicament. He saw her slacks and blouse on his chair and her bra and panties on the floor beside her shoes. He nudged her, "Hey, time to get up!" She was unconscious. Her breath and clothes smelled of alcohol. There was a half-empty bottle of bourbon on the dresser.

He left her alone to dress himself. What was he going to do with her? He couldn't even remember her name. Melissa? Melanie? He couldn't leave her there – what if she woke up? There were too many guns around, too much private stuff.

He opened her purse and began rooting through her wallet. He found his business card that he'd evidently given her. He removed it and put it back into his wallet. He found her Connecticut drivers license. Melodee Trammel. She was pretty, light-complected with curly yellow hair, and petite. Was she in Richmond attending college?

"Come on Melodee, time to get up," he implored, jostling her. She was unresponsive. Again he asked himself what he could do with her. He didn't know her local address, so he could neither take her home nor call a cab.

He pulled the covers back and exposed her motionless body. He wiped her damp crotch with one of his dirty t-shirts he pulled from his hamper, and then positioned her upright and slid her blouse, slacks and shoes on her. He grabbed his keys and wallet, and put on his coat. Then he wrapped her coat around her and stuck her bra and panties in her coat pockets. He grabbed an old blanket that he'd stolen from the airline on his only international flight years earlier from the hall linen closet as he carried her over his shoulder downstairs and out the door.

He sat her down gently on the edge of his lawn as he looked around to see if anyone had seen him. He put the blanket over her. He walked a few steps towards his car and then returned, realizing that he didn't want her to awake and realize where she'd been. So he picked her up again – thankfully she wasn't heavy – and carried her three houses away where the old couple, the Darvills, lived and set her down again on their lawn. He returned to his Hyundai and sped off downtown.

His meeting with Pasdon was largely a blur, something about redistricting that Pasdon wanted to impact. Danny walked, shivering, back to his car, fuming over the Governor's impertinence, and wondering what of any significance they had discussed that couldn't have waited until morning. He arrived home two hours later, dead tired, slowing at the Darvills' place to happily discover that his erstwhile lover, the stranger with whom he'd copulated earlier in the evening, was gone, hopefully with no memory of their coitus or his identity.

Tuesday, February 27

Sally was uncharacteristically buoyant on the way south on SR-20 towards Charlottesville. The day was sunny again, ultra-bright on the snow covered fields, and both women wore matching orange skull caps and thick down jackets. They sang along to several tunes on the radio. "I went down Virginia,"

Sally belted out, "Seekin' shelter from the storm…"

The routine was familiar to the twins now. They were amused when the nurse turned to Marjorie first, thinking she was Sally, confused by Marjorie's new hairdo. "I'm your patient," Sally insisted.

They watched the crimson toxicant drip into Sally's bloodstream, hoping it was the last time. As they were departing, they ran into John Jewett in the hallway. He shook his head gently and said only, "Not good."

The twins were back at Runnymede Meadow Estate before dusk.

Wednesday, February 28

"Hello," Marjorie said, answering the house phone. The caller ID said, "UVA Med Cen."

"May I please speak with Sally Bradley?" a female voice said, pleasantly.

"Who may I say is calling?"

"I'm Rebecca Ashe. I'm with the chaplain's staff at the UVA Hospital."

Damn, Marjorie thought. This would only be bad news. "One moment. Sally?" she yelled. As Sally arrived, Marjorie handed her the phone.

"This is Sally Bradley. Yes. When? Yes. I understand. Thank you for calling." She pushed the off button and returned the receiver to its receptacle.

"Selena Jewett has passed."

"When?"

"Just after midnight."

Silence.

"What's next?" Marjorie inquired.

Sally informed, "There will be a funeral in Fincastle in a few days. They said to watch the *Roanoke Star* website for the obituary. I'm sure I won't feel up to going, with yesterday's chemo kicking in…"

"I know that," Marjorie interrupted. "I'll go for you." Then she started laughing, nervously, spontaneously. "The minute I take off my hat, everybody will think I'm you anyway!"

Both of them laughed more, with sadness-tinged tears.

Danny Gold sat on the examination room table wearing nothing but his jockey shorts. After complaining about pain while urinating and penile discharge on his shorts, he had called his general practitioner who had sent him to a specialist. Doctor Allen Fink re-entered the room without knocking. Dispensing with ceremony or tergiversation, he blurted, "You got the clap, bub. Gonorrhea. Who you been sleeping with?"

"Lots of people," Danny admitted boastfully.

"Any men?" Fink queried.

"Fuck no!" Danny yelled impertinently. "I…"

"Shut up," the doctor demanded. "You can write anything you want on the Internet about my poor manners, but I'm not here to be nice. You have a sexually transmitted disease. STDs are a hassle at best and fatal at worst.

"You seem to think sex is a sport, but promiscuity can kill you. Within 48 hours, you will need to submit to the Board of Health over on Broad Street a list of everyone you've copulated with. My staff will send your record to their office.

"I'm going to prescribe some Rocephin and azithromycin for a couple of weeks, and then I want to check you again. Meanwhile, keep your joystick in your trousers. You're infectious and you'd be the biggest jackass in Richmond if you pass on this disease to anyone else."

Fink scribbled an unintelligible message on a prescription pad and handed it to Gold. "See my receptionist for your next appointment." Then he left the room.

Danny got dressed and appeared at the front office for his next appointment. He was given instructions on the risks of the disease and the treatment he'd been prescribed by a morbidly obese, sniveling black woman in a blue smock who seemed to be barking instructions loud enough for everybody in the waiting room to hear. He left and headed to the pharmacy for his drugs.

Five

"It is only when the people become ignorant and corrupt, when they degenerate into a populace, that they are incapable of exercising their sovereignty."
— JAMES MONROE, 12TH GOVERNOR OF VIRGINIA

Thursday, March 1

The morning news had the grisly headline of another state-supported execution, this time of a 42-year old woman the prior evening, also at the Greendale Correctional Facility in Sarratt. The woman had been on death row for eleven years for murdering her husband. She slit his throat while he slept, and then severed his penis and stuck it in his mouth. In the trial, it was proved that he had abused her physically and emotionally for years, and had likely been responsible for the death of their infant daughter. A jury of eleven men and one woman convicted her anyway. She was the first woman Virginia had executed in 58 years.

The Governor had signed her execution order at 10:00 p.m., and in spite of the protests of a group of 55 outside the prison gate, she was proclaimed dead at 11:23 p.m.

Even with the newfound work for Mr. Wattie, the electric chair, there was a malfunction that caused the doomed woman's hair to catch fire before she died. Witnesses said they were horrified by the gruesome nature of the scene they observed.

Sam Sebrell called Sally to tell her that he'd gotten word that another involuntary sterilization had taken place, this time on a 19-year-old man at the Waltons Ridge Correctional Center in Scott County. The man had been imprisoned three separate times since he was 15 and was often violent and delusional. Sam mentioned that the man was mammoth, extremely strong, and black.

Friday, March 2

For a change, Danny left the office early, at least for him, and was on his way to Rhonda's house by 6:30 p.m. as she had invited him over for a dinner date. His recent diagnosis of gonorrhea and the admonitions he'd gotten from his doctor were weighing heavily on his mind. He convinced himself that he'd speak with Rhonda about it that evening.

He was pleasantly surprised to find Alison Partlow, Rhonda's frequent tennis partner, sitting on the sofa nursing a goblet of wine. Jazz was crooning from the speakers. Three candles sat on the mantle, reflecting from a mirror, and an oil lamp burned on the dining room table.

"Nice seeing you again, Alison. How's your game," he commented to her, in his mind referring to tennis. She was as alluring as Rhonda, smaller but trim and pretty.

"I'm good," she retorted. "You, too?" She took off her eyeglasses and leaned back on the sofa, crossing her legs under her. "Rhonda has told me a lot about you."

"Some wine for you, Danny?" Rhonda asked, opening the china cabinet and grabbing another goblet.

He sat next to Alison and Rhonda sat on the other side. "How's *your* game?" Alison teased Danny, ricocheting his faux pas. She put her hand on his thigh. Rhonda unbuttoned the top button on her blouse. His heartbeat raced, and he felt sweat seeping from his brow. He fumbled in his pocket for the package of condoms that he'd brought along, but realized he must have left it in his car. He could go out to get it, but the mood would be broken. "I'm good, too," he said. "Better all the time."

Saturday, March 3

It was raining lightly when Marjorie did her barn chores. She took a quick shower and drove the back driveway towards the highway and began her two-hour trip to Fincastle for Selena Jewett's funeral. There was fog on Afton Mountain where Interstate 64 crossed the Blue Ridge, and traffic slowed to 45-mph, but otherwise it was clear sailing.

The grave-side service was short, with a preacher talking about what a good Christian woman Selena had been and an old family friend talking about Selena's volunteer work for the local library foundation. Marjorie wore a black stocking cap and a long black overcoat, suitable for mourning.

After the ceremony, John approached her and asked about Sally's condition. Marjorie noted that Sally's final chemo treatment had been successful and that Sally was entering her worst days from it. Surreptitiously, "I'll be there on Monday," and then he quickly walked away.

Sunday, March 4

Marjorie was half-way to the house with the morning paper when a front-page headline demanded her attention. It was a chilly, calm morning, but she stopped dead in her tracks to read it.

Whiston Corporation withdraws Virginia plans

The Whiston Corporation of Liverpool, England, announced today that the plans they made public in early November for construction of their first United States facility near Winchester, Virginia, has been withdrawn. The company had been lured to Frederick County by the prior Governor with the offer of $3.2 million in incentives from the Governor's Opportunity Fund, as Whiston had committed to adding 450 white-collar jobs to the payroll.

According to company spokesperson Christina Essex, "This was a difficult decision for our board, especially considering our earlier commitment. However, 54% of our employees worldwide are women, and we felt that the current government in Richmond has become increasingly hostile towards women and indifferent to their health care and reproductive concerns."

In a written statement, Whiston announced that they would be constructing their facility in nearby Hagerstown, Maryland, instead. The maker of medical diagnostic equipment for infectious diseases was on a rapid growth trajectory.

Preston Moreton, economic development director for Maryland Governor Prescott Action said, "We welcome the Whiston Corporation to Maryland with open arms. Maryland eagerly recruits companies that recognize that their employees, both men and women, are healthier, happier, and more productive when the company partners with them and supports them."

Neither Virginia Governor Brady Pasdon nor his communications director Daniel Gold were available for comment.

She continued her walk inside where Sally emerged from her bedroom and joined her in the kitchen. "Get this," Marjorie commanded. She then read the same article to Sally.

Sally sat at the table and crossed her legs, adjusting her bathrobe. "Situations like this are sure to happen with increasing frequency. It was only a matter of time."

"What do you mean?" Marjorie wondered.

"The Governor's actions will surely drive companies away. For decades, companies have been re-locating to Virginia and other southern states, drawn by cheap labor and lack of unions. The tide is turning. Companies are more enlightened now. They recognize that workers are real people and have needs that must be met."

Marjorie picked up the Metro Living section of the paper. "I'm sure this Governor thinks of himself as pro-business."

"All the Republicans do," Sally agreed. "Most modern companies, at least the good ones, don't want to pollute or subject their workers to unsafe conditions. They just don't want a tilted playing field. Commonsense regulations simply set the conditions where everybody can thrive." She pulled the tea bag from her cup and set it on the plate. "Good companies also don't mind being taxed. They understand that they are beneficiaries of roads, airports, educated employees, and police and fire protection that taxation provides."

Marjorie interjected, "The meme these days, particularly from the conservatives, is that corporations create jobs, so rich people shouldn't be taxed."

"It's one of the most pervasive and toxic ideas during my lifetime," Sally claimed. "It's an article of faith among the Republicans and even accepted by some Democrats. It's also emphatically wrong, as wrong as the earth is flat."

"Really?"

"Sure. Do you know why street vendors in Africa don't sell Rolex watches? Because their customers can't afford them." She uncrossed her legs and leaned forward, as if for emphasis. "Rich people don't create jobs. Hiring somebody is the last thing a businessman wants to do; employees are troublesome and expensive. Company owners hire people when their customer demand is great enough to support them. Consumers create jobs. The best thing we can do to stimulate the economy is to tax rich people, the people who have greatly benefited from the system, and spend that money on education and infrastructure, and let the people who work in those jobs spend their earnings throughout the economy. The states in the country where the taxes are the highest are the most successful; the same goes with countries around the world. Austerity is a death sentence. There's never been a successful recovery from a recession in the world in any nation that slashed government spending."

"Is that true?" Marjorie inquired.

"As far as I know, yes. How did we end the Great Depression? With a series of public works projects that fed massive amounts of money into the economy. Taxing rich people is good for everybody, even ultimately the rich people. Trickle-down economics is the cruelest myth that has been perpetrated on this country in the last fifty years . It has only made rich people richer."

"You know," Marjorie jibed, "You'd make a good governor someday."

Sally chuckled appreciatively. "We'll see."

Monday, March 5

As per their now normal Monday routine, Marjorie tacked up Gooch and Dawson and left Gooch at the Meadow site for John Jewett. Sally wasn't feeling well, but John arrived just after 10:00 a.m. and Sam Sebrell and Liza Randolph arrived moments later.

Sam and Liza offered condolences to John over the passing of his mother, condolences that John accepted graciously and politely .

John began the meeting, saying, "The General Assembly term ended yesterday. The Governor and his minions are pretty giddy about what they've accomplished."

"I'll bet," Liza snarled.

Marjorie asked Sam if his efforts had been at all fruitful. Jack explained that he had encountered obstacles at every turn. He admitted, "I'm not really sure what options you have – we have – especially until Sally is well enough to show herself publicly."

Sam added, "I think he's right. At this point, our side has

no titular head."

Liza smirked. Sally blushed.

"OOPS! Mea culpa," Sam stuttered, apologizing for his inadvertent blunder.

Jack continued, unflustered, "The Governor has always put a lot of effort into fund raising. But now with the General Assembly session over, he is putting that effort in full gear. I'm going to be really busy over the next couple of months driving him around. I'm sure his fat-cat donors will be pleased with the job he's done. And he'll be begging them to donate more money. He's talking about a permanent Republican majority and feels like within the next year or two, he can re-write away laws that would remove any fairness we still have in the democratic process."

Liza said, "I have some news. I've been coordinating with women across the state. We've had it up to here," she drew a line at eye level. "We're organizing a march on Richmond."

"For what?" Sam quizzed.

"We're going to march from the downtown mall in Charlottesville, down US-250, the old Three Notch'd Road, right down Broad Street, Richmond's main thoroughfare. We're going to stage a rally at the Capitol and demand the resignation of the Governor. We will accuse him of treason and give him three days to resign."

"Wow," Marjorie exclaimed, worriedly. "You don't think he will, do you? How will you convince him to resign?"

"We're not sure yet. If there are a few dozen of us, he'll flick us away like gnats buzzing around his head. A few hundred protesters might get him to think about it, though. We are calling ourselves 'The Women of Orange'. We will wear orange shirts that have the Seal of the House of Orange on it. It has a cut of two lions, symbols of our strength."

John said, "I'm pretty sure you'll need a permit to do that. First, you'll need a permit to block a lane of a highway. Then you'll need a permit to have an assembly at the Capitol."

"With all due respect, Mr. Jewett," Liza hastened with surprising formality, "it's a protest. I don't mean to be facetious, but there's something painfully askew when you apply for a permit to do a protest. We're assembling tomorrow. There are 38 of us who have committed to going and more by the hour. It's almost 70 miles, and we hope to be picking up new people on the way. We plan on doing it in four days and being on the Capitol grounds by Saturday for our rally at 3:00 p.m.

"Put it on your calendar and plan to attend," she smiled.

As the meeting ended, Marjorie was wracked in fear for her lover. She wondered how John Jewett, the State Trooper, was feeling about what Liza had planned and whether he was still committed to the cause.

Tuesday, March 6

Marjorie was doing paperwork in the morning on a warming day when she got the news over her smart phone that another execution had occurred the night before. This time, the Death Row inmate was a 78-year-old black man who had been convicted of the rape and murder of a white woman who was 19-years-old at the time in Lunenburg, 34 years earlier. The doomed man was being treated for a serious heart condition and was not expected to live much longer, but the Governor ordered his execution anyway.

Marjorie finished her chores and after getting Sally situated, drove to Charlottesville to send off Liza and her followers. Liza stood on the stage of the large, canvas-covered performing arts pavilion on the east end of the downtown mall, where she spoke to the crowd with a hand-held bullhorn. There were around 200 people in attendance, with seventy or so donning orange shirts and evidently planning to do the march. Liza thanked them for coming and spoke about the terrible actions of the Governor and how important it was to see him deposed.

At noon precisely, the chime sounded at nearby City Hall. Marjorie kissed Liza on the lips and said, "Please be careful." The marchers began their walk down High Street with approximately a dozen support vehicles ready to follow them. Marjorie walked back to her car and drove home to Runnymede Meadow Estate.

Wednesday, March 7

Liza called Marjorie late the next day with a progress report. "We're doing great," she exclaimed, enthusiastically. "We have over 100 with us now, mostly women but a few men. The weather has been good both days, thankfully, but we're expecting colder temperatures and some snow showers or flurries tomorrow."

"Have you been hassled?" Marjorie asked.

"We've had a few hecklers, but most people have been good. Last night we stayed at Zion X-Roads and tonight we're staying in Gum Spring."

"Are you camping?"

"Some protesters brought tents, yes. People are putting us up in their houses. People have driven here in RVs and campers to host us. There is a church here that is letting us sleep on the floor."

"I saw your march on TV last night," Marjorie beamed. You're getting lots of attention. You were on all the networks!"

"Marchers are calling friends from their cell phones while they walk, encouraging them to join us in Richmond," Liza beamed.

"Sweetie, do you know what you'll do when you get there? Do you even know if the Governor will meet with you?"

"No and no," Liza admitted. "We're going anyway. If the Governor will meet with us, great. If not, we'll raise holy commotion and get as much media attention as we can. How's Sally?"

"Better. She's been really weak since the last chemo. Each day, she seems a little stronger. I know she wishes she could be with you."

"I'll call you again tomorrow. Love you."

"Love you, too. Please be careful."

Thursday, March 8

Marjorie was playing chess after dinner with Sally when Liza called again, nearly breathless.

"What a day we've had!" she exclaimed briskly over the speaker phone. "Our numbers doubled since yesterday. Wow, what energy!"

Liza talked about the weather, which had tested everyone. It had dropped to a high of 41°F and the morning had blowing snow with sun breaks in the afternoon. She said three older marchers, two women and one man, had to leave due to physical problems. But with the doubling of their numbers, they were a formidable sight, marching towards the historic state Capitol. One marcher was an 83-year old black woman who talked non-stop about the civil rights battles she fought.

"Any hassles today?"

"Yeah," Liza admitted. "A State Trooper set up his car in front of us, with his lights flashing and all. He waited for me."

"What did he say?"

"He asked if we had a permit. I asked if we needed one. He said he wasn't sure, but he knew we'd need one to assemble at the Capitol."

"What did you tell him?" Sally inquired, listening over the speaker of Marjorie's phone.

"I told him that if we weren't doing anything wrong, he shouldn't be harassing us. Then I told him we'd sure like an escort. So you know what? He did!"

Marjorie interjected, "Are you going to get a permit at the Capitol?"

"Hell no! Like I told Trooper Jewett, this is a protest march. Do you think Dr. King got a permit to march from Selma to Montgomery?"

Sally laughed hard enough for Liza to hear her, and exclaimed, "Sure enough! It's not much of a protest if you have to ask permission. Anyway, you can tell them you have permission from the Lt. Governor."

Marjorie said, "I'm coming to Richmond. I want to be there for you. When will you be at the Capitol?"

"We'll spend the night tonight at Short Pump. We'll reach the Richmond City limits by tomorrow around lunchtime. We're planning a rally at Willow Lawn and then a final rally at VCU. We'll spend the night in the VCU area. We already have hundreds of offers to house people. Then on Saturday morning, we'll be on the Capital Grounds."

Marjorie looked at Sally and pleaded, "Is it okay with you if I go?"

"You bet," her twin agreed. "If I feel up to it, I'll go with you."

Friday, March 9

Marjorie took Liza's call late in the evening on a warmer day than the prior. Liza had excitement in her voice. "Another great day!"

"What's going on?" Marjorie asked, putting the speaker on again while finishing washing the saucepan she'd used at dinner.

"We did our rally in a parking lot at Willow Lawn. I screamed over the bullhorn so hard trying to get people to hear me that I almost lost my voice. Oh, gosh, there were a thousand people or more, I guess. People are carrying signs and waving banners. 'We want our Commonwealth back!' 'Pasdon must go.' It's crazy!

"The last four miles into the VCU campus area were amazing! An old friend of mine from law school works at VCU and she had set up a loudspeaker at Monroe Park. I felt like Martin Luther King, having my dream."

"What did you talk about?" Marjorie inquired.

"Oppression. Pasdon's take-over. How we needed everybody's support tomorrow. It's going to be a big, big day!"

"I'll be there!" Marjorie yelled.

They hung up the phone and Sally told Marjorie, "I'm not feeling well, Sis. I'm sorry; you'll need to go on your own. I'll be there in spirit."

Saturday, March 10

The next morning, Marjorie awoke early and did her chores, feeding the horses, the corgis, and Sally, and hit the road before 9:00 a.m. It was a fine late winter day. She made good time to I-64 and the Richmond city limits, but there, traffic was snarled by an accident. She lost an hour waiting and could only find a parking space for the Mercedes ten blocks from the Capitol. She trotted most of the way to the Capitol Square where a huge crowd had gathered.

She fought her way to the front, nudging people out of the way as Liza took the microphone, attached to speakers powered by a portable generator. Liza was still wearing the orange shirt she had on in Charlottesville, now stretched over a down sweater.

"Ladies and gentlemen, mostly ladies," Liza's voice rang over the massive crowd. "We are here today because we are taking back our government. Where are you, Governor Pasdon? Say with me, 'Where are you Governor Pasdon?'"

"Where are you, Governor Pasdon?" the crowd responded.

"Say it again!"

"Where are you, Governor Pasdon?" the crowd yelled, louder.

"Address the people!" Liza yelled. Liza saw Marjorie approach the edge of the rise they were using as a stage and winked at her.

"Address the people!" the masses echoed.

"Governor Pasdon, you are not our Governor at all. You have taken the office illegally. The people here and the citizens of the great Commonwealth of Virginia demand your resignation. You have 24 hours!"

The audience applauded.

"And if Brady Pasdon doesn't resign?" Liza got quiet for dramatic affect. "I hereby call on a general strike of all employees of the State of Virginia. If you are in a private-sector job, I want you to strike, too. If you teach our children, until Brady Pasdon resigns, stop teaching. If you run our libraries or patrol our streets or highways, stop! If you empty the garbage or mop the floors of our prisons, schools, nursing homes, or courthouses, stop!"

The crowd yelled, "Strike, strike, strike!"

"And to you women, to all the women of Virginia, you must take control!"

Cheers from the audience.

"Women, I ask you to join your sisters in a protest, a show of solidarity. Starting in 24 hours, if Brady Pasdon hasn't resigned, I call on you to stop cooking, or cleaning, or doing any of those things the men think you should be doing. I call on you to join a crossed-legs strike."

Laughter and cheers when up through the audience, mostly from the women. The throngs of police surrounding the crowd looked increasingly uneasy.

"Until Brady Pasdon resigns, there will be no sexual favors. Let the men have sex with each other. Let your man have sex with himself. But don't succumb to sex with them!

"Ladies, YOU have the power…"

POW! Gunshot rang out and Liza dropped the bullhorn, recoiling from the impact of a bullet that hit her above her left breast. She grabbed the spot as she crumpled to the ground, blood gushing out and turning her hand and orange shirt red. Marjorie lurched forward towards her partner as pandemonium broke out among the crowd, people screaming and shoving. Marjorie reached Liza and put her head on her lap, cradling her. Liza called out painfully, hysterically, "I've been shot! I'm hit! God, it hurts!"

Frantic people swirled around, rushing to and fro. A handsome young man reached Marjorie and bent down and said, "I'm an emergency room nurse. We need to get her to a hospital." He pulled a handkerchief from his pocket and covered the wound.

Marjorie began to sob. Liza started to convulse, mumbling painfully and gravely. The moments to follow were a blur. White clad rescue squad people began to appear, and they lifted Liza gently to a gurney. They strapped an oxygen mask over her mouth. Marjorie chased her partner to the ambulance where in a moment of inspiration she lied, saying, "I need to be with her. She's my sister," although she knew they could see they looked nothing alike. She also knew that if she had said, "She's my lover," she'd be denied access; homosexuals had no rights in Virginia.

The next hours were a fog of horror, pain, and disbelief. Liza and Marjorie were whisked away to the Medical College of Virginia where Liza was immediately taken into surgery. Marjorie sat outside, waiting, sobbing, with her world crumbling around her. Her long-term lover was fighting for her life. Back home, her beloved twin sister was fighting for her life as well. Her treasured state was being ripped apart, poisoned by madmen. She was ill with recrimination and rage.

Hours later – she had no idea how long – a doctor emerged from the operating room. Marjorie approached him, "How is she? Is she alive?"

"And you are?" the white-haired man removed his surgical cap. His badge said, "Dr. Greenman."

"I'm her sister. Is she okay?"

He looked closely at Marjorie, especially at her shorn pate. "She's still in critical condition. We extracted the bullet. It's a miracle she isn't dead. It smashed her clavicle and two ribs. It punctured her left lung and severed her axillary artery, the one to her arm. She lost a lot of blood. We've pumped six pints into her. She's sedated now."

"I need to see her," Marjorie insisted.

"How long have you been together?" the doctor called her bluff.

"Five years. Please let me see her!"

"I can't let you in; I'll lose my license. She's unconscious anyway. Please, you need to go home. If I'm guessing correctly, you have a sister to take care of, yes?"

"Yes." She knew by his comment that he knew who she was.

"Leave me your number, and I'll call you tomorrow. We have her stabilized, but we need to go in again to begin repairing the damage."

"If you're talking about going in again for more surgery, you must think she'll survive."

"She's a strong woman. I'm doing all I can for her, but her will to live will carry her through. She has more fight in her; I can tell. I admire what she's done. Everyone in Virginia does. That shot today will be heard around the world. Go on home. I'll call you tomorrow."

Marjorie gave Dr. Greenman her phone number and walked outside where she called a cab to take her back to her car. The driver, a Southeast Asian, mumbled non-stop about riots in the city, overturned cars and fires. People had gone on rampages after the shooting. Multiple sirens were still echoing. After several false directions from her — she couldn't remember exactly where she'd parked – she finally found the car and paid $38 to get it out of the lot. An hour-and-a-half later, she pulled into the back driveway, commiserated with Sally over Liza's assassination attempt, and fell into a fitful sleep.

Sunday, March 11

"Marjorie? This is Glen Greenman, the doctor at VCU."

Marjorie had just emerged from her shower to the sound of her phone ringing. "How is she?"

"She's still critical. I was hoping to do surgery today to do some repairs. But after evaluating her signs, I'm going to delay it for a day or two and let her body rest."

"I want to see her," Marjorie insisted.

"Not yet," Greenman fired back. "She's not ready. She's still unconscious. This is Sunday. We'll plan surgery for Tuesday morning. I'll call you afterward. If all goes well, I'll let you see her Wednesday morning."

"I understand."

"I'll talk with you then. Bye."

"Bye," Marjorie imitated.

"How is Liza?" Sally asked, entering Marjorie's bedroom. Marjorie recounted what the doctor had told her. Marjorie smelled coffee brewing in the kitchen, so she got dressed and followed Sally to breakfast that Sally had felt well enough to prepare.

Marjorie got an alert from her smart phone that an aide to the Governor would be holding a press conference due to air at 11:00 a.m., only 45 minutes later. The twins switched on their TV and found the public television station in Richmond to watch.

A man Marjorie instantly recognized walked to a lectern with the state seal, emblazoned with the female figure of the Roman virtue, Virtus, standing over a fallen foe, holding a staff of war and wearing a blue robe. Marjorie noticed that the image on the lectern had been altered from the original. Where Virtus traditionally had a bare left breast, it was now covered, apparently by the regime of the immodest, illegitimate Governor.

The man said, "Good morning. I am Daniel Gold, spokesman for Governor Brady Pasdon. I have a brief statement from the Governor's office regarding the tragic wounding of former dean of the UVA Law School, Liza Randolph, at the Capital here in Richmond yesterday."

Marjorie looked again at the seal. The area now covered in a blue robe, but formerly exposed, would have been the exact area where the attempted assassin's bullet would have struck her soul-mate. She could feel her anger rise; she was knotted in vitriol.

"Yesterday morning, while leading a small, illegal protest to the Capitol, Dr. Liza Randolph was shot in the shoulder. The weapon appears to have been a sniper rifle, fired from some distance away. Ms. Randolph's condition remains critical and if she survives will need extensive surgeries and rehabilitation."

Marjorie sensed that Gold had overtly and snidely emphasized the word "if." And she understood that by saying it was a small rally, he had intended to minimize its importance.

He continued, "The Governor expresses his deepest sympathies to Ms. Randolph and has pledged to avail all resources available to solving this heinous crime. That is all."

"Mr. Gold!" a man yelled from the small audience, outside

the camera's view. "Will the Governor be honoring Ms. Randolph's demands to resign?"

"No," Gold said flatly. "Ms. Randolph's demands are spurious and foundation-less. Brady Pasdon is the legitimate, sworn Governor of Virginia. Randolph's actions are contemptuous and unlawful. She organized an illegal protest without obtaining the required permit. The Governor considers her an enemy of the State and her actions treasonous. If she survives, she may face criminal charges. That said, the Governor does not condone her assailant's actions. That will be all." He left the lectern and walked away.

Marjorie turned off the set. "I'm going to kill him!"

"Which one," Sally smirked, "Gold or Pasdon?"

"Gold. Pasdon. Both the sons of bitches."

Sally wiped her hand over her baldness, "I feel stronger every day. Give me another week and I'll start re-asserting myself publicly. This war is far from over."

Monday, March 12

Without any communication with John Jewett, Sally and Marjorie assumed that he would be present at their weekly meeting, events the prior Saturday notwithstanding. So Marjorie ferried Gooch to the regular meeting spot at Eghamshire. True to form, the dedicated former soldier arrived right on schedule. Entering the house where he was greeted by Sally, Marjorie, and Sam, Jewett was excited to the point of hysteria. He said, "The Governor is in a panic. He's seeing riots all over the state. His advisor, Gold, is telling him to impose Martial Law. Pasdon issued an order to the National Guard units across the state to prepare readiness plans for controlling riots."

"Is he giving in?" Marjorie quizzed.

"Do you think he'll resign?" Sally proposed.

"No sign yet," Jewett professed. "I drove him and Danny Gold to a meeting of the Veterans of Foreign Wars last night in Williamsburg. I asked him if he planned any change in schedule, given the circumstances. Before the Governor could answer, Gold barked at me like my old chief petty officer, 'What fucking circumstances? There are no circumstances. We're doing what we're supposed to do; we're running a state.' It is almost as if he thinks he's the Governor."

"If I could ever get my hands on that bastard, so help me Hannah, I'd… I'd… I'm not sure what I'd do, but it wouldn't be pleasant," Marjorie screamed, pondering the possibilities aloud.

The room became quiet for a moment as Marjorie looked at the others.

"I may be able to help you with that," Jewett quietly volunteered.

"WHAT?" Sebrell shouted, his eyes bulging against the inside of his round eyeglass lenses. The huge man and the two bald twins stared a hole in the face of the young man. "What did you say, John?"

Jewett was quiet. He sniffled, threw his head back a bit, and took a deep breath, as if steeling himself to do the unthinkable. He whispered, "I didn't get much sleep last night. I took out one of my history books and read about an assassination attempt on Adolph Hitler. It failed. Afterwards, on Hitler's orders, almost 5000 people associated with it were executed by the Gestapo. I am about to commit the ultimate betrayal."

Sam, Sally, and Marjorie looked at him intently, awaiting

his admission, whatever it might be.

"Next Friday evening," Jack Jewett continued, "I am scheduled to take the Governor to a meeting with the President of Liberty University in Lynchburg. After that, I'm driving him to a fund-raiser in Fairfax. We'll go right through Charlottesville and Culpeper on Highway 29. If there is a diversion of some sort between them, I can easily detour up Route 20 through Orange."

"Holy shit," Marjorie put her hand to her mouth. "Holy, fucking shit."

"I'm already in danger just being here," Jewett complained. "I can't be seen as having anything to do with whatever might take place here that evening, or I'll be hung, figuratively or even literally. Whatever you want to do, please leave me out. But I can get him through Orange. His advisor, Gold, is scheduled to be with him, too."

The idea that hatched thrilled and frightened Marjorie to her core. The foursome talked about ideas and rejected them, and talked about more. They formulated a plan, rejected it, formulated another, and then refined it, becoming instant conspirators. Everything would need to work like clockwork, as they would have no communication with Jewett. Finally, they crystallized every detail and Jewett rode away, Marjorie close behind to retrieve Gooch.

Tuesday, March 13

The morning paper brought Marjorie more bad news which she shared with Sally. In a report from Radford, a nine-year-old girl had died from injuries received when several chunks of concrete flaked off the Interstate 81 Bridge over the New River and had struck her and the canoe carrying her and her father on Sunday. She had been wearing a life jacket, but was killed by the impact. The chunk that struck the canoe was as large as a beach ball, but jagged and sharp. It sliced the canoe in half severing the father's leg. He swam, bleeding profusely, to shore where he was rescued. The girl was found an hour later, 800 yards downstream, still floating but trapped under a patch of overhanging vegetation. An eyewitness said her face was largely collapsed and covered with blood.

Marjorie told Sally about it. Sally said that the prior General Assembly had appropriated money for bridge maintenance, but the current session had put the spending on hold, as several of the more conservative legislators objected to the $0.02 per gallon tax increase needed for funding.

Sally's reaction was harsh and emphatic. "Last time I looked, our tax on gasoline was 40th among the 50 states. It hasn't been increased in 25 years, while road maintenance costs have doubled and in some cases tripled. There is the blood of that poor child on the hands of those legislators."

Marjorie took a call that afternoon from Dr. Greenman at VCU. Surgery had gone well and Liza was in recovery. He still forbade Marjorie from visiting, but encouraged her to come the following day.

Wednesday, March 14

Sally and Marjorie were having breakfast when Sam Sebrell called. Sally put him on the speaker phone, and he told the twins that two more death row inmates had been executed on the prior two nights.

Marjorie then drove to Richmond where she spent two

hours with Liza, who was heavily sedated, too much to discuss events, prior or forthcoming.

Afterwards, Marjorie went shopping in Richmond for supplies, spending two hours at several downtown antique clothing shops, unsure she'd be able to find in Orange the items she needed for their upcoming event.

After she arrived at home, Marjorie got out some tempera paint for Sally who busied herself painting a royal coat of arms on a sheet of poster-board, twenty-eight inches across, with two lions flanking a royal emblem.

Thursday, March 15

Sam had more news for them the next afternoon. There were protest riots in Richmond and Norfolk. In downtown Richmond in particular, there was extensive damage, as several cars had been overturned and two businesses on Broad Street near where Marjorie had shopped the prior day had been vandalized. In Norfolk, an empty tenement building had been set on fire.

Sam said the Governor was on his way to the event in Lynchburg about which Jewett had spoken at their Monday meeting. Things were falling into place for the plans they'd made for the following day.

Friday, March 16

"Yes, Governor, Ken Bracey and Walter Boykins will be in attendance tonight in Fairfax," Danny Gold presented. He looked at his smart phone. It was 6:38 p.m., an hour after they'd left Lynchburg, and the sky was darkening. It was brighter to his left as they drove northward, outside the back seat of the

Cadillac SUV unmarked State Police car. It was painted black with darkened windows and a "1" on the license plate.

"What did they give me during the campaign?" Governor Brady Pasdon asked, wiping his nose on a white handkerchief, embroidered with his monogram. He pulled some papers from his briefcase.

The State Police radio chirped its usual noises, unintelligible to Gold. "Bracey gave your campaign $32,500 and Boykins gave $26,000."

"Excuse me, Governor," came the voice from the driver.

"What is it, Jewett?"

"Sir, I've gotten notification that there is an accident in the Northbound lane of US-29 just the other side of Ruckersville, before Culpeper. I've charted an alternative course on the GPS. At Ruckersville we can take Highway 33 over to Barboursville and from there through Orange and rejoin our route south of Culpeper. The detour will only take maybe ten or twelve minutes longer," the driver declared.

"Do what you need to," agreed the Governor, returning to his notes about the upcoming meeting.

Gold checked some e-mails on his smart phone and sent a text message to the contacts at the fundraiser in Fairfax, their destination, giving them an approximate arrival time of 7:45 p.m.

Pasdon interrupted Gold's thoughts a few minutes later as they neared Orange. "That's the entrance to Montpelier, James Madison's home over there." He pointed to his right. "Madison was one of my heroes. He was a rare politician who changed his views during his political life. When he was working with Jefferson, Hamilton, Adams, and the boys on the Constitution, he favored a strong national government.

But later on, he saw the light and realized the state should be stronger. My kind of guy."

"Didn't he know like a half-dozen languages?" Gold proffered. He bent back to his smart phone and looked up an encyclopedia article on James Madison on-line. Reaching the Orange town limits, the car began to decelerate, but it barely scratched Gold's consciousness. The car then slowed to a full stop and stayed stopped.

Pasdon immersed himself in his notes for the upcoming event. Danny looked through the windshield but didn't see any traffic lights. "Why are we stopped so long?" he snapped towards the driver.

"There seems to be some obstruction up ahead," Jewett reported. "Hard to see from here, but it looks like a couple of horse-drawn carts. I'm guessing it is some Amish farmers."

Satisfied, Gold returned to his smart phone again, checking for political articles from the on-line wire sources. The phone rang and Rhonda's caller ID appeared on his screen.

"Hello, Gold," Danny barked, positioning the phone against his cheek.

"Danny?"

"Hello Rhonda. Where are you?"

"Hey, Danny. My trip ended early. I'm back home now. I wish you were here. I really wish you were here. I'm wanting you."

"How was the trip?" he continued, looking towards Pasdon who continued reading his notes.

"Good," she crowed. "I got the McCanty order. I was feeling pretty good about myself so on the way home, I stopped and bought some chocolate-covered strawberries, a bottle of champagne and some scented massage oil. I'm sitting on the couch where we first made love, wearing that red negligee you gave me for Valentines Day. The negligee is open at the front right now."

"Yes, I'm with Governor Pasdon," he fidgeted, aching to change the subject. "We're on our way to an event in Fairfax."

"Oh, too bad, because if you were on Skype with me right now, you'd be enjoying the view of my panties. I've been tracing little circles on my thigh, spreading this new oil. It smells SO good! HMMMM! I bet if you take a deep breath, you can smell it yourself. Take a deep breath, Danny."

Danny squirmed in his seat and involuntarily took the deep breath Rhonda commanded. His face flushed red. Could Pasdon hear her? He held the phone tighter to his cheek.

"Listen," Danny pleaded, "I've got to go."

"Oh, no you don't," she whispered. "Should I remove my panties? Danny?"

"Er."

"Good idea," she continued. "I'm sliding my panties down my legs. Can you envision my legs, Dan? Can you see my tampon tunnel? My furry kitten? Are you there, Danny? Want to put me on speaker phone for the Governor?"

"Jesus!" Danny mumbled.

"What?" Pasdon said, not looking up from his papers.

"It's nothing, sir. Rhonda almost got sideswiped," Danny lied.

Pasdon said, "Tell her I said not to talk on the phone while she's driving."

"I heard him," Rhonda pointed out. "Tell the Governor I'm not driving. I'm lying back on the sofa now. I wasn't sideswiped, Danny. I want you straight-on. If you were here right now, I'd be rubbing your goods."

Damn, Gold thought, could Pasdon hear her, too? He must hang up! He felt a growing bulge in his pants.

"I'm stroking my clit right now Danny," she coaxed. "I'm wishing it was you doing it. Oh, it feels good. So good! So... so. Good. Yes. *Yes*. **YES!**"

POW!

Glass shards flew from broken windows on both sides, scattering across the car. Gold instinctively covered his eyes, and when he re-opened them, he saw a gloved hand reach inside and unlock his door that then flew open. His phone was ripped from his hand and thrown to the floor. The flash of steel of a large knife slid before his face, slashing his shoulder harness. He reeled from the impact of a hard object, slammed against his forehead. Dazed, he felt himself being wrestled out of the car and thrown to the ground by two or three people and shackled with handcuffs behind him. He felt a cloth bag being stretched over his head. He was lifted back to his feet and escorted to what felt like the back of a wagon, covered by a thin mattress. He felt another body being thrown against his that he assumed to be Pasdon. The wagon lurched forward, and he could hear the clopping of what he assumed were horses hooves on pavement. What the fuck?, he thought indignantly; we've been kidnapped.

He attempted to move, but he was rigidly bound. His hands were cuffed behind him, his feet were tied together, it was near dark, and he had a cloth sack over his head. Whatever fate awaited him was entirely outside his control.

Minutes passed. How many? He couldn't tell. He was furious and fearful. Fifteen minutes? Maybe twenty or more. He began to ache. He heard some voices, seemingly mostly female, and mostly in congratulatory tones.

The clopping of hooves gave way to a crunch as if on gravel, and then to what he thought must have been a dirt road, with more potholes, jostling him around painfully. He thought to call out in his agony, but no words came to him. His head throbbed, and he felt nauseous. He threw up inside the cloth bag. Moments later, the wagon stopped.

He felt several people pulling him from the wagon bed, and then upright.

"Gosh, what a mess," a female voice winced after pulling off his cloth bag.

He looked at her and was startled by what he saw. She was in some sort of medieval costume, with a Shakespearean theater eye mask. She wore an earth-tone maiden's cap and a flowing canvas peasant dress. He looked around and everyone he saw, maybe fifteen or twenty people, mostly women, were all in costume, all in earth-tones, accented in orange. Many of the women were completely bald. He and the Governor had been forcefully invited to some sort of demonic antediluvian ritual. Somebody slapped a cold, wet rag against his face and wiped away the vomit.

He looked again. They were in a grassy meadow, with a river nearby he could hear. Opposite him, a tall, costumed man sat alongside a woman on a makeshift throne. People stood around in a circle and behind them were several tethered horses. He looked beside him and the Governor was there, with the cloth bag being removed from his head. Gas torch-like lamps sat on several poles, illuminating the immediate area. There was the smell of incense in the air. There was a medallion, some sort of royal seal or coat of arms, two feet across, with two lions flanking a royal emblem, affixed to poles in the ground. Two small odd dogs ran around, yapping, like German Shepherds but with tiny, short legs. They wore orange bandannas tied around their necks.

He heard the sound of a bird, an owl, hooting nearby. "Who, who, who cooks for you!" it hooted.

Gold looked for what he thought might be his escape route in a nearby copse of trees and turned to run. He got one stride away when his ankle chains snapped tight, and he fell face-first, hard, on the ground.

"Oh, Mr. Gold," said a vaguely familiar female voice. "Stick around. No need to be on your way so soon. Let me help you up. But first, I've got something for you."

As he cocked his head, she walked over and kicked him hard in the ribs. His face, a mess of dirt, spittle, and residual vomit, contorted to a rictus of agony.

"Let's get him up."

Two women and one enormous man, all costumed, grabbed him by the arms and lifted his limp body to his feet. Somebody shoved a wooden chair behind him and pushed him onto it. They produced another chair and sat Governor Pasdon on it beside him. Four captors carried an old, large wooden table in front of them and placed two candlesticks with burning candles on it.

"Nobody is going anywhere for awhile. Make yourselves comfortable and enjoy the evening!" the female voice said.

"I demand that you release us immediately," Pasdon insisted. "Do you know who I am?"

"Absolutely!" she replied. "You fine sir are the illegitimate Governor of the great Commonwealth of Virginia! However, that will be no longer, in due course."

Pasdon snapped back angrily, "What do you mean by that? Let me go!"

"Pray tell, not just yet. Verily, we have some celebrating to do! Ladies?"

As Gold watched, several green bottles without labels appeared at the table. With old cork screws, corks were removed and wine was poured into earthen goblets. A woman picked up what appeared to be an old-fashioned stringed instrument resembling a guitar and began to play. She finished an instrumental tune and everyone applauded. Then four women stood alongside one another and sang a song that seemed to be in an ancient language. More applause followed. Wine was drunk and goblets were refilled. Merriment was all around, but Gold was overwhelmed with rage.

Pasdon snapped again, "Enough of this charade. Release me! I demand it!"

As Gold watched, the woman ringleader approached Pasdon, her eyes not six inches from his, and said, "I assure you, Mr. Pasdon, this is not a charade. And you're not going anywhere."

"Who, who, who cooks for you!" the owl hooted again.

"Then what is this about?"

She replied assertively, "Welcome to Runnymede. Verily, you may remember from your ancient English history that a certain King John was invited to the original Runnymede in England for a similar event in 1215 to sign a little document known as the Magna Carta, the Great Charter of Liberties. We've invited you here tonight and have brought along an updated version that we will thusly ask you to sign."

"Fuck that!"

"Tsk, tsk, Mr. Pasdon! Is that any way to behave? And such language! Are you not a good Christian man? Anyway, you seem to be in a bit of a hurry, so let's begin. Samuel of

Franklin, would you please approach the table and present Mr. Pasdon with his documents."

"Aye, Madam Margie," said the large, youngish man, fully dressed in period garb, with a flowing orange sash and orange theater mask. Comically, he had round-lens eyeglasses on, the ear-pieces cut through his mask.

"Hear ye, hear ye," he read from a parchment sheet. "'Article I, Magna Carta II. The issue of voting rights. Whereas, it is important for our democracy that every natural man and woman above the age of eighteen should be allowed and encouraged to vote. And whereas, on the thirteenth of February of this year, this Governor,' and that would be you, Mr. Pasdon, 'signed an executive order making voting arbitrarily restrictive. And whereas, Virginia has had a shameful history of voter disenfranchisement and intimidation. And whereas, in recent decades Virginia has had an equally shameful history of ethics violations leading to the conviction on felony charges of one recent Governor and his wife. Be it here now resolved that the executive order of the thirteenth of February is null and void. Furthermore, be it here now resolved that a new executive order is duly signed with the following provisions:

"'First, that there be an immediate redistricting of the entire state's Senatorial and Delegate districts, effective prior to the upcoming election, done by a non-partisan commission appointed by the Chief Justice of Virginia.

"'Second, that there be a strict limit on gifts to any current Governor, Lt. Governor, Attorney General, Senator, or Delegate of no more than $50.00 in value, and only from any natural persons.

"'Third, that there will be a strict limit on all campaign

contributions of $100.00, and only from any natural persons and exactly $0.00 from any publicly charted entity, including but not limited to corporations, political action committees, unions, and trade associations.'

"And finally, 'Fourth, our current system of winner-take-all elections will be replaced with a more modern, more truly representative system of proportional representation voting.'"

"Thank you, Samuel of Franklin," the woman the big man had called Madam Margie said. "Now then, Mr. Governor, you will sign here," she pointed at the document.

"You think I'm going to sign this?" Pasdon snapped angrily. "I don't do extortion."

"Yes, in fact we do," replied the woman. "If it would make you happy, we can use magic words. Everybody, let's ask Mr. Pasdon nicely to sign this document."

"Please, Mr. Pasdon," the chorus rang out. The dogs barked excitedly.

"Forget it," Pasdon yelled, angrily. "This will change everything. It will make mincemeat out of our election systems."

"That would be exactly the idea," she dabbed her quill pen with a long white egret feather into a black ink glass. She playfully tickled his nose with the egret feather from which he recoiled. Then she placed it on the table in front of him.

Gold looked at his fellow prisoner. He saw reflections of the fire-lights in his eyes.

"Fine," Pasdon said. "Unshackle my hands and give me a pen."

The huge man stood up and was joined by another equally large black man who unshackled Pasdon's hands from behind him and held them in front and shackled them again. Pasdon stared at them angrily, then picked up the pen and signed his name. "Now let me go, damn it!"

Gold fumed at hearing Pasdon say "me" and not "us."

"Oh, chuckles me," the woman hinted, "Not so fast. We've only just begun. We have more for you to sign. Mr. Samuel of Franklin?"

"Madam Margie…" he began. Then to the gathered audience, "Hear ye, hear ye. 'Article II, Magna Carta II. The issue of prayer in the school. Whereas, verily, our nation was founded on religious freedom. And whereas, that same freedom applies to any religion or no religion at all. And whereas, in our separation of church and state, the People have determined that in public institutions, including schools, any reference, including prayer, is inappropriate and in conflict with our great Constitution and the ideals of the Commonwealth of Virginia. And whereas, this governor has violated that sacred ideal. And whereas, this great Commonwealth has many extraordinary and sacred places of worship, notably churches, synagogues, and mosques. Therefore, be it resolved at this moment and forevermore, and by the Executive order of this Governor, the order of the seventh of February is hereby rescinded.'"

"Well?" Pasdon sighed.

"Well?" Madam Margie echoed.

"Is this it? If I sign this, will you set me free?"

Everyone laughed heartily. The dogs barked.

"Did I say something funny?" Pasdon insisted.

"Mr. Pasdon," Margie replied, "In fact we have several more for you."

"I'm not signing another goddamn thing. Release me now, and I'll ask for leniency at your kidnapping trial. Otherwise, you'll hang, all of you!"

"T'would seem that Mr. Pasdon has turned a bit, shall we say, circumspect," the giant man suggested.

"Reluctant," the woman added.

"Petulant," the woman on the stage offered.

An unsettling quiet hovered over the scene. Marjorie found herself smiling a wicked grin, devilishly enjoying the repartee.

"If you so please," the tall, sitting man offered, rising to his feet.

Gold thought the voice was familiar, but he couldn't place it.

"Yes, your Excellency, King Coriaceous," the woman recognized him asking him to continue.

"Perhaps, verily," Coriaceous suggested, "Mr. Pasdon might become more amenable should he hear at one time all of the provisions he's being encouraged to sign."

The audience nodded with approval. "Very well," Margie said. "Samuel of Franklin?"

"Yes Madam…

"Hear ye, hear ye. 'Article III, Magna Carta II. The issue of budgeting. Whereas, verily, the vital functions provided by our great Commonwealth, including but not limited to Education, Health, and Human Services, Transportation, Public Safety, Finance, Administration, Trade and Commerce, and Judicial, must be adequately funded. And whereas, public investment boosts the velocity and circularity of money, thus enhancing local economies. And whereas this Governor has by executive order of the Sixteenth of February of this year, arbitrarily and capriciously slashed these agencies of fifteen percent. And whereas the poorest of our citizens are disproportionately taxed through payroll, sales, and property taxes. Therefore, be it resolved at this moment and forevermore, and by the Executive order of this Governor, the order of the sixteenth of February of this year is hereby rescinded, and all state agencies will be enhanced, unless denied by those agencies due to lack of need, by an additional five percent, and a new tax of one-tenth of one percent shall be applied to all transactions made in commodities, investments, and stock market trading. Additionally, to reduce our state's energy footprint and greenhouse emissions, an energy tax on all carbon-based taxes shall be imposed immediately at the base rate of 25-cents per million Btu.'"

Audience members clapped. The dogs scurried around, nipping at each other. A horse neighed in the distance. A goat with a tiny kid walked around oblivious to the scene.

"So now you want me to wreck the economy by taking money from the job creators," Pasdon prophesied.

The woman next to the man they called King Coriaceous spoke for the first time. "Job creators! Bah! The trickle down theory is the greatest hoax perpetrated on the American people in my lifetime."

Her voice sounded to Gold much like the Margie woman.

She continued, "Economies flourish when poor and middle class people have money to spend. Consumers create jobs, not rich people. Feeding more money to rich people only makes them richer and does nothing to improve the economy. But this is not a policy discussion. Let us continue."

"There's more?" Pasdon protested.

"Yes," the big man cleared his throat, "Hear ye, hear ye. 'Article IV, Magna Carta II. The issue of involuntary sterilization. Whereas eugenics is one of the most reprehensible activities of mankind since time began. And whereas this Governor has ordered the involuntary sterilization of eighteen people since his executive order of Twenty-one February of this year. Therefore, by his signature, the Governor publicly condemns the practice of eugenics and issues an apology to the victims and their families. Also, therefore, the Governor offers reparations of $100,000 to each of the victims, payable from the Treasury of Virginia in not more than thirty days.'"

The big man looked at the crowd, many nodding approvingly. Then he continued.

"Hear ye, hear ye. 'Article V, Magna Carta II. The issue of abortion. Whereas this Governor has shut down all the state's abortion clinics in violation with the precedent set in Roe v. Wade in the United States Supreme Court in 1973, be it hereby resolved that all the clinics recently shuttered will now be re-opened with complete restoration of full funding.'"

"Fuck you people," Gold shouted.

Margie threw the wine from her goblet in Gold's face. Much of it dripped onto his white shirt, now soaked in sweat. "Shut up, you bastard," she yelled, "This isn't about you, at least just yet. If you have anything besides dead ants between your ears where your brain belongs, you'll stay really quiet so it doesn't become about you. Because if it does, you'll be sorry." She turned again to the large man, saying, "Mr. Samuel, please continue."

Samuel continued, "Hear ye, hear ye. 'Article VI, Magna Carta II. The issue of immunity. Whereas this Governor's activities have arrogated undue control to himself. And whereas he has brought on the necessity of drastic measures from these citizens of the Commonwealth to restore governmental power to the people. Therefore, the Governor offers complete immunity to those present for any crimes, misdemeanors, or felonies, committed on or about this day, March 16, in the year of our…'"

"What?" Gold vaunted. "You're asking for immunity to these crimes?"

Madam Margie jeered at Gold, "Well, kind sir, did we not instruct you to shut up?" Turning to Pasdon, "Let's be clear; we're not strictly asking. We're demanding. This is not open to prevarication, concession, or negotiation. These documents are before you, sir, for your signatures."

Gold looked at his boss, expectantly.

"Forget it," Pasdon said, flatly. "I'm not signing anything else."

A whip-poor-will sang in the distance towards the crepuscular sunset. Frogs chirped. The torches flickered. Nobody moved. One of the dogs barked.

"Mr. Pasdon, somehow, verily…" She thought for a moment and then lowering her voice in an impression of a man quipped, "What we seem to have here is a failure to communicate." People laughed. Turning to the man they called the king, she continued, "Some people are just hard to reach." Back to Pasdon, "Did I not mention that this is not optional or open to further discussion? I ask you one last time. Here's your pen." She pointed at the quill pen.

"Somebody is going to rescue me any minute." Pasdon took the pen from her hand and snapped it in half, pitching the broken pieces on the ground. He sneered at her.

"Very well," she acquiesced, taking a deep breath and exhaling loudly. She nodded at someone standing behind the prisoners.

Daniel Gold winced, feeling a sharp, spiking pain like a wasp sting in the side of his neck. "Damn-it. Jeez, what the hell have you done?" he yelped.

A hypodermic needle was extracted from his neck, its fluid already injected.

Madam Margie turned looked at Gold. "Mr. Gold, do you know what GHB is?"

"Hell no!" he screamed angrily.

"It's a muscle relaxer. People consider it one of the drugs of choice for date rape. You wouldn't know anything about that now, would you?" she scoffed. "It will take a few minutes to kick in, but the effect is significant. Mr. Gold, you can expect to feel some drowsiness and perhaps dizziness. Your body will begin to relax. You'll still be able to see, but not move. After a few minutes, you won't feel much pain. Given what is in store for you, you may wish you weren't able to see. In the meantime, I suggest we toast to the overthrow of the illicit Pasdon Governorship."

At that moment, Gold realized who his captors were. The woman conducting the ceremony was the woman he'd seen at the McGregor funeral in Richmond, Sally Bradley's twin sister. The woman sitting across from him was Sally. Who was the tall, sitting man? He tried to articulate his thoughts, to say something to Pasdon, but his head swam in a drug-induced fog.

Pasdon said, "Date rape? Are you going to rape him?"

"In a manner of speaking. You'll see," Margie grinned. "Please be patient."

A flute player played a Renaissance song and people refilled and drank more wine. The audience applauded. A helicopter flew low overhead.

"Let us begin," Marjorie smiled, realizing that time was of the essence.

The audience members began a lively dance as if from the High Middle ages. The music stopped and all the women froze in place. In near unison, they ripped off their peasant dresses. Below, each one wore pantaloons from their waist, and above, tight T-shirts, bright orange in color, with one shoulder and arm cut away, baring their left breasts, like Virtus, the Roman virtue on the Virginia state seal. They squealed in excitement and began dancing again.

The music and the dancing stopped, and all attention turned to Gold, who felt himself elevated from his chair into an upright position. He was turned and placed on his back on the smaller table. He struggled to move, but his muscles didn't respond to his frantic synaptic instructions. He watched while the masked, costumed woman before him took two rubber gloves from her pocket and snapped them onto her hands, and then drew a large knife from a leather sheath. His eyes grew wide, but he couldn't move. The woman, now with demonic eyes, grabbed his pants at the base of the zipper and slashed the fabric, exposing his underwear.

"Wait!" Pasdon yelled.

Madam Margie turned to Pasdon and glared at him, pointing her knife. "Stifle yourself. You had your chance. I need to concentrate."

She returned to Gold. She leaned over and grabbed his underwear, blue patterned boxers, and slashed that open as well. She snagged his penis and pulled it forward for all to see. She squeezed it hard, grimaced, and proclaimed, "Yuck. What an ugly dick." Then she slapped it aside and grabbed his scrotum, pulling it forward from the fabric. In one motion, she slit it open at the underside base. Reaching inside, she grasped his left testicle and pulled it forward and then slit the spermatic cord, severing the testicle, now loose in her hand. "Boo! Here boy!" She pitched it to the corgi. Then she grabbed the right testicle, pulled it forward similarly, and slit its cord. "Radley," she pitched the other testicle to her.

She stood erect and approached Pasdon, wiping some blood from the knife on her pantaloons. "Luckily for you Mr. Pasdon, I have a spare pen. If you break it, I still have my knife handy." She flashed the knife again in front of his eyes before waving it between his legs, slicing his pants at the crotch.

A woman approached Pasdon from the other side and brandished another hypodermic needle.

He shook in clear horror. He took the pen from her and hastily signed the documents he'd been presented, one after another, the quill quivering in his hand.

"You got what you want. Now release me!" he demanded again.

Gold writhed, as if trying to regain his motor controls.

"One more, if you please, Mr. Pasdon. Mr. Samuel?" she said.

Once more the towering man bellowed, "Hear ye, hear ye. 'Article VII, Magna Carta II. The issue of the governorship. Whereas this governor has cravenly and maliciously arrogated the office of Governorship from its rightful owner, Lt. Governor Sally T. Bradley. And whereas that arrogation is illegal and treasonous. And whereas Lt. Governor Bradley is now fully capable of holding and executing the duties and responsibilities of the office of Governor.'"

"She is?" Pasdon argued.

"That I am!" Sally stood up, throwing up her canvas dress, revealing her orange T-shirt. In the process, her mask, and hat were also removed. She was bare at the left breast area where after her mastectomy only a horizontal scar remained, and her head was entirely bald. "That I am!"

The crowd yelled enthusiastically, "Hail, Governor Sally! Hail Governor Sally!"

"I'm not resigning," Pasdon insisted.

"Very well. Your choice," Madam Margie said. She drew her knife again and flashed it in the light.

Pasdon looked at the knife. He looked at Margie. He looked at Gold, still reclining with a thin trickle of blood reddening his trousers. "Where do I sign?"

He lifted the pen again and signed the document.

"Do we have a notary public?" Margie queried.

"I am," one of the many bare-breasted women said.

"Please," Margie asked.

The woman stepped forward and signed, time-dated, and embossed each document, making them official.

Margie spoke to the notary, "Now that Mr. Pasdon has duly resigned, we can't very well go without a Governor for very long, can we?" and then smiled at Sally.

The audience cheered.

The woman stepped towards Sally, who rose from her chair. "Sally Bradley, are you ready to assume the office of the Governor of the Commonwealth of Virginia?"

"Yes, I am."

"Then please raise your right hand."

Sally did as instructed.

"Please repeat after me. I…"

"I, Sally Taliaferro Bradley."

"Do solemnly affirm."

"Do solemnly affirm," Sally echoed.

"That I will support and maintain the constitution…"

"That I will support and maintain the constitution…"

"And laws of the United States"

"And laws of the United States"

"And the Constitution and the laws of the state of Virginia;"

"And the Constitution and the laws of the state of Virginia;"

"That I recognize and accept"

"That I recognize and accept"

"The civil and political equality of all men before the law"

"The civil and political equality of all men AND women before the law"

Several women chuckled nervously.

"And that I will faithfully perform the duty of Governor"

"And that I will faithfully perform the duty of Governor"

"To the best of my ability"

"To the best of my ability"

"So help me God."

"So help me God."

"Congratulations Mrs. Bradley, you are now…" The notary wiped a tear from the corner of her right eye before continuing, "You are now the Governor of Virginia."

The audience erupted in cheers. Hats flew into the air. Boo and Radley barked excitedly.

Margie gave Sally a tight hug and whispered, "You go, girl!" She then collected all six documents from the table and held them firmly to her exposed breast. She nodded to her subordinates who unshackled Gold, who remained motionless, and then Pasdon. No sooner than Pasdon rubbed his sore wrists together, two dozen men armed in riot gear and shining bright flashlights burst onto the scene.

"Arrest these people, all of them!" Pasdon shouted to the man clearly in charge, a man who wore a name plate on his uniform that said, Broadnax.

"Yes, sir," he motioned to his troops, and they began to scurry forth.

"Not so fast," bellowed a voice from the man known thus far only as King Coriaceous. He stood tall and removed his mask and crown.

The owl hooted, "Who, who, WHOOOO?"

"Governor… I mean Senator Leathers!" Broadnax exclaimed.

"Mr. Broadnax, I believe it is Former Governor Pasdon you need to arrest," Tom Leathers instructed.

"Former, sir?" the officer disbelieved.

"He has admitted in a signed statement that he has committed high crimes and misdemeanors against the people of the Commonwealth of Virginia. He has also pardoned everyone here of any crimes they may have committed. And finally, he has, by a signed, notarized statement, stepped down from the Governorship. He is no longer in charge. Mr. Broadnax, please congratulate Sally Bradley, the new Governor of Virginia!"

A puzzled look grew on Broadnax' face. Marjorie showed him the parchment document that Pasdon had signed, relinquishing the office. Broadnax looked at Pasdon for some sign of what to do.

"Wipe that idiot grin off your face," Pasdon barked at him. "Take me home. And get that poor bastard some medical help," pointing at Gold.

"A pleasant night to you, Mr. Pasdon. Mr. Broadnax,"

Leathers said, bowing, and he and the audience quickly dispersed into the night.

Saturday, March 17

Marjorie woke early, well before dawn, flushed with excitement over the prior night's events. She contained herself only until a few minutes after 6:00 a.m. when she entered Sally's room to wake her. "Congratulations! Wow!"

"Tell me again what happened last night," Sally moaned, rubbing crusty bits from the inner edges of her eyes. "It seems like a dream to me now. Could it have been real?"

"Gosh, I think so. There's a document on the kitchen table that says you're our new Governor. What would be your first command, your highness?"

"Would you make me some coffee?" Sally laughed. "First, though, give me a hug."

Marjorie jumped onto the bed and hugged her sister affectionately and purposefully. "We did it! I can't believe we pulled it off. What's next?"

"Did we include in our planning that we might actually be successful?" Sally grinned.

"I'm not sure. Where do you think we stand?"

Sally wrinkled her nose, "Perhaps the morning paper will have some clues."

"I'll run and get it." Marjorie threw on some sweat pants and a hoodie sweatshirt and trotted down the driveway, making a mental note to herself to extract the tire traps as soon as possible. She retrieved the *Washington Daylight* and trotted back to the house, unwrapping the rubber band as she entered. She felt great running, her lungs having cleared themselves of most of the nicotine she'd poured into them for so many years. Sally had gotten up and was brewing her own coffee.

"Here's the headline," Marjorie noted, "'Virginia Governor kidnapped'." She read silently for a few moments.

"Well?" Sally interrogated.

"It says the Governor's official state vehicle was attacked sometime before 7:00 p.m. last evening in Orange. The Governor, his media assistant, and their driver, were kidnapped. As of press time, the Governor had not been found, nobody had taken responsibility, and an active search was underway. So I guess they needed to go to press before the police got there."

Sally noted, "I'm under the impression that the big city papers do several editions, and that the editions going out to the rural areas are printed first to get the trucks loaded and the papers delivered to the distant drop sites. I bet the on-line version is more current."

"Right," Marjorie agreed, opening her computer tablet and tapping busily at the screen. "Here we go. 'Brady Pasdon released' Hmmm. It says a team of special operatives from the State Police located and secured the release of Pasdon late last night, along with his 'communications director, Daniel Gold'. Oh, get this, 'Pasdon was unhurt, but Gold suffered genital mutilation and was hospitalized at Culpeper Municipal Hospital in stable condition.' Oh, then it goes on to say that Pasdon has resigned."

"Read it to me," Sally exclaimed.

"'As part of the release settlement with his kidnappers, Pasdon signed a specially prepared, notarized document that removes him from the governorship, signing over the office to Sally Bradley, who was present at the Pasdon captivity. It is unclear at this time whether Bradley was complicit in the kidnapping. However, in signing an additional document, Pasdon, prior to stepping down, granted blanket immunity to everyone present.'"

The phone rang. Marjorie walked over and saw the caller ID. "It says, '*Richmond Reporter*,' Do you want me to answer it?"

"No, let's talk first."

The phone gave ten rings and then began the outbound message. The caller hung up. Sally asked Marjorie to dictate a new outbound message, which she did.

"You have reached the home of Marjorie Taliaferro, sister of Governor Sally Bradley. We are not taking calls at this time. However, Governor Bradley will appear at a press conference on Tuesday, March 20. Details will be released by her staff. Thank you for calling. It's a great day to be a Virginian!"

Marjorie fed the corgis and fixed maple pancakes for breakfast. While Sally showered, Marjorie went to feed the horses and finish putting away the wagon and the tack that she'd left from the night before. She threw a saddle onto Jennings, her stallion, and galloped to Eghamshire to see if anything had been left behind. Nearing the site, she dismounted when she saw a flash of light reflecting from polished steel. She walked over and picked up her knife and the nearby sheath, which she'd evidently dropped during her departure. It still had some blood on it, which she wiped away with a tissue, which she then buried under some brush and dirt. She held the knife before her face, admiring it. A smile overcame her face as she thought about the emasculation she'd done the evening before.

She tidied up the area, putting the chairs and smaller table inside the cabin, leaving the larger table outside as it was too heavy for her to carry alone. She joked to herself that someday it might belong in a museum, like the table in the McClain house in Appomattox where Lee surrendered the Confederate Army of Virginia to Grant.

Returning to the house, Sally said she'd taken a call from Glen Greenman at MCV Hospital. Marjorie called back immediately.

"Good news," Dr. Greenman said. "Liza is more alert this morning and has asked about you."

"Can I see her again?"

"Sure. Come on down."

"I'm on my way."

Marjorie kissed her sister again and bolted from the door. She was at her lover's bedside ninety minutes later.

Liza was in a hospital gown, resting comfortably. "Hey," Liza whispered.

"How're you feeling?" Marjorie kissed her lips.

"Like broiled dog shit," not mincing words. Both women laughed heartily.

"I've got some good news." Marjorie told her about the prior evening's events in detail, including Pasdon's capitulation, relishing the eunichization she'd done on Gold.

Liza pondered aloud, "You know Gold better than I do. Do you think he had anything to do with my shooting?"

"I don't know. But it wouldn't surprise me. I have a feeling the new governor will employ the state's best detectives to find out."

Dr. Greenman entered the room. "Hi Marjorie. I hear there's much happy news all around."

"Doc, I'm just overwhelmed with joy. When can I take Liza home?"

"Liza, how are you feeling?"

"Great!"

Marjorie could tell she was lying to him.

Greenman looked at Liza while speaking surreptitiously to Marjorie, "Let's give her a few more days. Then we should be able to release her. At that time, may I release her under your care?"

"Absolutely," Marjorie agreed.

"My best guess is Tuesday or Wednesday. If she's still healing well, we'll get her out of here. Hospitals are awful places for sick people," he ruefully admitted.

Marjorie nodded and then looked at Liza, who nodded as well. Dr. Greenman took his leave and the lovers continued to talk about the recent events, feeling a special sense of satisfaction and vindication.

Sunday, March 18

First thing Sunday morning, Marjorie went to the shed and found her spade. She returned to the driveway and removed the tire trap. She hung it from a hook in an outbuilding intending to return it to Jack when she saw him again.

Upon re-entering the house, Sally told her that with her new position, she was soon to become quite busy, so she asked if Marjorie would walk the estate with her.

There were several robins hunting worms in the lawn, happy harbingers of springtime. Blue jays, mockingbirds, and cardinals sang joyously. The twins enjoyed being together, but Marjorie could tell that Sally still fatigued easily. They fixed a nice dinner of Asian noodles and link sausages, flushed down with a local rosé.

Monday, March 19

Marjorie was returning from her morning chores when Sally mentioned that Sam Sebrell would be coming by. The huge man arrived moments later, explaining that without instructions to the contrary, he was there for their regularly scheduled weekly meeting. It was an unseasonably warm day, and the three brought some orange spice tea to the outside patio to sit in the sun. No sooner had they done so when John Jewett drove up the back driveway. Marjorie had an instant anxiety attack, fearful that she'd forgotten to take a horse to Eghamshire for him.

"Good, good morning, everyone," Jewett exclaimed happily, explaining that with no further need for cloak and dagger activities, he'd simply driven up the driveway.

They got another tea cup and everyone exchanged congratulatory greetings. The sisters asked about John's experience on Friday.

Jewett began, "After the attack, I was dragged away by two of your conspirators. They were pretty attractive, actually! They took me down an alley downtown and tied me up."

"Were you hurt?" Sebrell asked with concern.

"I had a pocket knife. When we walked past a vacant storefront window, I used it as a mirror and I cut myself on my forehead to make it look more real. They put me down on some old corrugated boxes so I'd be comfortable and tied my hands and feet so loosely that I could have wiggled out any time, but I think it looked real. They kissed me on opposite cheeks, put some duct tape over my mouth like a gag and thanked me profusely for what I'd done. They were really sweet. I was 'rescued' within an hour, all bloody, but nobody was the wiser."

"Thank you so much for what you did, John," Marjorie extolled.

"Really, Jack, we owe you a great debt of gratitude," Sally agreed.

Sebrell nodded his concurrence.

"I was happy to help. I feel like I've done something good for my state. Still, I'm not sure my ensign in the Navy would be overly pleased if he knew what I did."

Sally said, "I'll issue you a pardon next week, regardless. I need to ask you something else."

"Yes, madam Governor?"

"Will you be my driver?"

"I'd be honored, ma'am!"

Jewett went on to explain that just as they'd planned, once the vehicle was abandoned, Marjorie's farm hand Wilson had disabled the GPS tracker, driven it to his barn, replaced the broken windows and seat belts that he'd ordered ahead of time, and left it under a cover at the Orange National Guard Armory where it was found by the police the next morning. So technically, there was no vandalism to the state. In fact, with Pasdon being unhurt and returned safely as well, the only lasting damage or injury was to Gold's goods, something everyone assumed little would be said or written about.

Sebrell conducted the remainder of the meeting, indicating that he had scheduled a press conference in the Governor's press room for the following day, Tuesday, at 3:00 p.m. Sally was eager to get to Richmond and meet the Governor's staff to see which members she would retain in her administration. Sebrell offered to taxi her to the Capital, but Jewett interjected, "That's my job now! I'm technically back on duty tomorrow. I'll get one of the Troopers to give me a ride to Orange to get the Governor's SUV and I'll meet you here. Say, 10:00 a.m., madam Governor?"

"Yes, please, Jack. I'll see you then."

After the meeting, Marjorie returned to Richmond to see Liza again, finding her in great spirits and rapidly improving physical health.

Tuesday, March 20

Moments after Jewett picked up Sally to take her to Richmond, Marjorie got into the Mercedes and followed ten minutes behind.

Just before 3:00 p.m., Marjorie entered the Governor's press room. She noted that the lectern had the seal of the Commonwealth and Virtus' gown had been restored to its original, breast-revealing form. Sebrell approached the lectern and introduced himself. "Ladies and Gentlemen, I am Sam Sebrell. I was Senator Sally Bradley's campaign manager last fall. Now I am the newly appointed Chief of Staff for Governor Sally Bradley. As you know, Governor Bradley has ascended to the Governorship at the recent resignation of former Governor Brady Pasdon."

At that moment, Sally Bradley entered the room. She wore a tasteful blue dress and a stylish, short wig of auburn hair. The audience rose from their seats and applauded.

Sebrell announced pridefully, "Without further ado, I give you the new Governor of the Commonwealth of Virginia."

Under the audience's applause, Sally approached the microphone. "Good afternoon everybody. Last time I spoke to you, I was the newly inaugurated Lt. Governor. The path to the governor's office has been painful and torturous. But here I am! I want to thank Sam Sebrell and everyone who has been with me through my illness and who has believed in me. I honor the memory of Miller McGregor and thank him for his service, albeit brief, in his role as Governor to the people of this state. I want to thank Senator Tom Leathers, a special friend who has been with me and supported me. But I especially thank the proudest, bravest, strongest friend a woman could ever have, my twin sister Marjorie Taliaferro. Marjorie, please come stand by me."

Marjorie got up from her seat and walked to her sister's side. At that moment, the twin doors at the back of the room opened, and Sam Sebrell re-entered the room, this time pushing slowly a wheelchair where sat Liza Randolph. Her left arm was in a sling, but she wore a flowing, bright orange dress. The wheelchair stopped and Sebrell picked up one, then the other, foot rests. Liza put the brake on the right wheel, and then slowly rose and stood upright, facing her lover and the new Governor.

One by one, the reporters in the room rose to their feet. One woman dropped her pen and notebook and began clapping. Soon everyone applauded. Liza looked at each of the twenty or so people and nodded in appreciation. When the applause subsided, Liza looked at Sally and said, "The world has been watching what you have done, Sally Taliaferro Bradley. I congratulate you."

Marjorie brought her hand to her face and her eyes began to moisten.

Sally showed the reporters the signed documents from Brady Pasdon's hand at Runnymede on Friday. She spoke of her urgency to see the reforms Pasdon had agreed to before his resignation the prior Friday and the healing and reunification of the strident political factions of the state. She entertained a few questions from the reporters, mostly about her health and the legitimacy of the actions that had taken place at Runnymede. Sally explained that her energy level was returning to normal and that she expected within a few weeks to be back at nearly full strength.

Questioned about Runnymede, she ventured, "What happened at the Runnymede in England is 1215 is part of the heritage of most of the people in Virginia today and an important landmark in human history. It is regrettable that the actions taken then were necessary for the maintenance of freedom as it is regrettable for that which happened in Orange last week. Democracy is ever-changing and must be practiced and protected forever. I pledge that my administration will conduct itself ethically and morally, and that every decision I make as Governor will be based upon a single, guiding principle, that it will make Virginia a better place to live, learn, grow, and prosper."

Two hours later, Marjorie and her life partner Liza Randolph were on their way back to Runnymede Meadow Estate outside Orange, Virginia. Marjorie had promised Dr. Greenwood that she would take care of Liza for the next few days before allowing her to be on her own at Keswick again.

Saturday, March 31

Eleven days later, Sally took her first break from her

duties in Richmond, spending the night with Marjorie at Runnymede Meadow estate.

"Let's go for a ride this morning," Marjorie exclaimed cheerfully as they finished breakfast. "Are you feeling up to it?"

"I'm still weary," Sally admitted, "But I'm sure it would do me some good. Where to?"

"Eghamshire," Marjorie pronounced unhesitatingly. "Let's relive our Magna Carta event."

"Sure."

The sisters went to the barn and got the saddles, bridles, and other tack for Gooch and Dawson. Marjorie helped Sally mount Gooch before getting on Dawson herself. They rode to the northwest at a trot. It was a fine morning, and the grass was beginning to turn green, pushing aside the winter browns. It was still early for the blossoms to begin on the area's cherry trees, but the first buds were beginning to show. The horses were eager to run, and the twins let them canter across the open fields.

They arrived to see two men sitting in chairs, their backs to the women. Sally rode in front of them and dismounted, exclaiming with surprise, "Brady Pasdon! What are you doing here?"

"G'day Senator Leathers," Marjorie said to the other man.

"Marjorie. Governor Bradley," the tall man said, smiling broadly and tipping his flannel hat. "Nice to see you again." He rose to his feet. Pasdon rose as well.

"What are you doing here, Pasdon?" Sally inquired again, still unable to contain her surprise.

"I've come to ask a favor," Pasdon ventured, taking a sip from a plastic water bottle on a table in front of him.

"Please join us," Leathers insisted, grabbing two more bottles from a nearby cooler and arranging two more chairs in a small circle. Sally and Marjorie sat where instructed.

"That was quite a show you put on," Pasdon admitted. "I'm guessing you think I was less pleased than I am."

"This has got to be good," Sally sighed to nobody in particular. "Please go on."

"I'm not going to say I knew what was going on, but I sensed you weren't going to take my taking of the governorship back in January quietly. I figured you'd be a bit, shall I say, peeved."

"Pissed. Peeved. Angry. Yeah. And?" Sally led on, looking like she was beginning to enjoy herself.

"Let's just say I had an epiphany a couple of weeks ago. Let me explain," the former governor said.

"I can't wait," Marjorie chimed.

"You may not know this, Governor Bradley…"

"Sally," she said, crossing her legs.

"Yes, Sally. For many years, I worked with your husband, Russ, in the Virginia Senate. Those were much different times. Russ was a fine man, and although we didn't agree on much, I had a lot of respect for him. In those days, things were more congenial and cooperative. Sure, there was some backstabbing, but it was nothing like it is now. These days too many of my colleagues will say 'black' if the other side says 'white,' even if they don't believe white. They do it just to obstruct. Nothing gets done on a bipartisan basis any more and painfully little gets done at all. Things only get done when one party is in complete control. While much of the recent legislation is to my liking, the process hasn't been."

"Really?" Sally quizzed.

"Really," Pasdon begged. "When Governor McGregor died and you were incapacitated, the Party, *my* Party, put lots of pressure on me to take over. They knew the political advantage they'd have if I did. I must admit I got swept away in the fervor. Who wouldn't want to be governor of Virginia? Patrick Henry. Thomas Jefferson. Heady company. You get your own mansion. You get your own cook. You get your own limo and driver..."

At that precise moment, John Jewett strolled onto the scene. "Hello everyone!"

"Right on cue," Leathers laughed.

Sally looked at him and said, "It takes no genius to guess that we've all been invited here. Whose party is this?"

"Mine," Tom Leathers said. "Well, it's Brady's really. But I put it together for him. Let's let him continue." He said, looking self-satisfied and taking a sip from his water bottle. A great blue heron flew over gracefully.

"Welcome, John. Thanks for coming. Now then," the vanquished former governor continued, "for many years, my singular focus in the General Assembly has been to eliminate abortions from Virginia. Sure, I voted on other stuff, but this is what motivated me. A few weeks ago, I had an experience that made me look at my actions more critically. John, do you remember when you drove me around with Pastor Lewis?"

"Yes," Jewett recalled. "He was the black minister."

"That's right. We left the dedication ceremony of the Virginia Slavery Museum together. His speech about the plight of the slaves was inspiring to me. I wanted to learn more."

"What did he say that got your attention?" Marjorie inquired.

"I guess I naively thought that Virginia's slaves had a

pretty basic but benign life. They got a place to live and a place to grow their food. They had their own communities. Pastor Lewis said it wasn't always like that. First, they weren't allowed to assemble, other than within their own plantation. Many of the masters were benevolent to a degree, but others were vile and vicious, treating them more cruelly and brutally than livestock. What really got to me were the stories he told about repeated rapes of the younger Negro women, girls really, by their masters.

"He said the girls were often sold away to other plantations, sometimes never to see their families again. Girls as young as 11 or 12 were no better than orphans, often sold into sex slavery.

"This was intriguing to me, and horrifying. My only daughter died when she was 12 from a rare pancreatic disease. It was the most devastating thing I've ever experienced. I cared more for that girl than life itself. I'm still not over it; I'll never get over it. My mind swept back to when she was only three or four days old. She had a touch of newborn jaundice, and I was in attendance when a big male nurse was pricking her heel to get a blood sample. He was not doing it well, and he was hurting my baby. I had an instinctive, animal reaction; I was going to kill him if he hurt my baby. It shook me to the core.

"I tried to imagine what it was like for parents to have their daughter sold away. I tried to imagine the horror the girls must have felt. So when the event was over, I invited Pastor Lewis to ride around with me in my government car. You remember, John?"

"Yes, sir."

"So Pastor Lewis and I talked for an hour or more, driving around the countryside near Fredericksburg. We rode out to the edge of the Potomac River. It's beautiful there. Small cliffs. Vacation homes. I started thinking about slavery and freedom. He asked me about my stand on abortion. I told him that abortion was wrong, unequivocally. It is an act of murder.

"He asked me to put my pre-conceived notions aside for a moment and consider that things may not be so completely clear-cut. He said women have always had abortions as a last resort to terminate pregnancies they didn't want. I argued that over 90 percent of abortions were for convenience. Rather than refuting me, he told me stories of slavery, focusing on abortions young Negro women had to kill the fetuses of their masters' sperm. Poisons. Sharp needles. Receiving punches or kicks to the abdomen. Douching with turpentine, lye, or other burning chemical. He actually reached over and put his hand on my abdomen. 'Governor,' he said, 'You're not a woman, but can you imagine a fetus growing in there that is the product of an act of violence and domination?'

"This was the first time I ever thought about it, I mean seriously. He said, 'Have you ever asked yourself why a woman would want an abortion?' I said I thought too many of them were simply promiscuous. But he really got me thinking about my stance. So even if they were promiscuous, did the State of Virginia need to punish them by forcing them to carry a baby they didn't want? My colleagues constantly bicker about the welfare state and the amount of money spent on the indigent. But the hypocrisy was suddenly clear. Why was the state so eager to force women to deliver babies into poverty that the state would then need to take care of? The only reason I could think of was for punishment. But who was really being punished?

"If abortion is wrong, and I still believe it is, rather than outlawing it, why aren't we trying to keep women from getting pregnant in the first place? He said to me, 'Roe v. Wade isn't about whether women can get abortions. It's about whether they can survive them'. I had never thought of it that way before.

"So how do we keep women from getting pregnant? I've always thought the answer was abstinence, but people are sexual animals and nobody waits for marriage any more. The moral integrity in this country has vanished. Pornography is everywhere. The days of courting are over. But the state of Virginia can't legislate that our kids return to platonic dating. I'm unhappy about it, but it's reality.

"And I realized that my Party was shutting down human health classes in the schools and women's clinics. That was hypocritical, too.

"So I got to thinking about my rise to the Governorship. I got swept away in it. You were too sick to govern, Sally. So I rationalized it, thinking the Commonwealth clearly needed a governor. It was easy to step up to the plate. I convinced myself it was the right thing to do. And I had the power to end abortions in Virginia.

"Then I made some bad decisions about my advisors. Danny Gold got involved and said and wrote the things I wanted to hear. But I got to thinking about him and started to question his motives. I was in military intelligence for much of my career. You liberals think that 'military intelligence' is an oxymoron like 'jumbo shrimp' or 'tight slacks'. But we were trained to think beyond the obvious. I started looking into the guy, his background and all, and the narcissism and arrogance started becoming clearer.

"I know what you're all thinking. You could have told me so. But by this point, I was trapped. My Party was drunk on power. I couldn't just say, 'Okay, Sally Bradley, is well now and the governorship is rightfully hers, so I'll just step aside.' I would have been drawn and quartered. So I needed a solution, something that would allow me to step down, would honor the wishes of the voters, would save my ass with the Party, and would enervate Gold and remove him from the scene, all without any suspicion or even a mere hint of collaboration."

"So you willingly walked into our trap?" Marjorie then deduced.

"Well, I didn't know exactly what you had in mind," Pasdon chuckled. "You were even more effective than I hoped," he wrapped his hands over his lower midsection. "Way more effective," he cried, in a high-octave falsetto voice.

Everyone laughed.

"You just figured if you got yourself nearby..." Leathers suggested.

"Right," Pasdon admitted. "I knew you were here in Orange," he nodded at the twins, "so I arranged a trip that would take me and Gold nearby. The rest was up to you."

"So you've been using us all along?" Sally chuckled.

"Let's say we used each other. You're governor, Sally, as you should be. Gold is gone. And the legislature is out of session so no more mischief, at least for now."

Marjorie stood and stretched. "Where is that bastard, Gold?"

Senator Tom Leathers said, "I heard that border patrol caught him trying to enter Canada from Michigan. He had a fire-arm with him. I'm guessing it will be a match with the bullet that struck Liza Randolph. I suspect Mr. Gold will be the ward of the state for some time."

Marjorie cracked a crooked smile, rubbing her hand over her head where a stubble of new hair was growing.

Sally looked at Pasdon. "You said you wanted to ask me a favor."

"Yes, Governor. Since the evening I stepped aside here in this meadow, I've been in official limbo. I'd like my job as Attorney General back. And I'd like to have a blanket pardon, like what Gerald Ford did for Richard Nixon. I'm sure there will be things that the citizens will find objectionable that I did while I was Governor. I'd like the record books to say that I was 'Interim Governor' awaiting your return. I don't even want a number associated with my term."

"No!" screamed Marjorie. "No. Hell no." Pregnant pause. "Sally? No, right?"

Sally didn't move. Marjorie's eyes darted incredulously from Sally to Pasdon to Leathers to Jewett and back to Pasdon. A crow cawed in the distance.

Sally spoke next. "You did some horrible things as governor, the executions and the sterilizations."

"May, I?" Leathers interrupted.

Sally nodded approvingly.

"Brady and I were talking before you arrived," he informed Sally. "He told me what he intended to do. So I've had a chance to think about it."

"And?" Marjorie usurped Sally.

"Two things," Leathers insisted, addressing Sally. "One, I think you need to make a decision soon, if not immediately. Two, although some of Pasdon's actions were abhorrent, none were technically illegal. And he did express some remorse to me."

"Brady?" Sally prodded.

"It's true. I did things during my short term as governor that I'll come to regret. Some I regret already."

Marjorie, unswayed, pleaded, "Don't buy that, Sally! Your supporters will never forgive you."

"One more point," Leathers offered. "Each side of the political aisle complains that the other lacks compassion, empathy, and charity. Perhaps we have an opportunity to set a better example. Marjorie, with all due respect, perhaps we can all use a bit of forgiveness these days."

Sally turned back to Pasdon. "So you're requesting a pardon. That's it?"

"Yes, that's it," Pasdon pleaded.

"Done!" Sally pronounced.

"So our meeting is over," Leathers insisted. "I've got work to do. I need to get back to Washington before the President declares war on Syria or Ethiopia or someplace."

"Before we go," Pasdon stood up, "What's with the King Coriaceous?"

The senator guffawed. "It means resembling or having the texture of leather."

"Damn," Pasdon laughed, chuckling with the others.

Pasdon exchanged handshakes with Marjorie and Sally, and congratulated Sally again. He shook hands warmly with Jewett. Leathers hugged Marjorie, shook hands with Jewett, and then gave Sally a long, heart-felt embrace. "Welcome back," he beamed.

Leathers and Pasdon bid everyone adieu, Pasdon picked up the cooler, and the two men strolled down the trail towards the river. "I guess I'd better go, too," Jewett offered.

"Wait," Marjorie implored. "There's been something on my mind since we met. I need to ask you about it. Your name always sounded familiar to me. The other day, I think I figured it out."

"Yes, ma'am," Jewett took over. "My parents were from Tennessee and Illinois. My name John is from my paternal grandfather. My parents always expected me to be called John or Johnny. Then my kindergarten teacher started calling me Jack. It sorta stuck. I was in high school when we moved to Virginia. In history class, I learned about an historic figure with the same name but a different spelling: J O U E T T."

"I remember that!" Sally exclaimed. "He did a midnight ride, like Paul Revere."

"Not exactly," Jack lectured, "but close. He was a handsome man, tall and heavy by the standards of the day."

"He was 6'4" and 220 pounds," Marjorie added. "I read up on him."

"You take it, then, for me," Jack said. "I'm not much of a teacher."

"Your namesake was a hero in the Revolutionary War. In 1871, General Cornwallis learned that Thomas Jefferson, Patrick Henry, Richard Henry Lee, and other revolutionaries had left Richmond and fled to Charlottesville. Cornwallis dispatched one of his colonels, Banastre Tarleton, to capture them. Jouett saw Tarleton's cavalry and correctly guessed their mission. He rode the back roads through the night, illuminated only by the moon, to warn Jefferson and the others. They were able to escape. Jouett is a hero in Virginia lore."

John Jewett claimed, "Since I learned about him, I've tried to live up to him."

"Perhaps you have," Governor Sally Bradley insisted.

"Perhaps you have. I'm starving; let's go get something to eat."

Six

Sunday, April 1

The next day, a couple from Kentucky arrived to pick up Tank. Under the watchful eye of veterinarian Dr. Angela Endres, they gave Tank a thorough evaluation and then presented Marjorie with a certified check. She gave him a hug around his head and helped the buyer load him into the trailer.

She held her emotions as her horse drifted away, accompanied by the fading crunch of tires on the gravel driveway. By the time the buyers' trailer receded from view, tears were streaming down her cheek. Boo and Radley jumped eagerly and lovingly against her jeans.

It was April Fools Day, but although it was her intention all along to sell Tank, the sight of his rump drifting away brought her no merriment. She walked inside and put the check in her pocketbook.

She put on a pot of coffee to percolate and then realized that she hadn't yet picked up the morning paper. So with Boo and Radley close behind, she strolled down the driveway that had just taken Tank away. Retrieving the paper from the box and unwrapping it on the way back, the front page headline stopped her dead in her tracks.

Virginia strikes down gay marriage ban

Her first thought was that it was an April Fools Day joke. But as she read, it quickly became real. Her eyes bolted down the page with frantic urgency and giddy excitement. A federal judge in Norfolk had ruled that Virginia's ban, backed by a state constitutional amendment, was in fact a violation of federal law. Her ruling said the ban unconstitutionally, "denied benefits to same-sex couples in violation of the equal protection and due process clauses of the Constitution."

The article went on to say that Virginia had joined California, Oklahoma, Hawaii, Illinois, and Utah in striking down gay marriage bans.

Further, the new governor, Sally Bradley had issued an order to all state clerks of the court to "begin offering same-sex wedding licenses no later than noon on Friday, April 6th."

Marjorie sprinted back to the house and gleefully called Liza. "What are you doing at noon on Friday?" she exclaimed.

Friday, April 6

Five days later, precisely at high noon, Marjorie and Liza stood second in line at the office of the clerk of the court in the historic 1859 Italian villa style courthouse in Orange, Virginia, awaiting their license. When their turn came, Ron Wolfe, clerk of the court, presented them with a marriage license where he had scratched out the words "Husband" and "Wife" and had replaced them with "Spouse" and "Spouse."

Marjorie was dressed in the same peasant dress she'd worn at the Runnymede event two weeks prior and Liza wore a beautiful gingham dress. Both dresses featured orange stitching and accents and both women wore matching rainbow wristbands. After watching Liza sign her name, then signing herself, and then watching Wolfe sign his name, Marjorie heard him say the words she never thought she'd hear as a Virginian. "I now pronounce you wife and wife."

The newlyweds kissed. They thanked the clerk, congratulated the other couples waiting in line, and departed.

The lovebirds returned to Runnymede Meadow Estate for the first connubial fun since Liza's wounding, lovemaking carefully since Liza's left arm was still in a sling.

Wednesday, April 11

Five days later, Jack Jewett took Sally to Roanoke first where she met with movers who arranged for her belongings to be transferred to the Governor's Mansion in Richmond. Then Jewett took her to UVA for tests and then to Runnymede Meadow Estate for two days of rest.

Marjorie and Liza were carrying dinner outside to the patio when Sally and Jewett arrived. It was an unseasonably warm spring evening, with a moon rising in the east. It had rained earlier in the afternoon after several dry days, and the sweet petrichor smell wafted across the yard.

After congratulating the newlyweds, Jack mentioned his urgency to return to Richmond. So he took his leave and drove away in the Governor's SUV.

As the three women sat for dinner of roast beef and spiced potatoes, Liza poured Merlot from Keswick Vineyards into three earthen goblets, the same as used weeks earlier in Eghamshire.

They chattered happily about the recent events, thanking Sally profusely for her help making gay marriage legal. Sally asked Marjorie about the recent return to Eghamshire. Marjorie admitted to Sally that, "Tom Leathers called and asked me if I could bring you back, telling me when he'd be there. He didn't tell me why, but I told him I would."

Marjorie spooned baked beans onto three plates followed by spiced potatoes.

"In addition to your marriage, I have more good news and some better news," Sally announced, lifting her goblet to her twin and her twin's lover. They raised theirs as well.

"First the good news. Sam Sebrell, my Chief of Staff, has proposed to his girlfriend in Blacksburg and he's now engaged."

"And the better news?" Liza queried.

Sally smiled broadly. "I'm cancer free!"

"Wonderful!" Marjorie and Liza said in duet.

The women toasted to the new Governor's health. A cardinal sang from the apple tree, "Pretty, pretty! Cheer, cheer!"

About Michael Abraham

MICHAEL ABRAHAM was born, raised and educated in Southwest Virginia. He is a businessman and writer. He is married and has an adult daughter. He lives in Blacksburg with his wife, two dogs, and four motorcycles.

For information on his books, excerpts, sample chapters, and upcoming presentations, visit his website at:
www.bikemike.name

Write to him via e-mail at
<bikemike@nrvunwired.net>

"I love hearing from readers!" Michael.

Also by Michael Abraham:

The Spine of the Virginias
Journeys along the border of Virginia and West Virginia

Harmonic Highways
Exploring Virginia's Crooked Road

Union, WV
A novel of loss, healing, and redemption in contemporary Appalachia

Providence, VA
A novel of inner strength through adversity

War, WV
A quest for justice in the Appalachian coal fields

www.ingramcontent.com/pod-product-compliance
Lightning Source LLC
Chambersburg PA
CBHW070109120726
47909CB00002B/543